Praise for

JAMIE IS

"*Jamie Is My Heart's Desire* is a book which, on its surface, makes very little sense (or what we construe as sense) but very good reading. Indeed, this book about Jamie defies summarization. We may go so far as to say that the novel opens in a funeral parlor in New York City and Harry Sutton, who assists the manager of this establishment in his mournful duties, is the narrator.

Harry has a great deal to narrate. He has a large circle of friends, among them Emily, a social worker who is good at her job but hates it; Wallace, a rather dim and semi-employed writer, beloved of Emily; Tess, who is simple and healthy and lovely and wonderful with men; and Tulley, a Roman Catholic priest of doubtful emotional commitments. Depending on how you look at it, there is also Jamie—that is, if you can see him. Jamie is dying and eventually dead—and those who *can* see him say he's beautiful. His presence seems to constellate Emily and Tulley, and make Wallace valid; it moves dark-haired, loving Tess to pity and reverence. But Harry cannot see Jamie: indeed, there seems to be some evidence that there is no corpse—no Jamie.

To take faith in the spirit world for the subject of a novel is rushing in where angels fear to tread, and Alfred Chester arms himself with a wry and saving humor that allows him to emerge at the end relatively unscathed by his dip into Acheron. For this book is funny—funny in the grain rather than in event or phrase. What goes on? The answer, gentle reader, is up to you."

—Martha Bacon, *The New York Herald Tribune*

BOOKS BY ALFRED CHESTER

Here Be Dragons
Stories (1955)

Jamie Is My Heart's Desire
A Novel (1956)

Behold Goliath
Stories (1964)

The Exquisite Corpse
A Novel (1967)

Head of a Sad Angel
Stories 1953–1966 (1990)

Looking for Genet
Literary Essays and Reviews (1992)

JAMIE IS MY HEART'S DESIRE

A NOVEL BY
Alfred Chester

AFTERWORD BY
Harriet Sohmers Zwerling

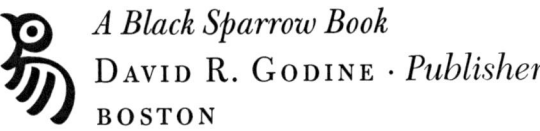

A Black Sparrow Book
DAVID R. GODINE · *Publisher*
BOSTON

This is
A Black Sparrow Book
published in 2007 by
DAVID R. GODINE · *Publisher*
Post Office Box 450
Jaffrey, New Hampshire 03452
www.blacksparrowbooks.com

Copyright © 1956 by Alfred Chester.
First published in Great Britain in 1956 by André Deutsch, Ltd., London.
First U.S. edition published in 1957 by Vanguard Press, New York.

The afterword first appeared in *Raritan*, Winter 1993, and was reprinted
in *Notes of a Nude Model & other pieces* by Harriet Sohmers Zwerling
(Spuyten Duyvil, 2003). Copyright © 2003 by Harriet Sohmers Zwerling.
Used by permission of Spuyten Duyvil, 42 St. John's Place, Brooklyn,
New York 11217.

All rights reserved. No part of this book may be used or reproduced in any
manner whatsoever without written permission from the publisher, except
in the case of brief quotations embodied in critical articles and reviews.
For information address Permissions, Black Sparrow Books,
9 Hamilton Place, Boston, Massachusetts 02108.

The Black Sparrow Books pressmark is by Julian Waters
www.waterslettering.com

LIBRARY OF CONGRESS CATALOGING-IN-PUBLICATION DATA
Chester, Alfred, 1928–1971.
Jamie is my heart's desire : a novel / by Alfred Chester. —
1st Black Sparrow Books ed.
p. cm.
ISBN-10: 1-57423-206-1 (pbk.)
1. Gay men—Fiction. I. Title.
PS3505.H679 J36   2006
813'.54—dc22
2006018110

FIRST BLACK SPARROW BOOKS EDITION
Printed in the United States of America

For
ARTHUR DAVIS

JAMIE IS MY HEART'S DESIRE

BOOK ONE

1

I have always felt at ease among the dead. This does not mean that I prefer their society to the living or that I am put to any discomfort when walking beside those who can walk beside me. It means simply that in this era of fright and squeamishness I am neither frightened nor squeamish, that I can face the total obliteration of so-called specifically human qualities with the same lack of concern I exhibit to those who yet retain them.

I am not an individual of philosophic calm, nor am I an incipient necrophile; I am only Mr. Trevor's manager or, more properly, the undertaker's assistant. The office where I sit, like any other anteroom of death, is formulated to austerity without being repulsive: I think it is ludicrous. The walls of this converted vegetable store are olive green, as is the worn unpatterned rug, and two plush benches stare vacantly at each other from opposite walls. Potted palms, whose burlap trunks and linen leaves sag with immortality, lean here and there about the store, and in the deep-set windows on either side of the glass door are two enormous bronze urns capped by laurel wreaths and a dry gray fuzz that must once have been pussy willow. My desk is toward the back; it is simple but impressively black and, except for a bulky ancient-looking ledger, there is nothing on its top. (The telephone is hidden in a drawer and although I have been working here more than two years I am still sometimes puzzled by the muffle of its distant ring.) On the wall behind my desk a faded print of Jesus Christ hangs, unsmiling, eyes half-closed, the gold of His halo so insipid it seems almost like a spray of hair standing comically on end.

The carved oaken door, hinged into the rear wall, is nearly always closed for it leads into an unlighted corridor that twists five yards and ends before the square, cold, white chamber where blood is drawn and exchanged for a more sustenant fluid. Sometimes I make jokes with Frank, our very serious embalmer; alternately I call him a vampire and a taxidermist depending on what he is doing at the moment. Without a smile, his small dreadful eyes fixed on his work, he always makes the same reply: "You ain't a bit comical, Mr. Sutton. You ought to show a little respect for the dead." It will never occur to Frank, I suppose, that it is he for whom I have no respect, that while I smoke a cigarette and lean my elbow on the ankle of a corpse, I am laughing at him, at his round little body, at the circle of bald flesh upon his head which he will, having completed the transfusion, cover with his panama as he leaves through the chapel. (With the exception of myself, all our employees exit that way because Mr. Trevor feels there may be a professional odor lingering upon them that would not suit the pathetic though congenial atmosphere of the office.) When Frank has gone I occasionally sit alone in the white chamber, for now in summer it is cooler there, and I enjoy looking at the *art* magazines that Frank invariably keeps on top of the instrument cabinet.

Seldom will I go into the chapel, and only when absolutely necessary into the waking rooms behind it, for there I often have the unpleasantness of seeing the bereaved people who, while not exactly dead, are not exactly alive either. And it is this half-state of noise and silence in which they grieve for another's life that has been or their own death that will be that I find so disagreeable. I do not care for vagueness and ambiguity; halftones and chiaroscuro are not to my temperament: I am impatient with twilights and dawns, with suggestion and deviousness, with *might I? can we? but is it* really *possible?*

So rather than wonder about their motives and to which degree of life or death they belong, I would sooner avoid the people in the waking rooms and stroll only between my office and the white chamber.

2

Uptown, glittering over the Hudson like a sequined cliff, is Mr. Trevor's elegant new funeral parlor (or *studio*, as he prefers to call it). Although the building has been open almost a year he is still too preoccupied with it to visit me more than twice a week. I suspect, however, that he sails his long black Packard by three or four times a day, but does not stop until he sees my shoeless feet relaxed upon the desk or a magazine propped in front of me or someone else in the office who is obviously not on business. This morning, drained by heat, Emily was here when Mr. Trevor pounced in, her blouse half-unbuttoned and crumpled into the top of her brassiere.

As my office stands close to the gray crowded slum area in which she works, she occasionally stops by and, while this was the third time he had found her here, he did not look at her, or at least I failed to notice, for his wobbly green-pea eyes are unbelievably quick, and while they seem not to move at all, I am certain they are turning very rapidly like the rotation of the earth. As always, he wore a black pinstripe suit (he told me once he owns seven of them), a shiny tie of pearl gray satin, and pointed black shoes. Mr. Trevor's clothes, like everything else about him, describe his devouring belief that a suggestion of formality makes the repugnant more bearable: I sometimes wonder what color his underwear is.

"Everything in order, Harry?" he asked me, reaching a thick hand across the desk to flip through the ledger.

"Yes."

I watched him slide his finger down a page. Mr. Trevor's carelessness is a practiced thing: it is too easy, too polished to be otherwise, and it can never overlook an error.

"Is Frank in the inner office?" he said, euphemistically referring to the embalming room.

"No, he's gone out."

"There, there, Harry." His loose damp lips paled as he pressed them together and, with effort, shaped them into a straight rubbery smile. "Maybe we'd better keep closer tabs on the——"

"I think he's gone to check on a delivery. But if you're interested you can ask the other men; they're decorating the chapel for the Campenella parade this afternoon."

"*Har*-ry, please...." he said demurely, turning to Emily for the first time. "You must forgive him, young lady: one gets hardened to things in our profession." Emily, wordlessly forgiving, nodded her head and smiled to me. "Well then, Harry, if everything is in order, I'll be getting back uptown." And he added nonchalantly: "You know, we're putting Charles X. Terninger to rest this afternoon—the Wall Street broker." After twenty years downtown, where he buried no one but immigrant laborers and the children of immigrant laborers, Mr. Trevor now is sharply aware of his *arrival* for he deals almost entirely with the remains of financiers, lawyers, and retired politicians. "Certainly is a scorcher today." (Putting a short finger under his stiff white collar.) "I'll see you in a day or two, Harry. Good morning, young lady." Leaving the office, he crossed the way and climbed into his Packard, which, as it drove noiselessly off, left the hot yellow street silent and empty; the large gray church opposite us was antique and abandoned in the sunlit quietude.

"I can't imagine why he's begun to part his hair in the middle," said Emily. "Doesn't he look insane?"

"He told me he feels cooler with it that way."

"I don't see how . . . but if he does I suppose he's not as mad as he looks. Isn't this the damnedest summer? It's worse than Chicago. Honestly, Harry, just imagine having to drag yourself through the streets on a day like this?" Her fingers, contrasting with the exhausted slump of her body, galloped across the small black notebook on her lap. "The city says if it's over ninety, we can take the day off, but I think their thermometer must start at ten below zero. I wish I could just drop everything and limp home to a nice cool bath."

"You can go upstairs and take a shower if you want. The place is a mess, but it'll——"

"I don't have time. I've got three more families to see before noon. Oh, God, I hate my job. But it's a blessing to come in out of the sun." Her shoulders dropped back emphatically. "Even if it is in *this* place."

Summer does not sit well on Emily: from the time she was very young the warmth nudged at and wilted her. Some women blossom during hot weather: they become ripe and lubricous, like Tess, and a lush pervasive smell exudes from them. But not Emily. As she sat on the green plush bench this morning her short curly hair was kinked and ragged, her face and breasts swollen with heat, and while her largeness is attractive in cooler weather, it was today only clumsy.

"Damn!" she groaned with sudden energy. "Do you know what I've got to do this afternoon? I have to see someone off to Europe."

"Anyone I know?"

"No, I don't think so. Some man I went out with a few times. How I dread the idea of getting on a mobbed liner in all this heat."

"It might be cooler over by the river."

"But the boat will be hot—everyone excited and running around and pushing." She paused, and then very quietly, "I wonder if I'll ever go; I think I've almost given up hope. Remember when I used to talk about nothing but a voyage to Europe?"

Uncomfortable, and in an effort to turn her away from the subject, I reached into the bottom drawer of my desk, took out the bottle of warm lemonade, and offered her some. But she shook her head.

"You know, Harry, I've even a list prepared of all the

things I'd have to take along: for the boat and for all the places I'd go. I've had the list made out ever since the war ended. Oh, I don't know..." she sighed, and again, "I don't know," as if she were responding feebly to the pressure of an important question. "Something always comes up to prevent me. I wish we could arrange our lives free of responsibility."

Turning to the window, she watched an old woman stop and gaze in at us, then walk slowly by. "Have you heard from Wallace?"

"He phoned last night," I said. "He wants me to come over this evening."

"Are you going?" She leaned slightly forward, her soft voice urgent but with an affectation of restraint so that I would think she was trying to conceal the urgency. I am seldom fooled by Emily.

"I think so. Will you be there?"

"No, he's mad at me again." Smiling sadly, that familiar expression came into her eyes. In the past, whenever Emily spoke of Wallace it was always with a look of longing, anxiety, and now, at thirty-one, that look is becoming transferred to almost everything she talks about as if a nervous old-maid quality grows within her. She and Wallace are always fighting, and they can permit themselves these frequent breaks only because I never argue with either of them: they have the security of a point of contact, a person through whom they can reach each other.

"Would you like to come along?"

She frowned and nodded her head. "Honestly, Harry, he's still such a child. Do you know why we argued?"

"He didn't mention it to me."

"You see," she began, "we went to the theater last week and during the intermission we met an old friend of his. I don't know if you've ever met her: her name is Dolores something. No? Such an awful person! You know the type —forty years old all over except for the face she puts on before going out. And nothing to talk about but who she knows and who she's going to know. Wallace wanted her to meet us after the play. I was just fed up; after all, Harry, I don't see him often and when I do I hate to have to share him." She caught herself quickly: "With anything like that. I told him I didn't want to, and I was really calm and reasonable about it. But he flew at me, said I was anti-social and that in spite of my job I wasn't even vaguely concerned with people and that the Department of Welfare ought to be warned against hiring cold-hearted females who pretend to be saints. Imagine! You'd think *I* had done something wrong. And do you know what he did? He tipped an usher and had his seat changed: just like that. Afterwards I saw him coming toward me, but there was such a crowd that . . ."

I shrugged; I never know what to say when Emily complains about Wallace, so usually I shrug. She has always been annoyed that he can find interest in people who either bore or irritate her and, although this interest has persisted since his youth, I think Emily does not really believe in it. Often when she and Wallace disagree, she makes it evident that she knows he is pretending, that he is indulging himself in one more extended fancy that will, like all the others, eventually end.

"What's the use of grumbling," she said wearily. "He'll never change, will he?"

"I don't think so," I replied, uncertain what she meant. Rising, Emily slid the collar of her blouse from her brassiere and absently straightened the wrinkles. "You're sweet, Harry." She leaned over the desk, to kiss me. "Sometimes I wonder what I'd do without you."

I laughed. "You'd get along."

"Perhaps . . . but not so well." Her head nodded slowly like the last exhausted motion of a jack-in-the-box.

We arranged to meet for a drink before going to Wallace's and she kissed me again upon the cheek, mildly, damply, with gratitude.

When she had gone I unlatched the oaken door and followed the unlighted corridor into the white chamber. Sinking to a cold steel chair I would have sat a while in the bright tranquility, but from the chapel I heard sounds of hammering and scraping. Walking across the chamber I opened the door and went into the carpeted foyer: a gold-edged Chinese lantern wired high in one corner stretched a fan of orange light across the ceiling. From there through a second oaken door into the small chapel whose fretted rose cornices arched over the sleazy biblical scenes kakemonoed on the walls. The two men worked lazily, pushing benches, nailing frames that trailed carnations and lilies round the altar, sweeping the floor. Above the altar, the sunlight dropped through the stained-glass windows and whirled tinted columns of dust upon the flowers.

"Morning, Mr. Sutton," said the older man, hammering beneath the lectern. On his knees, four long nails spiking from between his teeth, he looked as incongruous as a bucktoothed animal arranging stage sets.

I stood in the doorway watching them, drugged into motionlessness by their slow, ordered efforts. Finally the young man called, "Time for lunch, pop. It's after twelve."

And then I went back to the office.

3

When we circled from the landing this evening, he was leaning against the door jamb, his short-sleeved shirt unbuttoned almost all the way and clinging damply to his chest. As always, when he greeted us a small supercilious smile wavered at his mouth like a bead of quicksilver, not really annoying but rather unpredictable, unreachable, as if marking a conscious distance between Wallace and the rest of the world. Sometimes I fancy that age will never show on him in its ordinary way—that's silly, of course, but each year his body seems firmer, his eyes wider with surprise, his delight in everything stronger.

Standing between us, arms about our shoulders, he led us inside and urged us to seats. "Now sit down," he said, "and close your eyes."

"Why?"

"Never mind, Harry. Just do as I say." And he vanished into the bedroom. Opposite, her hands hidden behind the burly arm of the enormous purple club chair, Emily cracked her knuckles and a tense pucker drew her lips: familiar signals of disturbance which would remain until some mention were made of her argument with Wallace.

From the bedroom a metallic rustle shivered a warning and I shut my eyes.

"Don't look yet, either of you. Tilt your heads back and sniff deeply—inhale the ages." The slow rustling sound continued and suddenly a dry seedy odor began to needle my nose.

"Myrrh!" shrieked Emily, and I opened my eyes.

In the far corner, smiling broadly, Wallace rocked a small fuming censer before the window. From his hand a braid of silver chains unwound to a red glass globe caged in a thick silver frame.

"Isn't it wonderful?" And he shook out another blast of smoke.

"No," I said, sneezing. "Take it away. It stinks."

"*Stinks?* Harry, the odor is sheer poetry—but even if it wasn't, you might pause and consider that this is an eight-hundred-year-old stink." He caught the censer up in his hands and brought it to me. "How many odors, pleasant or unpleasant, can brag of such endurance?"

"How can it possibly be eight hundred years old?"

"It just is. The censer and the incense have been untouched all this time. And it's all hand-worked. Look here, do you see? Those tiny crooked numerals are the date. But

I suppose you think they're the manufacturer's serial number!" Then, turning to Emily: "I just bought it this afternoon. From the treasure of a Greek church: can you imagine?"

Emily looked away and nodded and I heard her knuckles crack.

"The incense is Russian, and I suspect it came to Greece during the . . ." He stopped abruptly, his mouth still open. "Aren't you people at all interested?"

"I am," said Emily, faintly.

Choking the beige fog that smoked from the globe, Wallace shook one sharp irritated clatter from the chains. "Two stones, that's what you are: two big lumps of concrete." He squinted and traced a finger lightly across the silver frame, then walked to the mantel, hung the censer before the fireplace and regarded it sadly a moment. Then, backing away, Wallace raised himself into the window seat beside and above the chair in which Emily sat.

Most of the people Wallace has met since he published his books believe he was different before, just as all those whom I have come to know during the past two years feel that Mr. Trevor's establishment must certainly have influenced my personality. There is no truth in their convictions, for people are born what they become; they are bound to themselves and create their whereabouts. I do not for a minute believe they can be anything more than what they are.

Even in Chicago, when we were children, Wallace did whatever he pleased: there were a few weeks every year that left his desk at school, his room at home, and Emily's square face—wherever it was to be seen—puzzlingly vacant.

And when he returned, it was with stories of the mountains to the south or of New York or, most often, of the Great Lakes where he roamed among the old sea-measled sailors. Occasionally he would attempt an explanation, long-windedly theorizing a simple need to move, but to those who believed him wrong he was incomprehensible, and ultimately he would only mutter a short apology: "I have to, that's all. Try to understand." That he grieved others may have grieved him but did not stop him from doing as he wished. He was popular at school, of course, as are all cheerful eccentrics because they give everyone else the feeling of superiority. This was especially so with Wallace, who failed class after class with merry indifference, although, when in the presence of adults, he would feign humility or sadness, but with deliberate inaccuracy. All our teachers, I think, must have hated him, except Mr. Bertram Larks of mathematics, who was later killed in the war. Mr. Larks arranged to have Wallace in his classes for three consecutive terms, each time giving him 95 percent, which, broken down, the teacher explained, was 5 percent for mathematics and 90 percent for calculated nonchalance.

But Miss Grace in English, typifying the opposition, forced Wallace to study with her for two years and became his most devoted enemy in the sense that she could consider a lesson well spent if she had, in her eyes, humiliated the boy. Wallace never troubled to answer her—that is, until the last week of school, when it was obvious he would not graduate and he was already old enough to leave.

"Pembrook," lilted Miss Grace; her voice was one of exaggerated sexuality, one that embarrassed rather than aroused. "Tell me, what have been the benefits of your education?" She always wore a large uncomfortable-looking hat in class, tipping the brim down her forehead to just above the eyebrows as if as soon as the bell rang she must fly from the room, which, in fact, she invariably did.

"Many," Wallace replied vaguely, standing at his desk, his face very serious. Tentative smiles already danced across the mouths of the students.

"Really, Pembrook? I shouldn't think they'd been many at this institution. Perhaps your devotion to scholarship"—pause for the laughter which obediently followed—"has led you to study elsewhere in the evenings."

"That's right."

"And may I ask you where?"

"No you may not." Wallace reconsidered suddenly. "Besides I don't think you've ever heard of it."

Miss Grace frowned and fixed her hat. "I'm not such an ancient schoolmarm as you might think, Pembrook. Do you consider yourself a student at the Institution of Life?"

Becoming impatient, perhaps angry, he shifted his feet, but said nothing.

"And what do you specialize in? Ignorance is usually the major subject."

Now unmistakably furious, Wallace lifted his books from the desk and said quietly, "I specialize in avoiding people like you."

"Come back here, Pembrook! Don't you dare leave this room without my permission!"

But he was already gone, so, without another word, Miss Grace returned to the lesson.

When the war came, Wallace would not let it touch him. He had ceased then even to attempt to apologize for his actions, and though the war was there, he wore it vaguely, transparently, like a scarf of chiffon, like something easily removed. He worked at many jobs, and saved a little, and went where one could during those years—and came back to apprentice himself to another trade and begin the cycle again. And all the time, very quietly and almost as if it were a secret, he was writing a book. It was published the year after the war ended and a lot of people read it: a comic little story that no one took seriously. His second novel, two years ago, was almost exactly the same; the same people read it and liked it, and no one took it very seriously.

"Wallace . . ." Emily called, her voice high and doubtful, as if awakening him.

"Yes?"

"I just thought . . . I mean, about last Wednesday . . ." She looked round weakly, her eyes grasping at mine for aid.

"Last Wednesday?" repeated Wallace. Wrinkling his forehead in recollection, he reached down to take her hand.

"Yes, at the theater. I'm awfully sorry for what happened, Wallace, really——"

"Oh, *that!*" His smile widened. "I'd forgotten all about it. What silliness!" Emily sank a little more deeply into the purple chair, the air of tension at last gone from her mouth. "Although," he decided suddenly, dropping her hand and sitting up straight, "I shouldn't forgive you at all after the way you've been ignoring my censer."

"I haven't been ignoring it."

"Well, you certainly haven't been showing any undue interest."

"I was distracted," she said softly, apologetically.

"You are the strangest thing, Emily. You always do that: you say, 'I was distracted,' as if it were some sort of excuse when actually it's the worst sort of excuse. Life and distraction are at opposite poles, and if you get muddled up and worried about one thing you never have a chance at anything else."

"That may be so, Wallace, but when you're distracted—well, it isn't the kind of thing you can control."

"Oh, of course it is. It's a question of habit. Imagine life presenting a series of traps in the shape of fairly obvious pits, some vast and almost bottomless, some not so deep. Within each one is a huge fat lazy old dragon who swallows you whole if you fall in. It takes fairly decent eyesight and only the smallest amount of brains"—he pinched his fingers together, indicating the quantity—"to avoid the traps, yet apparently most people find it easier to get caught than to go on. Sometimes the pit is shallow or the dragon is asleep, so you can, if you try, climb out and start the business of avoiding traps all over again. But often you fall very deep and even if the dragon is asleep, he'll wake up one day and devour you—and as often as not you forget all about escape and, snug and warm in the dragon's belly, you live blindly and dumbly and miserably ever after.

"Yes, I know, Emily, you'll say I'm heartless, but I don't care. Like anyone else who ever becomes one, I've had to shape myself into a human being and keep my eyes open for the ditches. So why waste sympathy on those who've been eaten up? They only irritate me a little with their stupidity."

Legs folded on the broad window seat, his pale trousers and white shirt were a brilliant relief from the night sky behind him. Tending to be serious, his face weakened childishly: his straight blond hair pasted round his forehead, his lips became small, his water-gray eyes turned down in a comic mixture of fright and whimsy as if he were about to reveal where the jam was hidden.

"It's not always possible to avoid the traps, Wallace," said Emily. "No matter how you take care. Someone will come along and push you in from behind."

"No, it can't happen." Wallace shook his head and laughed. "Not if you're watching out. You said you were distracted before. Why were you?"

"Well . . ." She hesitated. "I'm not thinking of myself now. I can give you examples——"

"To hell with examples. The only example you're concerned with is yourself."

"No, not necessarily."

"Yes, necessarily. Take your desire to travel. You've always talked about going but you've never gone. Why not?"

"Well—money. You know about my brother, Wallace. How can I let his family——"

"Nonsense. Let him worry about his family. But instead you let yourself, as you'd say, get pushed into a trap from behind. And I suppose you find it more comfortable than the effort to climb out."

"Anyway," she said with sudden firmness, "I'm not thinking of myself. I'm thinking of some of my clients, all of them, any of them. There's one—even her name is a calamity:

Mrs. Mussolini. She lives over on Crawford Street—and you know what it's like there—with two illegitimate grandchildren. Her daughter's dead; the rest of her family is dead. She's never had a single chance to avoid the ditches, not from the beginning, Wallace. In fact there hasn't been anything for her *but* ditches: they were always there and she always had to fall in."

"How do you know? Maybe it was stupidity and weakness that drove her in."

"No, she's not stupid." She paused, her head shaking. Her voice had eased back to softness. "She has almost no one to talk to but some kid next door, and me, when I can come there. And I've got to try to be maternal and terribly strong, to reassure her. Honestly, I'm like someone else with her; like a fountain of hope pouring out promises, saying, yes, yes things will be better soon." She sighed. "Who knows? Maybe they will."

She stopped speaking then, leaving a sad and pensive silence to hang heavily in the warm room. Emily loves to create this kind of mood, one of melancholy and impotence, and generally it is not unpleasant unless it goes on too long. But tonight, because it threatened to persist, I looked across at Emily and smiled: "Maybe your Mrs. Mussolini ought to have killed herself years ago."

But she pretended not to hear.

"Yes," whispered Wallace. "Maybe she should have." He said it with distant thoughtfulness as if the notion of suicide had never been suggested to him before. "Not recently. I mean, she ought not to have killed herself recently, but long ago, before misery became the chief characteristic of her life—when it was obvious she had been swallowed by a very tough dragon." He paused, then smiled. "I remember once I was on a train going from Paris to Rome. The first part of the journey I was alone in my compartment, but then at Dijon, the door opened and a man looked in, a thin monkey-faced little man, and asked if he might bring his things and stay. I said all right and he left, returning a moment later with his 'things' in his arms: a suitcase and a child—a girl, his daughter. '*Elle va mourir*,' he said apologetically as he put her on the seat. She wasn't more than seven and she didn't look as if she were going to die although her eyes were circled and her face pale. The father explained that he was taking her to her grandmother's in Naples. Well, nothing much happened during the day. We talked a little, and both of them appeared to be completely unconcerned about her impending death. The child never said a word, but her father told me a bit about their lives, and only with the simplest emotions did he mention the girl's disease, and when he did he would look to her for agreement. Sometimes she nodded her head; sometimes she did nothing.

"We crossed the border in the evening and afterwards I fell into one of those vivid nightmare-sleeps people have on trains, as if all their repressions are being pushed up by the rumble of the carriage. I awoke much later, possibly it was after midnight, and I saw the child and her father sitting close together at the window. I didn't move, but my eyes were open and I could see that we were passing through the Alps; it was a tremendous sight: those unreal mountains surrounding us, and the moon like a big white explosion. The man was whispering to the little girl, and for the first time she seemed alert and responsive, her eyes bright as the mountain peaks. I don't know when I've seen anyone happier—she wasn't delighted as a child is, or even as I was by the sight of the Alps, but she was rejoicing, lyrical, like a piece of the moonlight or the mountains. Her father spoke Italian, so I understood little of what he said, but one thing I could make out. 'It doesn't matter how long,' he whispered, 'but how deep. You can know it all in an instant, my apple.'"

Perhaps he imagined he was still speaking, for his face did not change expression, but he had stopped, and the three of us were again silent. Finally, Wallace burst into laughter. "Look at Harry. He's as bored as a fish. That's the luck of genuinely happy people—they need never interest themselves when others talk about how not to be unhappy."

I knew he was trying to bait me, but nevertheless, I said, "Who ever told you I was happy?"

"Well, aren't you? It's written all over your face."

I hesitated. "I suppose I'm indifferent."

"Indifferent!" He maintained a smile but a shadow of irritation deepened his voice. "From the vantage point of the funeral parlor, Harry can see life in its *true* perspective and so has the amazing ability of being objective about everything—even himself. Isn't that it? You can crawl out of your coffin now and then in order to examine your bodily remains."

"More or less. You know I don't care to talk about these things." Unnerved by the edge in Wallace's voice, I looked past him, over his shoulder at the sky. Had I not stopped him at once, he would have gone on to become red-faced and almost furious while we began the same old row again, with Emily echoing Wallace's points like a half-mute choir, feeble and indistinct behind the boom of the soloist.

"You know, I saw someone off on the *Queen Mary* this afternoon," said Emily in a rush of words; faced with tension that will not vent itself in argument, she inevitably becomes chatty. "I'd never been on it before: isn't that funny? And it was a horrible disappointment—as narrow and dismal as the subway. Honestly, when I come to think of it, I could write a book about all the boats I've been on but haven't sailed with. You know, often a bridesmaid but never a bride...." Her voice trailed into silence and she looked down at her skin in confusion as if all at once aware of having said a variety of wrong things.

"Who did you see off?" asked Wallace.

"Oh, you don't know him. Some fellow from my office." Her eyes fluttered by me, then dropped once more. "He's so damn blasé. Just the kind of person who, when he was in the army, would never say he was going overseas but always abroad. And there I was, sort of weakened by the heat and everyone laughing and crying, and so, stupidly, I told him how sad I was at the idea of saying goodbye. He said, very coldly, 'Oh, goodbyes mean nothing to me anymore: I've said so many of them.' How can he feel that way? I don't think I could ever get used to saying goodbye."

"No, of course not. Goodbyes are wonderful. They always imply something new."

Leaning my head back I closed my eyes and listened without interest to their continuing talk. I know that Emily feels she and Wallace sometimes exclude me from their conversations; if this is so, it doesn't matter. I find that I, like anyone else, become repetitious and predictable after a while, and it is silly to make pointless comments merely to sustain a pointless discussion.

I must have fallen asleep because I was surprised when I heard Wallace say, "We'll call the pit a ha-ha. How's that? Politely and ironically I tell the world that Emily's in a ha-ha." He turned to me. "But you're not in a ha-ha, are you, Harry?"

"I'm not in anything," I groaned, lifting myself and walking through the maze of furniture to the mantelpiece. "Except maybe a trance. I want to go home and sleep."

"You can't; it's much too early." He slid from the window seat.

"Don't go yet, Harry," said Emily, mechanically.

"I'm much too tired to hang around any longer. Do you want me to take you home?"

She looked at Wallace tentatively. "I suppose I'll stay a while. You don't mind, do you, Harry?" I shook my head and she asked, "Do you still love me?"

"Yes." I used to say no when she asked me that, but I have come round lately because it pleases her so much and because, while she asks it flippantly, she does not expect a flippant answer.

"And me?" Wallace made an awkward childish bow. I nodded and laughed. "Then phone me soon," he said.

The dense windless heat slumped over everything like the night, and from each areaway a monotony of sleepless voices buzzed. Along the streets I heard the dreary clump of the heels of heat-ridden walkers and the collapsed sighs of people drooping on brownstone stoops.

Although Wallace's apartment is in a better section, my flat (a room-and-a-half above the funeral parlor) lies only a short walk from his, so I followed the avenue south, emerging upon the noisy moonlit park. Here, the thin occasional breeze had attracted hundreds of people, and every path was swarming. To avoid the larger crowds I made my way along a small side lane where, toward the center, my eye was caught by the slight motionless figure of a boy sitting alone upon a bench. I could not remember where I had seen him before, but I knew I had, if only in passing, for his face, while unknown to me, was pressingly familiar. His large eyes were lowered, fixed on the line of blue smoke from the cigarette between his fingers, and through the branches of the tree above, a shower of moonlight sprayed over him. Walking by slowly, I thought he might be dead, that the element of familiarity in his face was merely death, but then—as if to reassure me—he stretched his leg, and his shoe crushed along the gravel of the path.

I strolled round a cluster of people and started south again, but turned once more to see the boy: his short thin body was stiff, and the moonlight fell like a curious dappled mask on his sad still face.

4

Kitty was lying on the bed when I came home, her round little body showing no enthusiasm other than the gentle purr that is there even when I go away. In the stale dismal heat of the room she was waiting for me to open the window; she would not leap out immediately: she would wait a while, nap a bit (head raised and eyes half-open), writhe across my lap, wander into the kitchenette, and finally she would go. From the sill, she would jump to the rolled awning above the funeral parlor, and from there to a thin ledge in the wall, and then down. On the walk she would sit a long time, observing the human and feline passers-by and, now and then, licking her orange hair. And when some special private moment arrived she would cross the street and disappear into her world of passageways and fences. When she returned, it would be the same way, at her own inexplicable pace, the jumps back to my room along the same path but with more judgment, with greater hesitation.

Life could not be simpler than it is for Kitty. Having no god but that of the flesh, she cannot be heretical; obeying no laws but those legislated in her blood, she cannot be criminal; and no thought can violate the pure and empty elegance of her mind. She has grown up to procreate; she will grow old to die. Romance and religion are remote from her, frills and niceties she has no need of. Kitty never makes love; she relieves a pressure that, though she may not understand it, takes her in the direction of relief. And when she dies, it will be alone in a corner, faraway from extreme unction, from weeping relatives, from the slop of the embalming chamber.

Occasionally I forget to feed her: it doesn't matter. She does not nag, nor does she take a shopping bag and a purse and hurry off to the butcher. She brings home a sparrow. Often I have seen her leap into the room with the dead fan of a bird in her mouth, its spread wings stiff before her, its pale beak frozen open, not in song but in horror. And quietly she finishes it all, except the feathers, and they float away, to be uncovered only on my rare cleaning expeditions under the rug, behind the breadbox, in the bed—frail reminders that the appetite is stronger than the aesthetic.

Ah, if only human beings could accept themselves as does my Kitty!

My Kitty? Not really; no one's Kitty, after all, certainly not her own, for she is merely a shape in space driven by desires to keep that shape in space and duplicate it; and so for a while she may be *my* Kitty, or when in the circle of a tom, *his* Kitty. Never is she her own; for she, within, is pressure and drive and compulsion: no more. Only without does she exist at all—and that is all she ever bothers with.

But now Kitty, or the part of her that calls for the night, meowed, and I opened the window; presently she went out, down the awning and the ledge, to her place on the walk. I turned away and straightened the unmade bed. I am not much given to tending house so, on most days, everything is a mess. Along the kitchen floor all the pots of the past week sit uncleaned and filled with water. The dishes too are cruddy (except where Kitty has licked them) and piled high in the sink like two ultra-modern bell towers leaning toward each other.

I opened a can of fruit salad and ate it slowly, looking through an old magazine. Afterwards I undressed, turned off all the lights and climbed into bed. It was then, with my eyes closed, that the boy's face returned to me, but its features were unnatural, caricatured, uncontrollable, the way it is when, attempting to fall asleep, one tries to fix something in one's mind. I could not grasp his face any more than I can force the sheep to jump the hedge when I am trying to count them.

I believe I fell asleep for a moment, but whatever it was, my mind suddenly relaxed and a face, not distorted or unclear, came back to me. It was a face altogether different from the one I had seen a few minutes before in the park, and yet I was absolutely certain it belonged to the same person for, while the notebooks under the arm were gone, the clothes were the same. I surprised myself with this realization and, disturbed, sat up in bed, switched the lamp on, and lit a cigarette.

A gentle heavy breeze shrugged through the window, calming me. And, sitting this way, I thought a long time about the disagreeable young man named Mark.

5

Now a funeral parlor is apparently a place of wonder to most people, because those pedestrians who do not ignore us fearfully as they rush by, stop before the store and gaze within, their rounded eyes wandering over the benches and potted palms and myself as if the furnishings and I had been displayed like freaks or waxworks expressly for their examination. And there is always a stupid detached curiosity or an unbelieving laughter in their faces—the curiosity and laughter one shows when viewing goods one expects never to buy or even to make use of. So, however often I notice people at the window, I look up impulsively, then back, and exhibit a lack of interest in direct proportion to the intensity of their curiosity.

Therefore I cannot say exactly when I singled Mark's

face out of the others. Although it was a slow process like a faint sigh that succeeds in being heard over the scream of traffic only because it persists, endures, I am certain there must have been a specific moment last summer when, looking up, I became aware that the boy with the tight tan jacket and the notebooks under his arm had been coming every afternoon to stare through the window. I could never tell at what he gazed: perhaps the heavy ledger on my desk, perhaps the picture of Jesus Christ on the wall behind me, for his dark deep-set eyes, long and intense and veiled with a shadow of lashes, seemed to regard not me but something near or beside me. And the expression in his face was not one of distance or humor, but rather consideration, as if at any time he might come in to price an article, make an arrangement.

But he did not—at least, that week or two I accustomed myself to his appearance each sun-dazzled afternoon. He would merely stand a while, staring into the store, and when I thought him most inclined to come in, he would turn and start rapidly across the street—with a little skip in his walk, favoring one leg—and either vanish round the corner or climb the wide gray steps of the ugly church opposite. Finally, one cool sunless day, I decided to speak to him.

He had been standing in front longer than usual, and I was becoming impatient. Lifting myself from behind the desk I started to the door, but he saw me, and by the time I had got outside, on the walk, he had already crossed the street and gone into the church. Though it was too cool for rain, the swollen clouds had turned dark pearl and solid; from a great distance I could hear a low rumble of thunder like the settling of earth. And I waited. It was a quarter of an hour before the boy came out again; eyes fixed forward, he walked in that quick jumpy way toward the corner.

Annoyed and unreasonable, I called, "Hey, you! Hey, there!" But he seemed not to hear me for, hurrying to the end of the block, he disappeared.

The next day rain fell and so I did not really expect him to pass, but nevertheless I waited all afternoon, my eyes moving over the rain-battered street, and I was slightly disturbed when the long black procession turned the corner from our chapel and rolled past the store blocking my view of the opposite side of the road. The day after that, except for an occasional drizzle that rapped suddenly against the walks, the sky was clear—but he did not come: I half suspected that, having acted upon his visits, I might not see him again. It is unlike me to be long anxious and, although this happened a year ago, I remember clearly as I watched the street that day, my interest was already weaker.

I am not in any way superstitious, nor am I concerned with what are known vaguely as *mysteries*: a riddle which cannot be solved quickly is one I will never trouble to solve at all, and had the boy failed to reappear within the next few days he would have gone out of my mind more quickly than he had entered it. Just once have I played with puzzles over a long period and that was ten years ago when Emily began a collection of clippings from newspapers and magazines— recent stories, touched with the supernatural, that were insoluble: the charred remains of a woman sitting in an unsinged chair, her apartment door locked from within; a ghost that moved furniture and soiled a spinster's bed by emptying a chamber pot upon it; a boy cured of brain tumor after being visited by John the Baptist's head; a Canadian farmer who had sunlight on his property while it was midnight in the world around; etc. I was in the army at the time and when Emily would write me of her latest item my pleasure would be to seek out, sometimes weeks later and in obscure places, the solutions to her insoluble clippings. Only one I could not find; I cannot now even recall which, although for a while I was as determined about my collection as she hers. I know that I did, finally, discover the article refuting hers, and I cut it out and sent it to Wallace, for Emily had just then, after four years' indecision—and only because Wallace intended never to go back to Chicago—moved to New York. Neither of them wrote of receiving it, and it was only recently I learned he never gave it to her. But it doesn't matter, for her hobby is long forgotten.

On the third day there was no rain, and the sky that first dry morning was a white blaze that folded stiff as meringue over the motionless yellow air; but the afternoon, released, went limp and humid and seeped under my office door to make everything soggy and unbearable. In my discomfort I spent most of the day in the white chamber, rarely thinking of the boy, and gave myself to the never-varying atmosphere, the cool dry restful constancy of mild refrigeration. At one point, having sat an hour thumbing the pages of an *art* magazine, I heard the tinny clink of the bell over the outside door, and going back to the office I saw, although the door was closed and no one had entered, that the boy was staring in at me through the window. Watching me closely his head was bent toward the right as if he had been trying to see behind the oaken door before I had shoved it closed. Our eyes caught, almost audibly snapping with the contact, and we gazed intently at one another until, breaking my glance, I crossed to the door and pulled it open: I had been too quick and only now did he turn abruptly and start away.

"Oh, just a minute, please," I called gently.

He paused and looked back, his thin dark face suddenly long with surprise as if I could not possibly be calling him.

"May I speak to you?" I said.

"I guess so," he shrugged, coming back slowly. He was about average height but appeared much shorter because of his narrow structure, and his hard angular body wore the tight tan jacket and gray trousers with a kind shabby indifference, denying any connection with rubbed-away elbows and knees. In his face there was something inconstant, more transient even than the baffled look of adolescence.

He shifted his notebooks from one hand to the other and kept his eyes lowered. "I hope you're not annoyed," he began timidly, "that I've been looking into . . ." He indicated my office with a quick gesture.

"No, not at all. I just wondered what it was that interested you. I've seen you stop by so many times. And you *did* start to come in now, didn't you?"

"Oh, no! That wasn't me."

Both of us looked up and down the empty street, and the boy smiled. "I . . . I'm awfully sorry. I wanted to . . . but then I thought . . ." Tilting his chin up, he drew his forehead reflectively. "Do you think it would be possible for me to come in?"

"Sure, if you want to. Everyone's welcome." I laughed but he was so unamused I wondered if he'd heard me. Apparently he had, for he turned at once and entered the store.

Following him in I closed the door behind us. He watched uncertainly, fear or suspicion tightening his face, until I seated myself upon the desk: then he relaxed. Like a child in a marvelous place his eyes circled the room slowly, resting a moment upon the urns, then upon the stale potted palms, then the oaken door, and at last upon the faded print of Jesus Christ where they remained. His lips moved faintly, not trembling exactly but as if he were murmuring something to himself.

"Do you know who that is?" I asked.

"Of course I do," he responded in a quick incredulous whisper; but when he looked at me he smiled crookedly, his face becoming awkward with the effort. "I didn't realize you were joking."

"Are you religious?"

"Not specially. I believe in God, if that's what you mean —but then I believe in everything."

"I saw you going across the street a few times."

"Oh. . . . Well, I go to church a lot, but more for the atmosphere than to pray." His words came out with a slow loud breath like a thick sigh, as though something fragile or holy were tumbling out and the breath eased the shock of its fall.

"One can learn from a church," he continued. "One can learn from anything. What can you tell me about death?" Recalling the way he said this there seems to be something disconnected and comic about the question; yet when he posed it to me it was so natural and so logical that I actually stopped to consider what I did know about death.

"Well, the body decomposes——"

"Yes, I know that. But what *happens* to it, I mean."

"To be honest," I said, recovering myself, "I'm not at all interested in speculating on things I haven't experienced. But from what I've been able to observe with others I'd say that the mind and body stop functioning and the dead individual is aware of nothing, not even himself."

My answer obviously relaxed him and, dropping his notebooks to the desk, he strolled slowly round the office and touched things. "I like the way you say it. You see, I hardly know anything about death, and I want to know a lot. I've never even seen a . . . body. I mean my parents died: but they drowned and they were lost. I want to know what *happens*, and maybe here——"

"Nothing happens here. All we do——"

"I thought there might be something in the air that would give me a clue. It's all so mysterious." Pausing he took a deep breath, attempting, I suppose, to inhale some of the mystery; as I watched I recalled Mr. Trevor's order that all employees except myself exit through the chapel to avoid the dissemination of professional odors.

"You couldn't have found very much in the air," I said, "standing *out*side the store."

"I wanted to come in. I started to today, but I was

ashamed. I thought you'd think I was crazy, because after all, it's only idle curiosity."

"Is that all it is?"

"Yes." His voice was flat.

And although I felt he wanted more than a cursory sniffing into the corners of the dead, I only shrugged. "Well, if you want, I'll show you around."

"That's kind of you. Do you own the ... business?"

"No, I only manage it. Mr. Trevor is the owner, but he's always uptown getting ready to open a new branch."

"What's he like—Mr. Trevor?"

I could see he wanted a detailed answer, or anyway a morbid one, for his face had the half-excited look of faces that expect to be terrified.

"He's a hypocrite."

"Is that all?"

"No, but he's mostly that. If you'd meet him you'd see what I mean. Well, do you want to look around?" I swung the oaken door open. "If you follow me through here, we'll come to the embalming room." Behind me, down the long dark passage, the sound of his heavy breathing was a quiet contrast with the sharp whistle of our clothes as we slid past the silver filing cabinets. Pushing through the steel door, I switched the light on: a frost of blue-white flooded the room and doubled its coldness. The boy's eyes shone and the black tumble of uncombed hair glistened fiercely, but his face went dull blue in the light. After a rapid survey of the room he moved toward the empty table in the center where he ran a finger or two across a corner as if testing its reality.

The back door, leading to the chapel, rattled open and Frank came in wearing his hat, his red cheeks puffed over his eyes. In each hand he clutched a handkerchief and, patting himself, he regarded us a long time through sweat-beaded lashes before he spoke. Unable at first to decide upon a reaction, he ground his teeth ambiguously, but realizing that the boy, a stranger, had intruded into his workshop, he settled his mind on anger.

"What's going on here?" Fury blossomed in his face and ears. "Mr. Sutton, I'd like to know why you go ahead——"

"Don't yell so, Frank. You'll wake the dead." But my remark touched neither of them, least of all the boy, who, eyes lowered, was terrified.

"I want an explanation, Mr. Sutton. There's such a thing as privacy in places and——"

"All right: calm down. I'm showing this gentleman around the establishment. He's interested in death."

"Then he can go to the morgue. This ain't no place for tourists. I'm sick and tired of the way you think it's a big joke here. Some respect is what they deserve, you know."

Turning, the boy appealed to me and gestured toward the door. "No," I said, and then to Frank, "Look, go around the corner to Rebecca's and buy yourself a beer. There's nothing to do anyway."

"But what about . . . ?" He shook both handkerchiefs in the direction of the three large drawers in the white wall.

"I'll see he waits till you get back."

Nodding doubtfully he left, closing the door behind him. The boy, staring at the wall that Frank had indicated, whispered, "What is it?"

"Here, I'll show you." But I think he guessed its nature for he drew back suddenly, then forced himself forward, bent his head, and watched as I pulled the bottom drawer open. As his eyes traveled across the body I thought he might faint, for his face greened and his fingers twitched like sputters of flame. The dry old head of the man lying in the drawer was lined with a fine network of cracks like an ancient leather mask; his eyelids and cheeks had slumped deep into his skull as if, at the instant of death, all the air had been drawn from him and his face had collapsed.

"Who is he?" asked the boy.

"I forget his name."

He clicked his tongue. "Poor man! Lying in a cold drawer in a strange place, and *you*"—he accused—"don't even know his name."

"It doesn't matter. I don't know yours either."

Nodding unhappily, the boy's lips quivered as they had in my office; I supposed he was saying something to himself or perhaps offering his sympathy and his heart to the thing below us.

"I often think about the soul," he said quietly. "But I don't know what it is. I used to believe that when the body died, the soul still went on existing somewhere. Now I don't know. Now I think maybe the soul can die before the body. Is that possible?"

I thought at first the question was rhetorical, but then he looked up at me, waiting for an answer. "I couldn't tell you," I said.

"Has it ever happened that you buried a soul without a body?" He smiled, and I began to suspect that all his senselessness was just a ruse to see how far my patience might be dragged.

"No," I said aggressively. "Bodies and souls come in here together; occasionally we get bodies without souls, but never to my knowledge have we arranged for the refrigeration and embalming of the soul alone. Nor," I added seeing his stunned eyes, "would we ever take the trouble to decorate the chapel, sweep the hearse, or dig a hole for the purpose of depositing the kind of nonsense that exists only in childishly silly imaginations like yours."

Bewildered by my loss of temper, the boy remained speechless, his eyes fluttering from the drawer to the wall to myself, unsure where they might rest safely. His narrow shoulders stooping and his small head turning pitifully away, I regretted my outburst. "I'm sorry if I offended you, but you see, in this profession"—I heard myself repeating Mr. Trevor's words—"one becomes hardened." I was lying, of course; it had nothing to do with *this profession*; there has never been a period in my life when I could tolerate frank idiocy.

"That's all right," he murmured glumly. "I know it sounds funny when I talk that way. . . ."

He turned to the drawer and shuffled uncomfortably from one foot to the other; I imagine he was trying to be polite by gazing intently at the cadaver. Finally I shoved the drawer closed and offered the boy a cigarette; then I suggested he come into the chapel.

There he was more at ease, less fearful, less tense, in fact, brazen in the familiar way he strolled round the room peering at the fraying kakemonoes ("Oh, *paper*," he said, his finger sliding down an edge), tracing lines in the unpatterned mosaic of the stained-glass windows and, in order to better study the altar, squatting below it on the spot where the coffin usually rests. I informed him of his location and he laughed apologetically but said nothing, as if afraid he might anger me again. At last I became impatient with the excursion.

"We'd better go out front," I told him.

Damp heat pervaded the office, and from my desk I withdrew the bottle of warm lemonade.

"Do you want some?"

"No, thanks . . . I think I'll have to be going."

"Oh," I said.

He took both notebooks from the desktop.

"Are you a student?" I asked.

"No. I write poems. Would you like to read some?"

"I don't care very much for poetry."

"They're not such good poems now, but beauty is all inside me. It's just a question of letting it take hold of me—and then do you know what will happen?"

"No," I said.

"I'll become another being: the Poet: the beautiful spirit."

The pleasure he took from this notion was so expansive I felt certain he expected me to applaud; instead I busied myself with more lemonade.

"That's why I believe in everything, because I believe in myself, in my potential. So everything for me is potential—there's nothing in life not to believe in." He then began to repeat all he had said, but suddenly his voice weakened and he finished stonily, without enthusiasm. "But maybe not," he sighed. "Maybe not. . . . Do you think I might come in again?"

"If you want. Are you in the neighborhood a lot?"

"Yes. I live nearby, on Crawford Street. Well, I guess I'd better be going." He backed toward the door. "Thanks very much for showing me around, Mr. . . ."

"Harry Sutton."

"My name is Mark."

Making a slight peculiar bowing motion, as if bending with a cramp, he swung round and opened the door. Outside, eyes narrowed, he observed the bright hot street a moment before starting his rapid broken walk in the direction of the church.

6

After that he began to visit me every other day in the middle of the afternoon when the heat was worst and my mind and body soggiest and most discomforted. Mark would enter with his soft medieval brain, which I sometimes felt he must have disimmured from a thirteenth-century tomb, and begin his speeches.

Astonishment is something I very rarely experience, perhaps because I have always been aware that order of life is dependent only on irregularities, that once you know you can anticipate nothing, you anticipate everything. If I were otherwise I might have been frequently startled by Mark's behavior, especially his entrances, which were now frightened, now unhappy, but most often inexplicably furious, as if it were at someone else's insistence that he rattled the door open and presented himself. But the moods in which he arrived lasted only until I greeted him, and then—shyness having disappeared during his original visit—he would reveal a continued interest in death, a solemn horror of all ideas that did not agree with his own, and an irritating persistence.

He showed his persistence first in his determination to witness an embalming.

"Nope, nope!" was Frank's reaction to the proposal. "It wasn't proper of you last time coming in that way and all without thinking to ask my permission."

"I would have asked you," said Mark, "but Mr. Sutton didn't tell me I had to."

"Mr. Sutton! Just like him."

"Couldn't I? Only for a——"

"Nope."

After a half-hour of flattery and respect, however, Frank came round and, during the embalming, found the boy's attitude so correct that he said it would be a pleasure to have Mark in his workshop whenever it was convenient to both and "as long as the boss don't hear about it because he wouldn't like it much."

So Mark's calls were generally divided between my office and the white chamber.

"I'm learning both the practical and philosophical sides of death," he said emptily, for if there is a philosophy to be taught, I do not know it, and even if I did, it would have stayed with me because the more Mark came, the less I cared to see him, and by his fourth visit I was adding only discouraging critical comments to his knowledge. He needed nothing else to carry on a conversation.

It is not strange that he continued to speak to me when I was so openly antagonistic or, at mildest, bored, for in his soft, vague, medieval way he found me fascinating not only because of my association with death but because, contrary to him, I did not interest myself in pondering abstractions of any kind. I find that I often attract—not necessarily in an active way—the very religious and those devoted to causes and beliefs: atheists and unattached people always do, just as the unturned field attracts the farmer. It must somehow soothe the zealot to know where, when he wants to, his challenge may be thrown. I have been acquainted with five or six fanatics; the last one was several months ago—a nervous young priest named Tulley, who had one eye of clear blue glass like a window in his head and the thinnest mouth I've ever seen, as if between nose and chin lay only a faint lipless slit.

Tulley and I had met professionally: at the funeral of his cousin, a young man for whom he was conducting a final prayer. Long, rather than tall, his body seemed inseparable from that shiny black suit, which ended abruptly at the white collar. And his head, detached, revolving, pale, had one single expression on its face, an expression which, in the following weeks, I came to believe was the only one he knew to make. It was like his movements: at once sharp, harried, irate, pathetic. It was that way at his cousin's funeral as, half-concealed behind a thin mound of flowers, he muttered his Latin songs; it was that way in the first weeks of our relationship when he talked of nothing but the benefits that faith would bring to my life. Afterwards I learned this was not Tulley's only face; the others were revealed gradually, in the course of friendship.

He would come over in the early evening while I was still at work, go directly up to my flat (the door is never locked), and relax while smoking expensive Turkish cigarettes. When we had known each other almost a month, he relaxed even further by drinking whiskey-glasses of gin. When I joined him we would drink together and I would watch his curious mouth clapping out a view, no longer only on faith, but on everything. In many ways he ignored church dogma—the very dogma he had nervously erupted at me a week or two before—but he seemed never to be aware of this except insofar as it might inconvenience him were it to be generally known. And so he would go on talking until his ideas floated away upon the stream of gin and his words blurred together and his tongue became too thick to move easily in the trap-like mouth; then he would say it was late and he must go. Our evenings together ended the time I came upstairs and saw him lying on my bed, his blue glass eye accentuated by the stretch of white flesh below it.

"Please, Harry," he kept repeating, each time more sadly, his face twisted miserably. "Be gentle and good to your father."

"Why don't you get dressed and have a drink, Tulley?"

"Oh, Harry. There is so much you have no knowledge of in this world."

"There are some things I'm just not interested in learning."

"It is cruelty and hardness."

"I don't want to." And I sat down to wait.

Not moving from the bed he wept heartily, the thick tears rolling out of one eye, down one cheek; the other eye expressionless, neither happy nor unhappy. The crying stopped suddenly and, muttering the word "Nevertheless," Tulley left the bed and dressed; he called me a heathen for a while and explained what would happen to me when I died. Then he went away and did not come back. As I am altogether ignorant about the clergy, I might have been more surprised at Tulley than I was, but years ago Wallace told me that such things are very common among priests, and the closest they come to being unfrocked for it is by one another. Wallace apparently knows everything about ecclesiastics. He mentioned once that each monk has beside his bed a small black sink into which he masturbates. I told this to Mark one afternoon, I remember, after he had talked of the heroism of those who purge all thoughts of physical gratification from their heads.

He turned completely red. "That's mean!" he said, his mouth barely opening. "It isn't true."

"I didn't say it was. It's just what I've been told."

"All those stories about monks and nuns are lies. And do you know who make them up? People who have nothing to live for, who can't believe in themselves or anything else: that's who. I don't say it's evil to have thoughts about the body and to . . ." Pausing, he shook his head until the correct word fell to his lips. "And to desire. But some believe in purity, and if they believe in anything that strongly it's noble to devote their lives to it, even though others who are jealous will gossip and make up lies. Don't you think so?"

"It doesn't matter."

Perhaps he was not, as he had said, especially religious, but he believed in God as he believed in everything else: as a kind of mystery. For not only did death puzzle him but also life, this earth, the sky, himself, and everyone around him. Mystic unscalable walls were these to him: and all were within his mind as ribboned, golden, evanescent confusion—over which presided the greatest confusion of all: the beautiful Poet: the force that drove Mark through life, that pushed his curiosity into places he was otherwise too shy to enter. For this Poet was an inhuman quantity, like a slowly dissolving vitamin tablet embedded in his stomach, which added to his constitution and which would eventually take it over: the part would swallow the whole. And *then*, the ribbons, the gold, the evanescence would be no longer confusion but would become explicit order and brighten the universe. Most of the time I think he really believed this, but once in a while he talked of it weakly, mechanically, without any conviction, as if the vitamin tablet had turned to stone and caused him nothing more than heartburn and, beneath the guilty superficial effort to keep it down, he would much rather have vomited it away. But these moods never lasted long although it was only during them that I said anything serious to him.

"The trouble with you," I told him one day when he was not convincing either of us, "is that you look at things crookedly. You make everything up. Why don't you walk up to life from the front, look at it, and take it for what it is?"

"But then there'd be no beauty," he cried, jumping on my statement before I'd heard it finished; and I knew I had caught him too late. Shrugging, I leaned my chair back on two legs and stared beyond him through the window. "Imagine, Mr. Sutton, that there's a crowded city built on a hill, and at the very top of the hill is a beautiful building, say a cathedral." His thin shoulders drew up and blocked my view to the outside. "And there are a lot of ways to get up to the cathedral: there's a large straight road in front, there are a couple of good roads at the sides, and there's even a modern way: an elevator that lifts you up the hill for a few cents. But in the back are dozens of dark little streets, complicated passages, twisting and mysterious and gloomy, and if you follow them you see all sides of the cathedral, the whole building before you reach the top: just as it ought to be seen. The other roads only give you one part to look at." He closed his eyes and murmured: "So many ways up, just as there are so many ways to heaven. But I wonder if heaven has such a cheap lift."

"I think it would be most sensible to take the elevator," I said. "And when you've reached the top, you can look around if you'd like."

But he had not heard me for, smiling anxiously, he continued: "Do you understand now what I'm trying to say—why I can't look at the world directly?"

I decided not to reply.

"Do you?" he pursued.

"It really doesn't matter whether I do or not."

"Why do you always say that?"

"Say what?"

"That it doesn't matter."

"When did I say it before?"

"The other day when I was talking about monks and nuns and I said that if people felt strongly——"

"Well, in that case it doesn't matter. If a man wants to spend his life in a monastery, there's no point making any more fuss about it than if he spends it in a grocery or a funeral parlor."

"I didn't mean in that case," he insisted, edging at me like a mosquito. "You're always saying it. Why?"

"I suppose," I said, my tone sharpening, "that I say *it doesn't matter* because most things don't!"

Always momentarily silenced when a shade of anger came into my voice, he moved his slight behind upon the plush bench. Then he crossed his legs, put an elbow on his knee, and rested his chin upon the palm of his hand. "I don't know," he mumbled to his fingers, his head shaking sadly. "Everything matters; everything has its meaning, its significance . . ."

He went on from there I suppose but I cannot remember; most likely I leaned back still further or lit a cigarette or sipped some warm lemonade, my eyes resting sleepily upon the silent street and Mark's gentle but interminable voice oozing through the quiet without interrupting it. Those frequent visits during the two weeks I knew him are as vague and indefinite in my head as his notions were in his. Each soliloquy I listened to or entered in upon is now inextricably entangled with the next and my memories are jagged and ill fitting. He cared about nothing really but his Poet, who would, he knew, some day take him over, and I would think the change in his face that I saw tonight was that of the final overtaking—but it cannot be. It is all silliness and idleness, the inability of the human being to reconcile himself to what he is. And even if it were the face of the Poet upon him, it would be very sad for Mark, for this face is not one of beauty or order, but of greater plainness than his own, and of emptiness, a full ripe vacuity of expression such as I saw on him at our last talk.

He had several times mentioned an interest in meeting Mr. Trevor, who he felt must be a much more formidable agent or associate of death than I. Yet, despite Mark's many visits, they did not meet until that last miserable afternoon in August when, while the boy spoke to me, I failed to notice the smooth black Packard draw up and park before the church. In fact only when the car door slammed and the squat, formally dressed man started across the street did I lean forward and say, "Here's your chance. The boss is coming."

Mark's eyes spread with terror and they did not turn from me. Through the glass door I saw Mr. Trevor's smiling face float upon the walk; at the window, his hand lifted to shade the sun from his eyes and lessen the glare as he peered within. After gazing for some time at each of us, he opened the door, the smile gone from his face, replaced by his standard interpretation of profound sympathy. He assumed Mark was a client.

Padding slowly across the room, he nodded and, reaching me, rested his hand upon my shoulder and asked, "Everything in order, Harry?" His small green eyes wobbled to the side and took a quick sharp look at Mark, whose head was now lowered.

"Yes," I said, bending out of his hold.

"And Frank? Is he in the inner office?"

"I suppose so. Business has been pretty slow lately."

He contorted his face to pantomime the instruction that I was to speak more carefully in the presence of the bereaved. Then he turned to Mark who, for the first time, had lifted his eyes. Mr. Trevor nodded slowly, deeply, his head sagging with wisdom, a sad but comforting, invulnerable wisdom. "Yes, young man," he sighed. "It must come to all of us sooner or later." Mark's shoulders jerked back violently and his face went absolutely white. "It knows not age nor previous engagement, this grim thing that takes our loved ones. I've gone through it several times; so has my assistant. And think how much worse it is for us; we earn our bread from these misfortunes; our children are fed on your bereavements. Can you imagine how tasteless our meals must be, how difficult it must be for us to swallow? Yes, young man, the world is a funny place."

Eyes fixed on the floor, Mark's head trembled in short rapid nods, hardly visible, as if on springs. One might have thought Mr. Trevor knew more about the situation than I, for the boy's face, no longer the startling sudden white, had a more even, a more permanent-looking paleness such as is found on mourners and other individuals who brood extensively upon things unpleasant to themselves.

"I'll go in and see how Frank is doing," Mr. Trevor said softly, and, on tiptoes, swung open the large oaken door and vanished behind it. A moment later he reappeared, whispering "Harry, may I see you?"

"Sure."

In the corridor his thick body was a wide indefinite form relieved, in the dimness, by the silver-pearl glow of his gray tie.

"Harry, I've been meaning to ask you about certain accounts that seem to be delayed in payment. I don't remember all the names of course, but some of them I think . . . There's Marconi and Graetz and those two Puerto Rican families with the same name and . . ." He continued to carelessly identify every backward account; I could imagine the delight that rolled in his disgusting little eyes, and as he spoke I heard a tight confident smile shape his words—obviously trying to bewilder me with information that seemed impossible for him to have. I assumed he came round from time to time during my lunch hour. (Later on I found I was correct, for I began locking the files whenever I left the office. It took two months before he made a point of it.) "I don't think you ought to let us fall so far behind. You know it gets progressively more difficult to pick up if we're not firm. Especially with these foreigners . . ."

The steel door of the embalming room clanked open and a wave of blue-white cold rushed over us. Frank stood in the doorway, the remnants of a smile fading from his mouth. "Oh, I thought," he said.

Nodding to him, Mr. Trevor went on. "You'll try to keep more up-to-date in the future, won't you, Harry?"

"Yes."

"That's a good fellow." He reached up and patted my shoulder.

When I returned to the office the pallor had left Mark's face, and it was then I saw the expression of emptiness in it: not merely the lack of emotion, but total blankness as a positive thing.

"What do you think he meant?" the boy asked.

"He didn't mean anything. He only——"

"But he must have. The way he went on...."

"He thought you were a customer and he was pulling his routine. I told you he's a hypocrite."

Turning to the picture of Jesus Christ, his lips trembled, but he was silent and did not change his position until Mr. Trevor emerged from the corridor, then he lowered his eyes, the pointed chin still tilted upwards.

"Everything seems to be running smoothly," said Mr. Trevor sadly. "I'll be getting on now, Harry. You won't forget the little matter we discussed in the inner office?"

"No."

He touched Mark's arm. "Can I drop you anywhere? My car's just outside."

The boy did not move, and Mr. Trevor continued to stare at him expectantly. Struck by the peculiar picture they made, I laughed aloud and Mr. Trevor, dropping his hand, frowned. His mouth twitched as he said, "I'll see you in a day or two, Harry." And, without turning to Mark, he added, "Good afternoon, young man. You have my sympathy."

When he had left, I watched his dumpy figure strut to the other side of the street, where he scratched something off the windshield of his Packard before climbing in. Then the car drove off with smooth soundless grace.

"Well, what do you think of the terrible Mr. Trevor?"

He had not yet moved, and only when I repeated my question did he turn, as if having forgotten all about me, lift his notebooks from the bench, and go out the door into the street. His unequal pace gradually increasing its speed, he was almost running as he went up the wide steps into the church.

Although that was the last time he visited my office, I saw him now and again in the fall and winter, and once in early spring. Generally I noticed him on a subway platform, often waiting for the same train as I; I was always careful to take another carriage, for during none of these encounters did I want to speak to him.

Once, traveling uptown with Wallace, we saw him putting a penny into a gum machine just as we were riding out of the Fourteenth Street station. I was rather surprised when Wallace jumped from his seat, pounded on the window, and called the boy's name. It was too late, of course, but on that journey I learned for the first time that Wallace had also been briefly acquainted with Mark.

7

Always, on my way to Tess, the world falls away; what surrounds me vanishes and reality is shaped by a concentrated drive. My eyes cataract with the texture and shades of her body, my ears clog with grunts and pulsations, and the walk beneath me yields to my step like a carpet of flesh. Now and then, going toward her place, I become aware of my cold fists opening and closing, damp with anticipation, my fingertips raw and tender and alive to anything they touch: the silk of her thighs, the sponge of her nipples, the moist, the dry, the cool, the hot, the everything. And when I have come to the building, not knowing how I have got here or how long it has taken, and have climbed the stairs slowly, my breath snagged as I stand before her door, my senses are already spent from desire, exhausted by memory and need.

Between the croak of the buzzer that rings me into the littered lobby and the *puff-puff* sound of her shoeless feet as she comes to the door, there is a moment when senses are asleep, when I remember with relief that it is Tess I am facing—Tess who is sloppy with clothes and sloppy with words, whose apartment is cluttered with underwear and incomplete sentences, who likes to eat and laugh and dress up and undress, and who never talks about afterwards, after the ooze, after we have lit our cigarettes and rolled apart to opposite sides of the world.

A surprised but full smile broadens her round face as she opens the door, and the thick bright lipsticked mouth sags a little with the weight of her pleasure. Her gleaming black hair, usually long, has been tossed up and stacked high on her head where it is held in place by a small tortoiseshell dagger.

"Harry! Jesus, I was just thinking about you." Closing the door behind me, she turns her chin up to swallow my kiss. This is no ordinary kiss of greeting but one tentatively passionate, which does not go through the heart but rather down the throat and the hot cave of the belly. Pushing apart, she grumbles, "Hell, you should've phoned me. I told Madeline I'd be . . . I guess I'll call her up and explain. You know Madeline? The blonde with the big nose." She puts her fingers to her face descriptively.

"No, I don't."

"You're not missing anything. Listen, I'll run down to the lobby and phone her. If you want to wait in the kitchen, there's some stuff on the table you can eat." Opening the door, she turns back. "Oh, say, Harry, give me a dime, huh?

My money's in the— Thanks, because I'd ..." With an indefinite wave of her hand she hurries into the corridor.

From the pink and yellow foyer I wander into the pale green kitchen where, upon the table, three or four brown paper bags have been torn open hastily, revealing pasty looking potato salad and cold meats and small decorated cakes that Tess has picked up at the delicatessen on her way home from work. On the stove the glass cap of a boiling percolator taps rapidly and a brown necklace of bubbles runs down one side of the pot. Turning the flame low I drag one of the chairs to the window and look down through the copper screening at the wide lot behind the house. Half a dozen children, their pale skins gold in the late sunlight, are gardening a few yards of deserted dump. One little girl with red hair and steel-framed glasses refuses to weed because no one else wants to plant roses; the rest, shoving her impatiently, are furiously convinced that onions and sweet potatoes will grow better.

"Onions stink," the little girl cries. "And sweet potatoes make me constipated."

"But you can't eat roses, can you?"

"Who says I can't? And even if I can't they smell nice and they look beautiful."

"How do you know they look beautiful? You can't see anything anyway, Four-eyes."

Four-eyes walks away from them to a corner of the lot and, in the angle of a broken wall, she lowers her panties, squats, and pees. Having finished, she returns to the others and continues the fight. It occurs to me that their argument has been going on for weeks and the fighting and arm waving will not be resolved tonight.

"They're cute, aren't they?" Tess has come quietly up behind me and put her hands on my shoulders.

"Do you think anything will grow?"

"Why not? The other day I heard them screaming something about lettuce coming up. Say, you should've heard Madeline, Harry. I told her I got my period and was going to bed, and she said, you just had your period last week, my God, I bet you have a man there. So I told her I'm very irregular because . . . Don't laugh, Harry. As a matter of fact I am, you know. Last year I went four months without . . . But then it came."

"Maybe you were pregnant."

"No, stupid. But I had a girlfriend once who was five months late and she went to so many doctors. They couldn't find anything wrong with her: *nerves*, they all said. I told her, listen here, Patricia, if you want my . . . Anyway, nervous or not, four months later she had a baby." Sailing her fingers through my hair, she kisses the tip of my ear and then goes to the table. "You eaten, Harry?"

"No, but I'm not hungry. You don't want to eat now, do you?"

"Sure I do." Smiling, she moves her head in a slow lazy circle. "I have to have a little energy. I guess you wouldn't like me if I got all dried up and there wasn't . . ." She gestures with her hands and curves her shoulders forward until her chest seems hollow and fleshless. "Anyway, just a sandwich. You sure you don't want one?"

I like the way Tess eats: she is not concerned with nutrition or social grace. Her large white teeth descend only on what tastes good, and she does not measure her bites. I have pulled my chair opposite her, and occasionally, infected by her appetite, I pick at a piece of meat or a cube of the potato salad. From below, the continuing scrap of the children rattles through the screening and, while Tess looks at me, she seems to be half-listening to the voices and with an air of seriousness weighing the arguments. Suddenly she jumps up, turns off the percolator, and looks out the window.

"Ah, for crying out loud, why don't you let her plant a couple of roses!" she bellows. There is silence below, and Tess leaves the window. "That won't stop them. They'll just go on like that. To hell with it!" She drinks a glass of water. "We'll have coffee later. Come on, let's go in the bedroom."

There, the pale walls are washed with orange sunset; her hair is released upon the sheet and glitters round her head like long star points, and a half-asleep look of excitement softens her face: she is waiting for me, for anyone. The open windows are striped by the elevated in the distance and now and then the roar of the train makes the building tremble.

We should not be here.

We should be upon rough damp earth, under a tree, near a river, in a jungle, covered with mud and mosquitoes, flushed beneath a screaming sky. We should be unaware of the special sensitivities of each other's body—the lips, the eyelids, the raw delicate flesh—and discover them by accident not by memory, in the hurry-frantic race for our own pleasure. Lust is made by selfishness and in discomfort in swamps, in marshes, where everything adds and disappears, in our crawling rush to glide away from ourselves into the flushest swampiest part of ourselves into a motion of slipping and losing. And pressing closer I am pulled further away, past the suffocating scratch of the jungle, above and insensitive, hung by a chain atop myself, wriggling to descend yet raving to be tugged higher.

Then swoop and gulp and loop-de-loop of falling to no more. The chain has shocked and snapped and all is over.

I am here: toppled back into myself: and slowly, gradually, sluggishly, all surfaces are defined—and we, Tess and I, are drenched with sweat.

The sun has almost disappeared and the orange walls are hushed with violet. A network of shadows folds into the wrinkles of the sheet, and as the room darkens Tess's damp belly glistens. She opens her eyes and smiles and it is only then I can see her mouth for it has been twisted crazily by the paint that streaks to her nose, her cheeks, her jaw. "It was nice," she says contentedly and strokes my thigh. Climbing from the bed her long legs take large strides to the dresser where she finds a package of cigarettes.

"Here." She thrusts one into my mouth and lies down again beside me. For a while we smoke quietly, readjusting ourselves to the bed in the bedroom in the city, and then she begins to talk, mostly gossip about the girls and salesmen in her office. She is apparently the plumpest fruit on the office grapevine for all news travels through her; and although she is incapable of keeping anything to herself, no one seems to mind. "I like most everybody," she often says to me. "But I can't see any harm in exchanging interesting stories about them with other people."

"Did I ever tell you about Max Turnip?" she is saying. "He's the fattest thing you ever saw and he's at least sixty—but is he crazy about girls! You would die, I swear, to look at the way ... Every month he comes in with a new stock of women's hats and he's always trying them on for us. If you ever saw him in a cloche! Oh, you know, he gave me a hat as a present last Friday. I've got to show it to you. And he gave me a necklace with a cross on it—with fake rubies."

"Why did he give you that?"

"I don't know. He gave them to all the girls, even the Jewish ones; he's a little nutty, but he has his serious side. I told him I didn't go in much for wearing crosses and he said, 'What, Tess, don't you believe?' So I told him no. But then, I don't know." She leaps once more from the bed. "Say, don't you want to see the hat?" Swinging the wardrobe door open, she reaches her arm up until a hatbox shakes from the top shelf. It tumbles to the floor, falls open, and a white and green corkscrew hat rolls toward the bed. "Dammit! Dammit! It'll get filthy and I haven't even ... Just wait until I put it on for you." Picking it up, she plunges it upon the back of her head. "Isn't it sweet?" But she is so comical standing naked at the foot of the bed with that long twisted thing curling out of her head that I cannot contain my laughter. "Oh, you men," she pouts. "What do you know about style?"

In the deepening blue light of the room she walks back

and forth before the triple-mirrored dressing table admiring and rearranging the hat.

"He's studying to be a lawyer," murmurs Tess, quietly, respectfully.

"Who is?"

"Max is. Max Turnip. What do you think of that? Isn't it marvelous that a man of sixty can ... Just imagine, after a hard day's work he comes home and reads law books. He gets them by mail, and are they hard to understand! But in six years he'll be a lawyer."

"Do you think he'll live to see the happy day?"

"Well, why not? And even if he doesn't ... It's always been his ambition, but he never had the time before. Now his wife's dead and his children are grown up. I think it's beautiful. Everybody at the office thinks it's beautiful."

"I think it's beautiful too."

"Oh, aren't you funny," she mutters, peeved, and sinks to the stool in front of the dressing table. Staring at me through the mirror, she says, "You're a louse, Harry. I don't mind telling you it would be a lot better if there were more people like Max. So what if he doesn't become a lawyer!" She swings round angrily and faces me. "It's better to want to be a lawyer than to be satisfied working in a funeral parlor all your life."

The connection between subjects is so tenuous that I begin to see her scraping at a resentment I had no idea existed. "And what's wrong with working in a funeral parlor?" I ask calmly.

"Hmmph!" is all she replies.

"Someone's got to bury the dead, so why not me?"

"I just don't like it, that's all. Oh, I know all right, Harry, that you keep coming around because I don't bother you. I give you what you want and you can go away free. But don't think you drop as clean out of my mind as I do out of yours. Maybe you think I'm a hoo-er; maybe that's what you think, that I'm a hoo-er." As if aware she has mispronounced the word, she rises indignantly and strolls through the room. Her flesh ripples as she walks; she is made for desire, for kneading, for penetrating. Her voice drops suddenly into a hoarse raucous bass. *"I'm getting' in tonight, boys. Gonna bang up Tess the hoo-er.* Well, I'll tell you what, Harry. You're the hoo-er, that's what. I guess you won't . . . Sure you wouldn't believe me, but you're the only man I sleep with."

"That's not true."

"Sure it's true. You think I'm so crazy for it that I'd . . . Oh, I don't care. Yes I do so care. I swear you're the only one."

"It doesn't matter, Tess."

She has stopped walking and stands now at the foot of the bed, her eyes lit with tears, the corkscrew hat rolling back of her head. Flinging the hat away, she grunts angrily, then grabs a chain from the dressing table.

"Here. I'll swear on sweet Max's cross. I swear that——"

"Cut it out, Tess. That's enough."

"What's the matter, Harry? Don't you like me to swear on a cross? You think I don't believe in it?"

"That's enough, Tess, that's enough!"

"Well, maybe I do after all," she persists. "Anyway I don't right away say no to everything around me." She comes to the edge of the bed, clutching the necklace in her hand, the rubies glittering black in the darkening room. And the way she holds it out to my face reminds me of the Vampire legends, how they were destroyed by being stabbed with a wooden cross. I can no longer recall how the argument started and I am annoyed because this kind of conversation has no place in the jungle: it has cut away the tangle of underbrush and cooled the sky.

"It's really true that you're the only one, Harry. Honest."

During the long silence that follows, Tess's round face lengthens unhappily and the tears continue to float in her eyes, but do not drop. "You're mad at me, aren't you, because I didn't mind my own business. Maybe you won't . . . I wish I kept my mouth shut. I'm sorry, Harry. Will you visit me again? Will you still come, Harry?" Her voice is soft and generous, her lust-voice without the lust-words.

"Sure I will, Tess. It doesn't matter," I whisper, pulling her down to me and kissing her while her long black hair falls like a curtain of night round our faces and exudes a cheap heavy odor of toilet water.

"Let's do it again," she says, lying down beside me.

All light has gone except for occasional flashes that flicker from passing trains, and as I bend over the silent motionless body, I become aware of the drumming of my heart, and I forget exactly who she is.

8

There was no sun this morning, or rather a purple-gray quilt of clouds kept it from shining, and so until noon the day was chill and breezy. From behind my desk I watched passers-by shake fretful heads at thick gusts of wind that scooped dust in their grim determined faces. Moved by the briskness in the air I felt like working, but there was nothing to do except type a couple of sympathy letters (bills enclosed) and file their smudged carbons in the cabinets pressed against the dark walls of the corridor behind the oaken door. So I spent some time round the corner at Rebecca's and had three beers and thought of Tess. But to think of her as I used to, within a single context, was impossible. They all eventually turn out the same way, for no woman can be satisfied with occupying only one area in a man's life. She will intrude, extend her influence, take it upon herself to fulfill other needs—whether the man has them or not—and so force him to look elsewhere for the thing he wants. Perhaps it is because in the artificial condition known as society a woman is ridiculed if she is simply a man's hoo-er or a man's friend: both functions must for some reason overlap. That, I suppose, is why Emily, who I have never really believed wants Wallace in bed, persists in giving the illusion. To her mind a frustrated woman is more respectable than an unambitious one.

I would have stayed at Rebecca's longer but three college boys came in, ordered Chartreuse, and began talking noisily about modern art. I left the bar and went back to the funeral parlor, entering by way of the chapel in order to talk a while with the men, then I went into the embalming room where Frank told me he also felt like working.

"Why don't you get a gun and drum up a little business," I suggested.

His dry staring eyes bulged with horror. "You're a funny fellow, Mr. Sutton." (He meant funny in the sense of odd, peculiar, as he rarely finds me droll.)

"As funny as anyone else," I said, offering him a cigarette, which he put behind his ear for afterwards.

He was quiet a moment, scratching his bald head genteelly with his little finger, then he asked me, "You don't take anything seriously, do you?"

"Sure I do. I take you seriously."

He looked at me with indecision, wondering whether I meant it. "I'm grateful for that," he said at last, and I could not help smiling; he became irritated. "See what I mean?

That's very bad, very bad. There are some things in life that one just shouldn't joke about."

"What, for instance?"

"Listen to me, Mr. Sutton; I'm a lot older than you are." He leaned forward confidentially. "And I know that life is a deadly serious thing. I know what kind of . . ."

I had turned my face away and so he stopped abruptly; when I looked back his lips were pursed and his head shook dismally like a priest dubiously appraising someone's soul.

"Say, Frank, do you remember Mark, the kid who——"

"I certainly do."

"I saw him the other night."

"Is that so? How was he?"

"I don't know. I didn't talk to him."

"Oh, that's too bad. Such a fine character. It was a genuine pleasure to have him here. No funny business about him: very respectful. You know, Mr. Sutton, he used to take the bodies to heart like each one was a relative."

He probably would have gone on describing Mark's virtues had I not interrupted him. "Got any new *art* books, Frank?"

His scalp blushed. "They're all up on the cabinet."

But I changed my mind and instead started to the door.

"Oh, I almost forgot, Mr. Sutton," said Frank. "The postman brought a package for you while you were out. I left it on your desk."

In my office I found the long thin box wrapped in green tissue paper. The return address was Craven Ties. I did not open it because I knew what it would look like and I knew whom it was from.

✦ ✦ ✦

After lunch a pale but constant sun heated away the wind, and the rest of the hot colorless day made me glad I had no work to do. At six o'clock I hung the *Please Phone* sign in the window; this would be removed later on by Samuel Pry, the old bowlegged attendant who takes my place (and Frank's as well) at night. Having locked the office I went next door to the staircase that leads up to my flat and, on the landing, Mrs. Collini, who has the apartment in the back, swept the floor, her little boy behind her leaning against the wall with a small bony finger in his nose. A flowered chintz housedress wound round her body like sausage casing; with every motion her breasts heaved against the dress, and when she leaned over, the glazed cloth caught between her buttocks and stretched across the balloon of their outline. For a few minutes she swept the corridor as if there would never be anything else for her to do, but then suddenly she looked up and saw me; she frowned and I went into my room.

Kitty's eyes drew open, regarded me vacantly as I walked into the kitchenette, and finally closed. The flat was still disordered, of course, so I steamed a can of sausage and beans and shared it with the cat, then I drank the last of the vermouth. Afterwards I went downstairs with the thought of going to Emily's, but because it was still so early, instead of walking directly over to Third Avenue, I turned north and strolled toward the park. Although the evening sky was clouded, the static air was warm and uncomfortable, and already people were beginning to fill the park. Crossing the street, I started into a side path and made my way to the bench where I had seen Mark the other night: this time two girls sat there staring into dim space, their fingers frantically peeling oranges. I nodded to them as I passed but they merely continued to gaze dumbly.

On a bench before the north railing I saw Wallace. Beside him sat an old beggar whose sleazy yellow beard was ripped in places and whose large furious eyes peered like separate living entities through the dead blue mask of his face. He was speaking with great seriousness and with great decision to Wallace and his toothless gums chomped down powerfully on each word as if it were a peanut. I decided to remain where I was for I am not interested in hoboes' conversations: round here they regard themselves as prophets or philosophers and I hate to give them money because they make me feel it is not charity but tuition. Wallace enjoys talking to them, but I find their conversation repetitious and broad; they speak in unrelated generalities as if, having themselves fallen into a general, unrelated division of mankind, they are no longer capable of anything specific. The old man shook his finger occasionally in evident warning, but aside from that he made no motion and his tight blue face never altered. Wallace, listening speechlessly, moved with excitement, his face responding constantly, the pale pugged features now vibrating with disagreement, now drawn in thought, now relaxed with laughter.

For about a quarter of an hour I leaned against a railing and watched them continue in the same way. But at last Wallace put something in the beggar's hand and the old man stood up stretching his arm out, dropping his palm on

Wallace's shoulder, obviously giving him some sort of benediction. Wallace smiled, shook his head, then seemed suddenly quite angry and jerked his shoulder in an attempt at release, but the beggar retained his grasp. Finally, with terrible impatience, Wallace shoved the man away and I heard him say, his words clear and exasperated, "No, I will *not* go, so will you please leave me alone? I won't be here, I promise you." His tight face still expressionless, the old man tugged at his ragged beard, the persistent scowl frozen in his eyes; he wagged a crooked finger reproachfully and turned away. When he had started down the path, I left the railing and walked to Wallace.

"Where did he want you to go?" I asked.

His sharply squinted gray eyes had been intently following the beggar through the park, so he jumped slightly when he heard my voice.

"Oh," he said, still frowning. "To the aquarium. He wanted me to meet him tomorrow for lunch, and then he would take me to the aquarium."

Unexpectedly his face widened and he burst into laughter. Wallace seldom remains angry for more than a few minutes and although I am aware of this it is always a surprise to see his passionately outraged face open into a smile of pleasure without any apparent reason.

"Why there of all places?" I asked.

"He's got some notion about fish. Really, what people will dream up! But never mind that. What are you doing wandering around parks at twilight, Harry Sutton?"

"I'm on my way to Emily's."

"This is the wrong way."

"I know. I thought I'd take a little walk first. Do you want to come along?"

"I can't," he said. "I've got an appointment at eight. Oh, damn, there he is again."

He nodded toward the end of the path where the fury-eyed old man had turned to stare at us.

"What's so important about going to the aquarium?"

"I won't tell you because you'll think it's crazy."

I said nothing and, after a moment, Wallace went on. "He believes fish are what people become when they die, and he claims to have a pile of evidence to prove it. Or, rather, *had* a pile of evidence: it's all been destroyed. He says that years ago he owned a goldfish that was Oscar Wilde. Did you ever think of Wilde being the goldfish type? Anyway, it died—and what became of it then? My old friend doesn't know. I suppose it's not a bad thing to think about if you believe you're going to be a whale or a shark; but what if you turn out to be a clam or a sardine or something like that?"

We looked up as the beggar walked by and paused a moment directly opposite us. When he started on his way again I noticed the slit cuffs of his baggy trousers trail behind him.

"He was so obstinate. 'You must talk to them,' he kept saying. 'They understand you.' So I told him they didn't seem very understanding last time."

"Last time?"

"I forgot to tell you," he laughed. "I went to the aquarium with him the other day. He wasn't as pushy then. He was so innocent and sincere that I suppose I was carried away.

And I thought, well, it's been so long since I had a good heart-to-heart talk with a herring."

"I think you're crazy," I said.

"I told you you would. But it was really fun. For fifteen solid minutes I confessed to a tank of tropical fish; they just looked at me blankly and blew bubbles, and they weren't nearly as interested in listening as were the old man and two fat school-teacher types who stood thunderstruck at my left. They were horrified, but they didn't leave until I was quite finished. The old man claimed it was their fault I had no results from the fish: they're supposed to respond and reply and make signals and do all kinds of things. But as I say they did nothing except twist their tails in my face and bubble. But it was interesting. You ought to go sometime, Harry."

"And confess?"

"That's you!" Wallace complained irritably. "You take everything so damn seriously."

"*Seriously?* You know I couldn't care less——"

"Yes, I know. But you're so serious about not caring less that you contradict your whole point of view. If an old beggar gets a kick out of telling dirty stories to a slew of lobsters and dreaming of the day he'll be floating among them, why the devil should it bother you?"

"It doesn't bother me. I just don't think it's as funny as you do."

Down another lane I saw the old man shuffle until he reached a bench. Seating himself, he stared over at us and then began to talk to the woman beside him.

"You know," I said, "I saw someone who might interest

you. The other night when I was coming back from your place I passed Mark, that pesty little——"

"Mark? Did you? Where?"

"He was sitting here in the park. But I didn't recognize him until I'd got home. His face was altogether different."

"What do you mean?" Wallace laughed. "Plastic surgery?"

"No. I suppose his features were the same, except that he looked kind of exploded. I can't explain. At first I thought he was dead."

"You would! I know, maybe he's become his Poet. No, I guess not."

He began to press me for details, but I could repeat only the little I had observed while passing the boy in the park, so eventually Wallace dropped into thoughtful silence. That was a good sign because generally when either of us mentions Mark, Wallace insists upon going over all we know about him—which is actually hardly anything.

The afternoon I learned he knew the boy, we rode the subway twice from Forty-second Street to Coney Island without leaving our seats because Wallace not only had to hear what I could tell but had his own story to relate.

"I used to see him over at the wharves on the Hudson," he had begun as the train chattered out of the tunnel onto rickety Brooklyn elevated lines that pass beside housetops, over busy streets, and through the winter-dead carnival of Coney Island. "I'll never understand what it is about ships that gets me; I've been on them so often now you'd think they'd lost their novelty. But they haven't. It's not only being aboard that excites me, it's even being near them or seeing them: especially in harbor on a white-hot summer day when the water is spraying up at you and a little way off a tramp or a liner is loading. I think the greatest thing man's ever done is the taking of the sea: it gave us the world. Just look at it, Harry." Beyond the blue-red plaster world of Luna Park, the boarded custard stands, the canvas-covered carousels, there was the flat gray stretch of ocean. "Here we are, land animals, and without natural equipment or mutation we've learned to live on and under the water.

"Anyway, last summer I used to go down to the quays very often. I'd spend an hour or so watching the boats, talking to the sailors, idling on the dock. A lot of people do it, you know, but nobody was as much a regular as I—except Mark, and although I saw him almost every time I came we didn't pay any attention to each other. That was at first before I noticed what a funny little character he was. He used to walk around with his chin raised a bit and his nose in the air as if sniffing something out. Sometimes he'd sit down, not far from me, wearing that old jacket even on the hottest days, and he'd open one of his notebooks, moisten a pencil on his tongue, and every few minutes jot something down. He was always interested in what was going on around him, but I don't think he cared very much to become involved with it. I remember that once in a while a sailor or a dock-worker would come over and talk to him; he would answer them politely, but it was plain he was happier when undisturbed. I suppose that's why I spoke to him first, just to discomfort him a little; but there was another reason. His writing was obviously some kind of imaginative work: even if only love letters. A boy of twenty-one—I'd guess that to be about his age—won't dawdle so dreamily over homework or a business account. He'll come out of the dream with a determined sigh if it's not a creative thing he's doing; but if it *is* he'll work in the dream—and that's the way it was with Mark. I felt it was wrong to be writing there; life is too advanced on a waterfront; you may be excited with what's going on but it's not elemental enough to internalize with. So one day when he was sitting not five yards from me, I went over to him.

"'Generally speaking,' I said, 'you'd be much better off if you could find a good high cliff or a wood or something that overlooks a deserted part of the ocean. That's where passion really comes out.'

"He said nothing.

"'That is, of course, if you need to write outdoors. I do it in my bedroom with the blinds shut.'

"Closing his notebook, he put the pencil into his breast pocket; he looked at me briefly, then away, then back to me.

"'Are you writing poems?' I asked.

"'Yes. They're not very good.'

"I continued to explain how I felt about writing under complex situations but apparently he was not interested because his eyes had the wide dull look you'll find in people who pretend they are not ignoring you.

"'Do you write poetry?' he asked.

"'No, prose. You may have heard of me. My name is Wallace Pembrook.'

"He blushed. 'No, I'm sorry, I haven't. But if you can tell me what you've published I'll——'

"'Oh, just two little books. You probably wouldn't care for them. I always annoy poets.'

"'But I'm not a poet,' he said quickly. 'The Poet's within me.'

"'Well then, perhaps I would annoy *him*.'

"'No, you don't understand. You see, the poet I'll become is inside me——'

"'Like an embryo?'

"'Not exactly—well, kind of. I've got to work in order for him to develop, and when he does I'll disappear and instead of me there'll be the Poet.'

"'That's interesting. But I don't like the idea of vanishing in favor of someone else. Do you know anything about your Poet?'

"He thought a while and I sat down beside him at the edge of the wharf.

"'He's very beautiful,' he said. 'I can't tell you what he looks like or how he is, but he's beautiful in every way.'

"'Even so, I'd resent being taken over that way.'

"'You keep thinking it's someone else, but it isn't *really*. It's the figure you've created that takes you over; maybe you would say it was just one aspect of yourself that makes everything else shrink before it. And when this one aspect becomes so developed you are really another person, although not *really*.'

"'And what will happen,' I asked, 'when this—I don't know what to call it: union? transformation?—takes place?'

"'I'll be a great poet, and I myself will be a universal. That is, you'll be able to see life through me: a whole vision of it through my work and through me.'

"He was very excited when he said this and I couldn't argue with him even if I'd wanted to because what he believed was all feeling and no logic, and yet I think he expected me to consider his notion the way I would a rational one. The only thing I could say was, 'I can understand that your poetry might be universal, but not yourself.'

"'Well, Shakespeare is a——'

"'When people say "Shakespeare" they mean his work.'

"'I don't know,' he muttered. 'Maybe it's something that never happened before.'

"He became suddenly silent, withdrawn, his face miserable.

"'Is anything wrong?' I asked.

"'Maybe it won't happen at all,' he sighed. After that we said nothing for a long while.

"'I'd really be most interested,' I told him at last, 'to see your poems. Do you think'—I gave a tentative tug at his notebooks—'I might take a look?'

"'If you want to. They're not very good.'

"The first thing that struck me was his small neat handwriting, completely unadorned except for large fancy capitals, each of which was just like the next. And then I noticed the name Jamie in almost every poem; when I had gone through about fifteen or twenty of them, I realized that the quality of each poem—some were rather good and some were very very bad—depended on how he felt about Jamie at the moment he wrote it. You couldn't call them love poems, they were more like religious ones, and whoever Jamie was, the boy certainly worshiped him. I've never seen form and content so closely connected in any other work, and as I continued to read, it became more like testing a hypothesis than judging a poem. I wish I could quote some of them (they were all very short), but I can't remember any perfectly except a stanza of one that was dated about two years ago:

> *Contrive to nest my verse upon a mountain, where*
> *Its woven wicker heart pastels*
> *Within the frozen morning air.*
> *And you, from out the sky, an Eagle,*
> *Jamie.*
> *Vanquish it!*
> *Make me larger than life!*

"In the end I became much more interested in finding out who Jamie was than in examining the poems, so I asked him. He pretended not to hear and I repeated the question.

"'My brother,' he said.

"'Such queer feelings toward a brother!' I laughed.

"'What do you mean?'

"I explained. I've never seen anyone so offended by the insinuation. 'How can you think a thing like that?' he shrieked, and several sailors turned to look at us. 'There's nothing in the poems that's anything like that. I never——'

"'All right. Don't get upset.'

"He was much more tensed, and even moved a little away from me. When I handed his notebooks back to him, he stood up and said, 'I'm glad to have met you. Goodbye.' And as he walked across the quay, I noticed his limp for the first time.

"I suppose I was slightly surprised the next afternoon because I expected if he would not completely ignore me he would at least have displayed some sort of coldness. But there he was when we met again, apparently delighted to see me coming along the wharf.

"'Hello, Mr. Pembrook.'

"'Why don't you call me Wallace?'

"'All right . . .'

"I waited then for him to introduce himself, and though the pause was obvious, he said nothing. Finally, I asked.

"'Mark,' he said, and then quickly, 'I read your books yesterday.'

"'Both of them?'

"'Yes, they didn't take me long.'

"'And what do you think?'

"'They were very depressing,' he said.

"'Depressing?'

"'Yes. I always expected something fine was going to happen, but it never did.'

"'Never mind what you expected, did you *like* the books?' I think I was becoming angry.

"'I don't know. They confused me, I guess. I mean, I always felt I was going to like them, and when I was finished I felt that I might have. But I'm not sure I did.'

"'I think they're both splendid novels.'

"He was becoming frightened and perhaps would rather have dropped the subject, because in a small uncertain voice he concluded, 'They're pointless.'

"'*Point*less? That's no criticism at all,' I stormed. 'Pointless! Well, for heaven's sake, what isn't?'

"Although he had retreated, now he looked up, his face

as shiny and convinced as when he had told me of the Poet he would become, and he said, '*I'm* not.'

"'Do you mean *you* personally, or is that the *I* through which we're supposed to see all the world?'

"'Both, I guess. Writers must see a point to life or else they mustn't write.' And, come to think of it, Harry, the next thing he said was probably a reference to you. 'You remind me of someone I met recently who doesn't see anything in anything—not even in himself. It's all right for him to walk through a dead world, but not for you: not for a writer.'

"'Now, look here, Mark. Can you say I describe a dead world in my books?'

"'I don't only mean dead that way. I mean a thing is dead when it has only one level of existence, when it has no life beyond itself. If *you* write about a flower, it's really only a flower.'

"'Well, what would you like it to be?'

"'I don't know: maybe a symbol or a reflection of something or someone.'

"'All right now, listen to me. Do you see the river? What is it? Water—moving a bit, sometimes splashing, sometimes rainbow-colored from oil: mostly it's a steady greenish-bluish substance. You want this river to *mean* something: and it doesn't. Some people get emotional about it—I do, perhaps you do—but I'm not interested in anything as a cause, but as an absolute. There's enough in the river from a physical point of view to satisfy me in every way; its value isn't less if it doesn't have anything to do with the brain of man. You want everything in the world to relate to your life:

but it just doesn't happen that way. And you mustn't be afraid to understand that you're a stranger here in a large sense, just as you wouldn't be afraid to know you could be a stranger in a distant city. Look around and have fun, but don't fancy non-existent meanings into things, and don't believe they have anything to do with you. This river lives as a river and dies as a river—and it's marvelous enough *as* a river not to need to be anything else. That's what's wrong with most people, you know; they can't be satisfied by what exists. Even this life isn't enough for them; they have to hallucinate other ones. Oh, don't think I condemn them for a minute—it's a tribute to their imaginations. And if they want to ignore this world for one less certain but possibly more beautiful, I think it's fine. But I'm glad I don't. And, you see, Mark, in my books I glorified the certainties in relation to themselves; it's the same thing nature's done.'

"He had been jumping through everything I'd said, ready to pounce on each word, thought, sentence, but when I finished, all he said was, 'If you're going to put down just what is, I guess there's no point to writing in the first place.'

"But I let the argument go at that. I was more curious about him personally than about what he believed, and what I wanted most was to bring him away from this kind of talk to conversation about his life. But it was impossible: he wouldn't tell me a thing. I don't know where he lives, what he lives on, what he does when he's not writing poetry; I even tried to lead him around to things more private. Once, in complete disgust with his secrecy, I said that it was just the kind of day one would like to put his hand between the thighs of a woman, didn't he think so? 'It would depend on the woman,' he said. And, as always, he turned the conversation right back to his Poet or to my novels or to a critical examination of his latest poems. Several times I asked him to have a drink, come over to my place when I was having friends, or meet me for dinner. He apologized a great deal but never accepted, although most of the time I felt he would have liked to. Oh, yes, twice he did say he would come—I'd almost forgotten. I asked him over alone in the evening, and he said he might be able to make it—that was the first time—in fact, he was *sure* he might be able to make it, but wouldn't I give him my phone number just in case. Half an hour before I expected him he called to say he was all tied up at home. The second time—I'm not sure, he might have come. I invited him a day in advance, he said he would certainly be there, but I left town in the morning. You remember how I went away suddenly at the end of last August? So he may have been at my place: I don't know, there was no note."

We were back at Fourteenth Street, once again headed uptown, and both of us leaned forward looking out the window. He wasn't there, of course.

"And you haven't seen him since?" I asked.

"No, not a bit—except for just now. It's funny both of us knowing him at about the same time, isn't it?"

The train started up, tunneling us out of the station, carrying us to an appointment, an hour and a half late.

The old beggar seated in the other lane had been deserted by the woman to whom he had spoken and, in the thickening twilight, he grew vague, his face settling into shadows.

9

The tie is a whip of orange, and large black mosquitoes with long legs rest upon the edges. It is disgusting to see and, although it would undoubtedly go well with my single pale blue suit, I shall never wear it.

Even before I tore away the tissue paper, opened the box, and recognized the handwriting on the pink card in the shape of a bowtie ("Just because it's you!") I knew it was from Emily. Two or three times a year she will do that: an extravagant plaid handkerchief, a tie so embellished it would set Mr. Trevor's nerves quivering, a pair of socks ringed with color.

She is generous I suppose, and yet I suspect her generosity is based not on kindness but on sentimentality, a crass, changeable sentimentality that varies with her moods as her indefinite green-hazel eyes vary with the color of the sky. She is generous with what she has most of and to what will make her cry, to what suggests her own frustrations. The card that came with the gift might more appropriately have read: "Just because it's *me!*" I imagine she walked by a haberdasher's yesterday and thought of me, creating a picture of my life that paralleled her own, that had me veiled with loneliness and confusion, draped with self-pity, blanketed with unattainable desires. And so, to ease the pain she had forced upon me, she bought the tie as a reminder that I am not without sympathizers. Often she has pleaded, "Harry, why aren't you more open? After all, we've been friends for so many years, we've gone through so much together. Can't you let me know what's underneath that unemotional surface?" When I try to explain that I am surface from my depths, she cracks her knuckles impatiently or throws her hands into the air. And perhaps that is best, for she has decided what I am like underneath and even I could never change that image.

Occasionally on a dry evening I will wander toward Third Avenue and turn uptown among the dazzle of neon and the blur of jukebox voices to Emily's fourth-floor apartment, the door usually open, herself lying in the dreary-neat living room lit only by the slowly vanishing gray light that slants from the courtyard upon which her rooms face. A scratched rasping half-dumb recording of Bach's *Arioso* will be unwinding on the phonograph and, before she notices me, I will hear her sighing as she is rocked, caressed, carried away by the wave of deep religious sadness. And even in the dimness, although her back is to me, I can see her eyes.

What is that look in Emily's inconstant eyes? I have

thought of it as anxiety and longing, and yet, as I recall seeing her tonight lying on the sofa, her arms flopping limply to the floor, I think it is more like resignation. Still—and this is one of the reasons I sometimes feel disgust for her—I know that she is not resigned to anything: not to herself nor to the palpable realities nor to her feelings toward Wallace nor to the god she talks about amorphously and with terror. No, Emily is resigned to nothing, except perhaps the knowledge that she will never be resigned, that she will linger tearfully, weakly, upon her sofa, driven by the most painful and futile of all motives: a vague hope that can never resolve itself into action. And her eyes, if this is what they say, are beaming neither anxiety nor longing, but a quiet, flaccid appeal charged with fright: *come to me, I am too weak to move.*

When I entered her apartment this evening, the *Arioso* sobbing from the machine beside the windows, I stood a moment listening in the doorway. It is, I think, a piece of music I might have liked had I not come to feel it had been misused into a backdrop for masochism, that Emily can hear it only as an echo of tortured self-pity.

"Turn it off," I said flatly, coming into the room.

She jumped up immediately, smoothing her rumpled hair back. "Oh, you startled me, Harry . . . I had a headache and the music was so relaxing." Each time I find her this way she pretends it has never happened before and usually offers the same explanation. I switched off the machine and asked if she wanted the lights on.

"No, it's nicer this way, don't you think? Soothing and intimate."

"It doesn't matter to me." I looked through a window

across the dim gray courtyard into the apartment opposite. A naked bony middle-aged man was lying in a lighted bedroom; he lay facing the window and, except to scratch his chin now and then, rarely moved. "You have a good view," I said.

Raising herself slightly, she peered out the window. "Oh, *him*. Haven't you ever seen him before? He's always doing that." She stood up and walked across the room to the mantelpiece where there was a dish of sweets. Stuffing an enormous chocolate into her mouth, she offered the candies to me but I refused. Returning to the sofa she placed the dish at her side. "In the summer," she said, choosing another one, "I look so damned awful anyway, I don't feel very guilty about eating all this stuff. Do you think I've put on any weight, Harry?"

"I can't tell without the light on, but you looked a little heavier the other night at Wallace's."

"Did I?" she asked, disturbed. Then, reconsidering: "So what! Who the hell is there to look nice for? And if I'd take the trouble for someone, he probably wouldn't even notice." She stared out the window absently and scratched her head. "I spoke to Wallace this afternoon. He said he's writing another novel. Isn't it funny the way you never can tell when he's writing? Honestly, his energy is inexhaustible: always flying around no matter how the weather is!" She sighed noisily and in the dimness I could see her silhouetted hands flitting over the sweets.

"Emily," I said, remembering my thoughts at Rebecca's this morning. "Do you still feel the same way about Wallace?"

Without a word, she finished chewing the chocolate, and I believe she was very startled by my question, for it is a subject we have not touched directly since adolescence, having then, after years of discussion and analysis, let it melt gradually into the form of insinuation or assumption.

When she spoke her voice was flat enough to betray suspicion. "What do you mean, 'feel the same way'?"

"You used to say you wanted more from him than just friendship."

"I still do."

"You want to sleep with him?—marry him?"

"It's not just that. You know, Harry, feelings change: mine have. I don't know what I want from Wallace, but I think love is a way toward it—toward being together."

"Love is much too general a word. You mean sex."

"No, I mean *love*—loving each other. But that's only part of what I want. No, don't ask me what the rest is: I don't know—maybe *sharing*."

"Sharing what?"

"I don't know, life I suppose. He has so much life, I wish I had some of it." She was silent a moment, then she asked, "Do you think it's wrong to feel the same way?"

"Personally," I said, my tone harder than I had intended, "I don't believe anyone goes on wanting something twenty years when they know from the beginning—or soon after—that they'll never get it."

"But no one ever knows they'll never get it, do they?"

"I think you can be pretty sure that if——"

"I don't want to hear any more," she said quietly. "You can go on wanting something you'll never get. I've wanted to quit my job for years, but I go on with it—and I still want to quit. And some day I *will* quit. I know I'll quit it: it's a horrible job. You see one miserable side of life all day long, and you have to be another person to survive it. Sometimes on my way home from work, I stop and repeat to myself, you're Emily Morrison, you're Emily Morrison. I feel like that after I leave Wallace now and then. It's even worse with Wallace, I think. Isn't it funny to switch identities on and off like that? But I don't get so exhausted with Wallace; I can sit back and let him carry me along. At my job!" Her sigh was deep. "My God, Harry, it seems everyone gets poorer during the summer, or anyway they have more complaints."

I assumed she would begin describing, as she often does, her latest cases, and generally I am interested in hearing about them. Each poverty-stricken family *is* Emily, and the sympathy she expresses toward it is, in a way, a demonstration of her feelings toward herself. Their hungers on one level are hers on another, their fear of cold is hers, their diseases too, and their insoluble dilemmas are the mud hills of frustration in which her feet have stuck over the years. And when Emily gives her clients an old dress or a package of Christmas toys or a few cans of meat when they are particularly hard up, I cannot help believing her action is reflexive. But this evening, having entered upon her reverie, I did not care to hear an extension of it, even though she would have talked of others.

"Well," I said, "people don't die as much during the summer."

"Don't they? That's odd. I think if I had my choice I would much rather die during the summer. I feel half-dead in the heat anyway." After a pause, she began again, slowly at first, but gradually increasing the speed of her words as if leading to something of undelayable importance whose pressure became every instant more forceful. "You know, Harry, my vacation is coming soon and I've been wondering where I might go. I don't want to spend another holiday in the city, but I don't want to go to New England. Someone at the office suggested Mexico. But why there—for souvenirs? And then I've realized it's been five years since I was home. Maybe I ought to go to Chicago."

"It's much too hot to go there in summer," I said.

"But it's the only time I have. Awful, isn't it: the only time I have." She breathed a deep noisy sigh like the shriek of some peculiar living thing inside her chest. "Something terribly depressing happened to me this afternoon. It wouldn't have bothered you, Harry, but it upset me enormously."

She interrupted herself, waiting for me to press her. After a moment of silence, she repeated, "It upset me enormously," and then paused again.

"What was it?" I asked finally.

"I was walking up Fifth Avenue after work; the street was crowded and it was rather warm, but I felt good for some reason. I was looking into shop windows, examining the fall clothes—you know, just wandering around. Then I passed a travel agency. You've seen those really smart ones on Fifth Avenue, haven't you—a million *papier mâché* little worlds, and scenes painted on glass and plaster. This was like most of them, but I stopped because I saw the shop boy inside the window arranging a new display. He was a tall, thin, blond fellow, in fact he reminded me of Wallace a little

—that funny smile, I mean; but his features were finer than Wallace's. Well, he was fixing a paper palm in one corner of the window and he tacked a long yellow drape to a branch of the palm, and on the cloth, in great big paint strokes, was written: TWO WEEKS IN THE YEAR ARE YOURS—MAKE THE MOST OF YOUR VACATION.

"Reading the sign, I was frozen to the ground. You can't know how sick it made me, and I don't know why it should have: it wasn't anything new to me. After a while, I noticed the reflection, on the window, of the crowds passing behind me. The head of a woman was cast on the glass painting of the Eiffel Tower, and this or that man was thrown on a *papier mâché* beach or a plaster mountainside. All these people rushing by in a mad blur on Fifth Avenue—and I felt superior. No, that isn't it! Feeling superior is a good sensation, but this was unpleasant: more detached than anything else, as if I were solidly on earth and the passers-by were stupidly floating in space and I had the terrifying power to see where they were going and to see their images, their dreams, falling for an instant across the display. It was a remarkable experience."

I laughed. "Not *that* remarkable."

"I wouldn't want to live if it were something that happened every day."

"It wouldn't matter because you'd get used to it."

"I wouldn't want to get used to it."

"What did you do?"

"It was the shop boy. Suddenly he rapped at the window, but very softly, and I looked up; he was smiling—you know, like Wallace, but infinitely more tender, and although he was quite young he seemed somehow wise. And he was beautiful: that's just the word for him. We kept looking at each other and I can't explain what the look was—something mystical, I'm sure: no, I don't mean that, I mean it was something tangible, as if I could pick up his gaze like a small warm bird and hold it to me until my body warmed. Then he motioned, but I couldn't understand what he meant; he seemed to want me to turn around and face the street, and I did. At first I was puzzled because everything seemed ordinary. And that was just why, Harry, because everything *was* ordinary again; I was together with the world and it was a relief and I felt my warmth run out of me and reach to the passers-by: I loved them, all of them—I wanted to cry from my love. Oh, it was good! Then I became excited and turned back to the shop boy; I smiled or perhaps laughed—I wanted to go inside and talk to him. I put my hand on the door, but at the same moment, he frowned through the window and shook his head. I stepped back and so did he, back to the palm tree where he finished tacking up the yellow drape. We didn't look at each other again, and finally I went home."

I said nothing. The room was now dense with darkness and I peered once more across the courtyard: the naked man was standing beside the window putting on a pair of shorts.

"Marie," I heard him shout. "How about supper?"

"Oh, Christ!" cried Emily. "What time is it? I'm sure it must be——"

"I don't know. It's too dark to see my watch."

Lifting herself from the sofa, she lumbered toward the wall and switched the light on. "It's almost nine," she said, glancing at the clock on the bookcase. "And I'm expecting someone. Just look at me!" Her skirt was wrinkled and a small smear of chocolate ran at the neck of her blouse.

"You look fine," I told her.

"No, I don't," she decided after seeing herself in the mirror hanging over the sofa. "I look awful. I'm going to take a shower and change my clothes. Will you wait?"

"Is it all right?"

"Yes. You can entertain him if he comes."

Through the splash of the shower I heard her low pleasant voice moaning a love song. One of the things that amuse me in Emily is the way she can sing these absurd songs and make them sound as if she means them. But this time she stopped in the middle of a word.

I was very warm because there is rarely a breeze from the courtyard and, while the door was open upon the landing, nothing drifted in but heavy dinner smells and the clatter of footfalls up and down the staircase. Emily's living room is crowded with furniture, but it is unbelievably neat, for most of the pieces are smaller than ordinary; this exaggerated daintiness does little for the room and only makes Emily seem twice as large when she walks through. But I suppose the things are easier to push round and this is important because Emily is always arranging things. Many times I have found her reorganizing her orderly bookcase or her meticulous closets.

"Excuse me," I heard a man say. Looking up I saw him standing in the doorway, a shiny panama spinning in his hands.

"Is this Miss Morrison's apartment?" he asked, apparently

more uncertain of me than the location. He was dark and thick-looking, as if incompletely molded out of clay. And his voice was thick too.

"Yes," I said. "Come in."

"I have an appointment with——"

"That's all right. She's inside, dressing. Why don't you sit down?"

"Thank you." He sank beside the dish of sweets and fingered his hair into sharp black waves, his eyes resting upon me expectantly. "Are you waiting for Miss Morrison also?" he asked unpleasantly.

"No, not really. I'm her uncle."

"Her uncle?" He smiled and relaxed against the back of the sofa. "You certainly look awfully young to be her uncle."

"That's what everyone tells us. The fact is, she's older than I am."

"Is that true? I've heard of cases like that but I've never actually met one. It's amazing, isn't it?"

"One gets used to it."

"Imagine that!" he repeated three or four times in a whisper, his fingers running along the rim of his panama. Then, after a moment's silence, he said, "It was some game today, huh?"

"What?"

"It was a swell ballgame."

"Oh, yes, it was," I agreed and turned my head to look out the window again, but the light was off in the bedroom opposite. The man was now in the kitchen talking quietly to a fat gray-haired woman whose breasts were dumped into a green halter that teetered as she spoke.

"I think St. Louis was cheated," the thick young man was saying. "It's not just because I'm a St. Louis fan. As I was telling Emily the other night, a lawyer learns to be impartial about everything. But I know St. Louis was cheated. Lionel should've been walked his last time at bat, and that would have sent the run in. But, as they say, the umpire was blind."

"Is that so?"

"Sure. Oh, I guess you think I was at the game. No, I saw it on TV. We've got a set over at my office. Here's one of our cards." He crossed the room and handed it to me, then returned to the sofa. The card read: *Dominick & Warsaw, Law Offices,* and was surrounded by telephone numbers and addresses.

"I'm Irwin Dominick," the young man said. "And my partner's Steve Warsaw. I want him to change his name or else everyone will think we're communists." He laughed. "We're not, though, you know. See, Steve's father-in-law is in the TV business and he gave us a set when we became partners. That's how I saw the game today: and it was certainly exciting!"

"Yes," I said.

"I'm telling you that the umpire struck Lionel out when it was really a walk. Don't you think that's true? Oh, but then——"

"Isn't what true?" asked Emily, coming into the room. Her face shone and her short damp hair was pinned back. She wore a coarse-looking chartreuse-colored dress.

"I was just telling your uncle"—puzzled, Emily looked across the room at me, but said nothing—"that I think St. Louis was cheated out of today's game."

"Are you talking about baseball?" she said, her tone light with removed contempt.

"Sure. Don't you care for it?"

Frowning, she stared over Mr. Dominick's head at her reflection in the mirror. "No, I don't. I think there are better things to be interested in."

"There sure are," he drawled. Then, smiling, he winked.

"Excuse me," I said, standing up. "I'd better be going."

"So soon?" he asked. "Just when we were getting warmed up for a nice discussion. Well, maybe some other time."

"Yes."

"By the way, what did you say your name was?"

"Harry Sutton," I told him.

"Well, so long, Uncle Harry!" He laughed.

Emily walked with me across the landing. "Awful, isn't he?" she said, indicating her apartment with a nod of her head. "He really forced me into seeing him...."

I shrugged, then leaned forward and kissed her on the cheek. "Oh, I almost forgot," I said as I was turning away. "Your tie came in this morning's mail."

BOOK TWO

10

(*In the fall I will be thirty-two years old.*)
As I lie here the thought persists and resounds, laces through my mind its pointlessness. Why this notion continues to circulate round the images and memories of such a disturbing day I can only vaguely understand: there is large soft comfort in it like this bed—something I can rest back upon. Thirty-two times I shall have journeyed round the sun, thirty-two times I shall have come by the same places without stopping at any of them: the planets and stars, the fixed constellations. Each year I roar alongside them, offering nothing new but the greater, more intense stink of progressive decay. Ultimately I shall ride by as dust, my constituents flinging, flying, spouting—until there is no more left at all: then will the journey end and peace come to my particles.

Perhaps the inevitability of all this—my age, my death, my disintegration—is now not only a matter of acceptance, but one of great attractiveness. For in these things resides certainty: they are freed from *perhaps* and *maybe*. And uncertainty is ringing in my ears tonight.

Should I lift myself from the bed and cross to the window to look out over the warm moonless street, I should see whatever was visible. Opposite me would be the church, unlit but open; below, a derelict or two—a nervous girl hurrying home late, alone, afraid—a crowd of youths screaming up to sleepers. I could if I desired sit at the window the rest of the night until Kitty and dawn padded slowly across the pavement and entered my room, and I would observe everything the human eye can see. But yet, and yet, there is a place they would tell me I am blind, that upon an empty davenport a deadnotdead boy is lying with two candles burning at his head, their flame blackening the lowered shade behind them. And *they* in hushed voices, with murmurs and sobs, with terrified eyes are seeing what I cannot see, and through it all. (*In the fall I will be thirty-two years old.*)

On Saturdays at noon, all summer long, Sarah Trevor comes into the funeral parlor. This year she is twenty, a junior at the university she attends, but there is no real change between her now and last year or even the year before. Her breasts may have grown, her thin mechanical laugh may be slightly more metallic, and her lipstick may extend beyond the outline of her mouth—but she is the same. Pretending still to believe the funeral parlor haunted, she shudders when I prepare to leave soon after she has arrived, and says, "Ooh, Harry, you're not going to leave me here alone with all these dreadfully ghoulish corpses?" and opens her manicure set and a history text, and alternates between them. Thus, I suppose, she remains until five o'clock. And for these hours every Saturday, her uncle pays her the equivalent of one-fourth of my salary.

Today when Sarah entered, her breasts carefully formed beneath the taut pull of her jersey, I spent a few minutes with her, smoking a cigarette. She talked about love, pressing me for personal information. I shrugged in reply to each question.

"Don't you want to talk about it, Harry? Or maybe you don't want to talk about it to *me*," she said, putting a studied resistible tease into her voice. "Do you think I'm inexperienced?" Her artificial mouth stretched, then rounded.

"I don't know if *you* are," I told her. "But I am."

"Ha ha ha," she said. "You can't pull that with me, Harry Sutton. I'll bet you've got dozens of women pining away for you. Sometimes you're real cute! Should I tell you something, Harry? But you've got to promise not to say a word to Uncle Clark. There'd be hell to pay if it ever got back to my family. Promise?"

"Cross my heart," I said.

"I don't know if I ought to tell you. . . ." Considering the problem, her face was blank, but then she drew a deep breath and her breasts rose. "I made love this year at school."

"In which class?"

"Oh, that's not what I mean, nutty." She giggled in her dry unwinding way. "I'm not a *you-know* any more. Aren't you surprised?"

"Yes."

"You're not at all surprised!"

"Is that why you did it—to surprise me?"

Angry, she flipped open her textbook, pounded the pages flat, and pretended to read.

"So long, Sarah," I said. "I'll see you next week."

"Are you going already?" She shuddered. "Must you leave so soon? I'll have to spend the whole afternoon locked up alone with all these spooks. Oh, stay a while, Harry."

"I can't. I've got an appointment for lunch. And anyway, you won't be alone. Frank's here—why don't you go back and talk to him? He'd be happy to entertain you."

"In *that* room? Never. I'd sooner die." She paused, thought over what she had said, and giggled.

As I opened the door into the street, I heard her call after me, "Remember your promise, Harry."

By the time we had finished lunch, a full beam of sunlight had moved round to the living room where it broke into color through each glass and crystal object. The red globe of the censer, hanging before the fireplace, was orange in the sparkling light, and it swung slowly, evenly, in the fine breeze that sailed through the windows. Rolling a glass of iced coffee between his palms, Wallace sat on the arm of the purple club chair, his shoes upon the seat, his back leaning against the window seat.

"Do you think she was really serious about it?" he asked.

"I don't know. She said it's been five years since she——"

"Even if it were ten, I couldn't imagine going back there —certainly not in summer. And she hasn't got a soul there but that villainous old brother. Remember him?" After a pause, he continued. "Maybe she wants to check up on the money she sends him. Doesn't he work?"

"She's never been very exact about it. I think he works, but he's got more children than he can support."

"Well, she must send him tons of money; she says if it weren't for him she'd have saved enough to spend years and years in Europe. I really can't think of anyone less deserving than Sidney. Remember when he beat me up?"

"No, I——"

"Of course you do. 'I don't want you near my sister,' he said and smashed me in the nose. You can still see the bump here." He leaned forward. "You see? the little dome on the side? And you were really the guilty one, weren't you, Harry?"

It was a curious thing for Wallace to recall and even, in fact, to know. For so long now I have not thought about it, and I feel certain Emily would not remember even if it were mentioned to her, because I believe she went with me only that I might tell Wallace. I never did, of course—and until this afternoon I was not aware he knew the boy jumping over the garden hedge had been me. It had been a fine thing at first, in warm damp summer grass, and the surprise of drawing over Emily. But after the beginning, after she had unloosed her large tear-shaped breasts and started whimpering, it was primarily a ritual of sadness, something I would have gone through only out of obligation just as I tell her yes when she asks if I still love her. But at the final moment, the garage light leaped over the garden and reached our legs in the corner near the hedge and Emily whispered in a scream *run run run*. As I jumped I saw her sitting up, the flesh tears heaving into the light. Except when Wallace told me of his encounter with her brother a few days later, none of us ever mentioned it; but I have always believed the error was not a mistake in Sidney's judgment, but something he was deliberately led to believe.

"All your coffee's gone," said Wallace. "Shall I get you some more?"

"No, it's all right. I'll get it myself. Do you want some?"

When Wallace cooks even an egg, he believes it necessary to have all four burners going on the stove "just in case," and so, because he had heated some peas for lunch, the kitchen was still hot and the bowl of ice, fixed only a few minutes before, had already turned to water. Chopping another tray from the refrigerator I filled the coffee-glasses and, as I shook the sugar in, I heard the telephone ring in the living room. After a moment Wallace said "Speaking" and then he was silent.

He was still on the phone when I returned and he was still silent, his face intent, his head nodding slowly as if in thoughtful reply.

"Very little," he said suddenly. "In fact almost nothing.... I hardly know him at all.... Just one other ... Yes, I do.... Frankly, I don't understand it. What makes you think anything is there?"

He continued to nod at the telephone, then looked at me, raising his eyebrows and his shoulders. Covering the receiver, he said to me, "The most peculiar thing ..." And he spoke once more into the phone. "Yes, all right, if you'd like. No, it wouldn't be any trouble. No, no, I assure you of that. Yes, really, if it were too much trouble I wouldn't come, so please don't upset yourself. Now what's the address? Yes, 32 Crawford: I've got it. No, I wouldn't call the police, I'd tell the neighbors to go fly a kite. Yes, fine; you go on back again. Goodbye." He put down the phone and took the fresh coffee-glass from the mantel.

"It was about Mark," said Wallace, and began to laugh.

"What's so funny?"

"Nothing. It's not funny at all." His laughter ended abruptly. "The man who phoned is a priest who's from somewhere in Mark's neighborhood. He told me that an old lady who lives in the apartment next to the boy came to the church a couple of hours ago and asked that a clergyman come over to assist in some great catastrophe which she couldn't explain very clearly. Well, when this man got there, he found the whole tenement—it's over on Crawford Street—reeking with a smell of putrefaction, and the tenants were making a big racket about it. The smell obviously came from Mark's place where the door is wide open; the boy is there, sitting in the living room, apparently out of his head, and not saying a word to anyone though the flat is filled with people. The priest says the door leading to a second room is locked and the corpse, or whatever it is that's stinking up the house, is there. He can't get any response out of Mark, so he doesn't know where the key is; he's gone through everything in both the living room and the small kitchen, but has come up with nothing. It isn't very funny, is it?"

"How did he find out about you?" I asked.

"Oh, my phone number. It was in Mark's notebook with my name. He called because none of the neighbors knows anything about the boy except that he's lived there about a year and a half. The woman who came to call the priest says she's a good friend of the boy's, but he's told her very little of himself. And there wasn't a letter or any kind of document around, no photographs or addresses, no way of finding out about relatives. So the clergyman called to find out if I knew anything. I told him no, but he asked if I might come over and try speaking to the boy. I said I would. Do you want to come along?"

I frowned. "I don't know."

"Oh, come on, Harry, perhaps you can do a little quick business for Mr. Trevor."

11

They are all the same, the streets down there: Crawford, Anderson, Peasdale, the rest: they grow gradually behind the blocks of gray-windowed factories as if the soft constant hum of machinery indicated their steady and eternal production. The streets are characterized by the scream of children and women in a dozen languages, by sloping fire escapes, by chalk-scrawled asphalt, by a smell of straw and onions and urine and chicory, by faces that reveal primarily exhaustion, and by the plain enduring grayness stamped on everything even in the sunlight. And the people are as indistinguishable, one from another, as the buildings and the stores and the proud chalked penises whose erections will dissolve with the next rain. As seldom as possible do I come down to that neighborhood; the lives it holds are not pleasant ones, and their only consolation can be that they will end soon. Why, I wonder, have they begun in the first place? Oh yes, there is always hope: when there is nothing else or even too much, there is hope, as inheritable as idiocy, as congenital as syphilis.

Wallace and I did not speak as we drove toward Crawford Street in the taxi. Along Wimple Road the factories surrounded us, and perhaps due to their insistent monotonous rumble Wallace turned to the window; but his eyes were too fixed to have been observing what we passed. I supposed he was thinking of Mark or of the telephone call. There is a contradiction in Wallace's personality which I have seen evidenced to every acquaintance of his but myself; and it is this: he is as volatile as summer rain and yet as constant as the moment of storm. With me he is neither —or perhaps both, but always together, and this is so, I believe, because on all things basic we agree. His feelings toward me never become as passionate as toward others, nor do they—at the height of their passion—vanish. Today in the taxi I am certain he was devoting himself, above all else, to Mark; tomorrow, with equivalent sincerity, he might not give a damn.

Thirty-two Crawford Street is gray, of course, and where it is not gray it is soot black. The fire escapes zigzag up the façade, and the windows that were open throughout the building this afternoon seemed to have been never closed: but that is the air of everything: permanence. Above the door, the brass 2 in the house number was inverted, and below it, upon the small stoop, sat a neat little boy with straight blond hair.

"It's the sixth floor; the top, I think," said Wallace as we entered the corridor.

He must have noticed the smell at the same time as I for an instant later he looked at me uncertainly, his eyes narrow with concern.

"Yes," was all I told him because it was obvious that the thin persistent odor was not one of life. As we climbed the staircase, the smell was sometimes obscured by cooking and hall toilets, but only briefly, and then it returned, neither stronger nor weaker. At the top of the house it intensified suddenly and carried with it a rush of cracked whispering that ran along the landing.

There were perhaps thirty people grouped together round that one door, and easily as many within. Most of them were women in florid housedresses and their unified undulations gave me the impression of watching the blurred panorama of moving wallpaper. Some of the women held complaining children by the hand, and a few silent men nodded and listened and looked grave.

"That would probably be him now," a man's voice came from the center of the room, and all the ladies hushed, turning round, each automatically sliding her hand up the neck of her dress to make certain it was closed. The talk began again, no longer in whispers.

Maybe there'll be an end to this—
I'm only hoping so—
Something should've been done—
Ma, I wanna pee—
Mother of God, didn't I say call the police—
What's he got in there—

And as my eyes traveled through the flood of voices, I saw midst the women, like a stiff black kernel, the serious-faced young priest. His lipless mouth was flapping up and down, uttering indecipherable words. Waving the women aside, he pushed his way through to us.

"Hello, Tulley," I said, but he pretended not to recognize me, and his single eye regarded me with indifference.

"I do not believe I have had the——"

"Harry Sutton," I told him, but he continued to affect forgetfulness.

"Are you," he asked Wallace, "Mr. Pembrook?"

"Yes, I am."

"Ah, I am so happy you've come. It has been all I could do to keep the ladies from calling the police. Perhaps you have noticed the . . ." He sniffed noisily several times. "Yes, I imagine you must have. And you understand the neighbors have been very resentful. I may be stepping out of my place by keeping the police away, but I believe the law should be kept from such things until absolutely necessary. Nevertheless. Whoever he has in there must be dead quite a while. And in all this heat! But I have persuaded them, you see, to wait until you arrived. I do hope you can do something to make the young man come around."

Tulley was much more nervous today than he had been at the end of winter when we were friends. His eye slopped round as rapidly as Mr. Trevor's, and seemed in fact worse because of the other, stolid, translucent, gazing everywhere and nowhere in its fixed calm. His thin tan hair had a touch of green in it like an alley cat's, and his long fingers ran restlessly among the strands.

"Are you also an acquaintance of the young man?" Tulley asked me.

"Not a very close one. I've only spoken to him a few times."

"I hope you understood," said Wallace, "that I hardly know him myself, and that we've never talked about anything more intimate than poetry."

"How unfortunate," Tulley moaned. "It seems as though no one knows anything about him. All these ladies were hardly aware of his existence. Until now he's lived most quietly, troubling no one. . . . Isn't that so?"

Certainly is —
Quiet like a church mouse —
You never can tell —
Ma, I wanna —
Such a thing I never heard —
Don't bother me now, Angie —
We ought to call the police —

"Perhaps you might speak to him, Mr. Pembrook," said Tulley. "We must find the key."

"I'll try. Where is he?"

The women broke apart suddenly into smaller groups, and among them I could piece the room together. Although it was fairly large there was little furniture in it: an unpainted table, two or three wooden chairs, a couple of lamps, several shelves half-filled with books and copy-pads, and, against the far wall beneath the window, a large square armless couch with a sleazy purple coverlet—and upon the couch sat Mark. His head was resting on his fists, and his eyes, if they were not shut, were so lowered they appeared to be regarding himself. Except that his tan jacket was gone, he looked as I had seen him that night in the park dappled with moonlight. And if his face were different from what it had been a year ago, this one, on second glance, suited him as well, seemed as fitting and as natural for, actually, it was only the *removal* of expression rather than, as is most common, the substitution of it.

Seating himself beside the boy, Wallace stared at him a while before he spoke, then he began softly, "Mark, can you hear me? It's Wallace. You remember me: Wallace Pembrook; you used to see me at the river last summer. Can you hear me, Mark?"

He waited several minutes. The men mingling among the women breathed heavily, and now and then coughed or cleared their throats—and the ladies shushed them.

Putting his arm round Mark's shoulder, he began once more. "Listen to me, Mark. Try to hear me. Is there anything I can do for you? Would you like me to get in touch with anyone for you?"

Without looking up or moving perceptibly, the boy sighed, a deep quiet sigh, and the room was terrible with silence. At first they waited for more, but when it seemed that nothing else was likely to come, Wallace continued to speak.

"Now listen here, Mr. Pembru," a loud female voice broke out.

She was a fat woman in her forties and paper curlers trembled in her kinked hair as she spoke. Her right hand squeezed the neck of the housedress secure over the split between breasts, but the dress was wide at the thigh and a thick dark bristled leg stretched out.

"Now you just listen here to me, Mr. Pembru," she said again. "We're all getting tired of this foolishness. It's been going on for three hours and more, and we don't like stinking bodies stinking up our house. Maybe it's not such a fashionable place as you might live in——"

Maybe it's not—
But just the same—
And even if it ain't—

"——but that's no reason we got to stand for it. Now I'm gonna go right downstairs and fetch a cop. You hear! That kid ain't gonna open that door and how long——"

"Just a moment, Madame," Tulley interfered.

"Isn't there a passkey?" I asked, and they all turned on me, incredulous.

"*'Isn't there a passkey?'*" the loud female mimicked. "Where do you think you are, Fifth Avenue? I'm going right down now and call the cops." And she swung round, preparing to do so.

But Wallace jumped up and took hold of her arm. "Don't you dare," he said flatly.

"You take your goddam hand off me, Pembru."

Releasing her arm, Wallace made a deep comic bow and when he stood up his lips were shifting with a supercilious smile. "I think it would be most unkind, not to say stupid, to bring the law into this," he told the woman. "Most of us —possibly even you—have experienced the death of someone close to us. And we all know that such a thing may temporarily put a person out of his mind. Perhaps that's happened to the young man. Now, could you, *Missus*, take the responsibility of adding further pain or possibly something *more* serious to this boy's condition? *I* couldn't!"

"Mr. Pembrook is quite correct, my dear lady," said Tulley. "We ought to be generous to our neighbor in a moment of crisis, not try to wound him further."

"I don't know, Father," the fat woman muttered. "You been standing here and telling us to be patient for——"

"Look," said Wallace. "If all of you will get out of here for five minutes and leave me alone with the boy, I'm sure I'll get him to open the door."

No one was willing but, at last, guided by Tulley, the crowd moved in a slow unconvinced line out the door. I was the last to leave, and I closed the door behind me.

Just five minutes and no more—
Not a second—

Separating himself from the squirming print-flower mob, Tulley came toward me, his lips set parallel in a smile. He did not speak at first and I also remained silent, alternating my gaze between his embarrassed face before me and the chaotic ladies beyond.

"Well, Harry," he said finally. "It certainly has been a long time."

"Yes, it has."

"How have you been? Ah, I suppose all right; you are always all right." And, facetiously, he added, "Are you still sinning?"

"Yes. And you?"

A dry uncomfortable little laugh choked from his throat.

"What do you think of all this?" he asked and, as he gestured toward the crowd behind him, I realized for the first time how delicate his movements were. "I wonder what he might have in that other room. The ladies told me he lives alone."

"His parents are dead. That was almost the first thing Mark ever said to me. They were drowned, I think. Aside from that I know nothing about him except that he writes poems."

"So I discovered. I found some of his work in the notebook that had Mr. Pembrook's telephone number. Of course I did not have the presence of mind to read any, but some of them seemed very religious: I saw God on almost every page. Well, he has that much on his side. *You*, Harry, are still the same, I take it. Yes, there is no look of vitality in your eyes, and that only comes with faith."

"You've told me that, Tulley."

"I know I have. But it is not something one can say too often. Nevertheless." Suddenly his face softened. "Do you still have your cat, Harry? A charming little creature, indeed. I'm reminded of you every time I see an orange cat."

"That couldn't be very often."

"More often than one would imagine. Can you have forgotten how fond I am of cats? I have three of my own at the moment; none of them orange, of course, but one is Siamese."

"Don't your colleagues mind?"

"Ah, no, I don't keep them there. You see, I now have a room uptown: a small one with limited comforts. But I find it convenient to have a little place of my own where I can live unknown as a clergyman and rather keep in touch with the people as a layman. And it is easier to have acquaintances there. I try to get up to the room for a while at least every other day, to feed the cats and so on."

Tell the father—
That's the best thing—
All right, I will—

"Father!" It was the fat woman with paper curlers who came forward, and Tulley spun round to her. "We've come to a decision. We're gonna let Pembru stay there for ten minutes, but if the door ain't open by that time we're gonna call the cops."

"I assure you, my dear lady, that Mr. Pembrook will be out in plenty of time, and things will have a more peaceable end than if the law were involved. And besides we have the good fortune to have with us a person from a funeral home. The gentleman to whom I was just speaking...."

Pressing close to the wall, I edged past them and walked the long gray corridor to the opposite end where a greasy window looked out upon the wall of the building across the narrow alleyway. On either side of me an apartment door was open and I became aware of two women speaking softly at my left. Their words were indistinct, but the tone of one older and with a foreign intonation was broken and miserable, while the other, smooth and warm, comforted. When I realized whose the younger, the comforter's, voice was, I turned my face to them. Both women stood in a yellow kitchen that was half living room apparently, for two figured plush chairs of red were pushed close together, only a mirrored ash-stand between, beneath the window. Emily was before the chairs, her hand on the old lady's arm, and as they spoke, I saw Emily's largeness put itself to a strange use.

I have always felt that her body was the wrong one, that it was an exaggerated contrast with her personality, and that one must disregard it in order to know Emily at all. It is her fault I have believed this so long, for in all her ways she has negated the strength and bigness her figure shows, and substituted weakness and dependency and fright, so that one imagines Emily within as a small powerless girl turned eternally selfward, incapable of offering anything. Even when she has told me stories of her work I felt her clients could expect no more genuine comfort from her than a painful unrealistic identification. Yet today, the power of her build was true: she was a fortress to the small dry woman whose flash of white hair dripped across a wasted face and a wasted unhappy mouth. From the way they stood together in the sunless yellow kitchen I could see Emily giving everything the old woman needed. Emily now did not droop, did not lie flaccid, did not lose herself: she was, those moments, present and enormous and indestructible. And I had never seen her so before.

But when she noticed me outside the door, her arm dropped from the woman, and her mouth started first in surprise and then into a smile: and she was the same as ever—asking, not offering. Raising her finger, to the white-haired lady she said something and backed into the corridor, not turning until she reached me.

"Harry," she whispered. "For God's sake, what are you doing here?"

"There's something going on in the apartment down the hall."

"Yes, I know. It's got poor Mrs. Mussolini all unnerved. She's kept me here over an hour; she wants me to go into that place but I won't. But how did you happen to . . ." She paused, her face shocked. "Business . . . ?"

"Not exactly. Wallace knows the kid who lives there, and the priest found his number in a book."

"I thought I heard them say Pembrook, but I didn't think it could be Wallace."

"Yes. And I was at his place when the call came."

Looking down the corridor we saw the crowd moving, murmuring, Tulley still trying to pacify the loud fat woman.

"But where's Wallace now?"

"He's in the flat trying to get the key from the boy. Everyone else has been thrown out."

"Honestly, it's weird, isn't it? I can't imagine what he's got in there. I'd rather not wait around except that she keeps begging me to stay."

"Do you know him—Mark?"

"I've seen him once or twice. I've got a dozen cases in the house, so I'm here pretty often."

"Miss Morrison, Miss Morrison," said the old lady coming to the door. "Why you don't ask your friend come in for a cup of tea?"

"That's sweet of you, Mrs. Mussolini," Emily began a standard refusal. "But I'm sure he wouldn't want to trouble you."

The old woman seemed momentarily undecided, but then pursed her lips and made a gesture of indifference.

"They still waiting, eh?" she said. "Poor little Mark." Her thin head nodded many times. "I don't know what he's do with things in his house smell like that. You know him, mister?"

"Just slightly."

"You do?" asked Emily.

"I've only met him three or four times and that was a year ago."

"And he's look so different now," said Mrs. Mussolini. "His face change like that. All of a sudden. He's be good friend it's now a year: and so nice to my little children—my daughter children. She's dead, poor thing; better off. She's never have a husband. Then all of a sudden, it's a couple weeks ago, I don't see him more. He's no more come visit, and he never like when I come knock at his door. But anyway I gone and knock, but never answer. The other day he's was in the steps when I took Paulie to the toilet. Don't talk or make laughs. 'Come to read me poems, my friend,' I say. No answer; nothing. And his face change just like that—all of a sudden. You think he's have an operation?"

Her head nodded again.

"Mrs. Mussolini was the one who called the priest," said Emily.

"He's good boy, believe truly in his heart. They was wanna call the cops. I say let me bring a man of God, and I gone. Poor Mark."

It was then the door began to open, very slowly, and as it drew further back, a hush grew in the corridor, so that when Wallace stood in full sight, there was not a sound.

Although we were only a few yards away I could not determine his expression; he seemed to be smiling but his face was half tired, half serious.

"We go," said Mrs. Mussolini, taking Emily's arm.

"Oh, no," she said. "I'd really rather not. Maybe we ought to wait here until——"

"Miss Morrison, you come with me, eh?"

"It's not that I don't want to. But it's so late and I've got . . ."

The three of us left Mrs. Mussolini's doorway and walked to the rim of the crowd, waiting with the others. Behind Wallace I saw Mark sitting exactly as he had before, his eyes still with the air of being set upon himself.

"It's all right," said Wallace. "You can come in now, if you'd like."

He went back of the room and opened the door that had thus far been closed: and the fine smell of wax blew along the corridor.

"It's all right," Wallace repeated. "You can come in now and pay your respects."

The procession began slowly, by twos, like a curious unhappy dance, led by Tulley and the woman with curlers in her hair, still clutching the neck of her dress. The men, the women, the children followed, and Emily and I entered last, preceded by Mrs. Mussolini, who wept and spoke Italian to herself. Tulley and his partner paused before the door to the room and waited, apparently for a signal from Wallace, but before he gave it, Mrs. Mussolini broke forward and crossed to Mark. He did not move while the old lady held him and sang consolations, and after a moment she rose and came back to her place. The smell of wax had thickened, and if there were any intensification or even remnants of the odor of decay, it was obliterated by the better smell of burning candles.

"Go on in," said Wallace to Tulley, and the procession started once more.

And as they entered, there was wailing and coughing and sighing, so that those still without pushed hurriedly and expectantly.

So young—
And such a face just look—
Have mercy on this—

Until at last I entered behind Emily, seeing her face go white as she looked at the davenport in the corner of the room. And then I peered, over the heads of the ladies weeping round the couch, nodding their heads to it, muttering to it. And although I rolled my eyes and squinted I could not make it out, for, so far as I could see, there was no one on the davenport. It was empty of everything but a rose silk pillow at the head.

12

Back of the davenport, behind the silken pillow, two pale candles as thick as arms stood burning upon heavy bronze stands. Their tall flames jetted into the air, then bent backwards from the breath of the crowd and drew lines of carbon upon the drawn window shade. When the original noises of shock and unhappiness had subsided, only gentle murmurs and soft prayers purred from the observers. Tulley, now standing beside the vacant bed, moved his lips rapidly and lightly up and down like two threads blowing against each other. Leaning over, he held his hand above the couch and lifted it several times, wavering, alternating, exactly as if he were shifting something.

Alongside me Emily's breasts heaved with distress while a line of tears, sparkling with candlelight, ran by her nose, past her lips, and dropped from her chin. Every few seconds she poked a small embroidered handkerchief to her nose.

"What are you crying about?" I whispered, but she was not able to speak. Several times she opened her mouth to answer, but she stopped and instead lifted her hand to her throat as if indicating pain.

So ridiculous was it that I wanted to burst with laughter at these dozens of people drenched with tears and tragedy. They reminded me of a crew of actors at the climactic moment in a play. But the prop, the symbol of the tragic has been lost, destroyed, misplaced, or forgotten in the wings; yet the cast with surpassing valiance goes on, pretending there is still reason for the intensity of the performance.

"Harry," whispered Emily. "Listen. It's so hard for me to talk. Do you know who he is?"

"Who?"

"The boy lying there. He's the shop boy. Remember, I told you the shop boy at the travel agency. See the smile?" She paused, swallowing. "It's faint, but can't you tell it's like Wallace's in a way?"

"What are you talking about?"

"The boy. He's the same boy. He was fixing a sign in the window of——" Breaking off, she jerked forward, her face wild, and she shouted: "No, don't you do that! Don't you do that! Are you crazy?" She pushed through to the end of the room, beat her fist on Tulley's shoulder, and dropped to her knees. "Why are you doing that?" she screamed, her voice hoarse and cracking. "He isn't dead, you fool. He's not dead."

Out of her mind poor thing—
Isn't she the welfare—

Who can blame her such a shame—
Ma please can't I—

I looked round the room for Wallace, hoping to find reason in his eyes, or the quick vacant smile that would deny all this nonsense; but he was not there. Stepping back I gazed between two sobbing women through the door into the other room, and saw him sitting beside Mark, his legs crossed, his expression far away from either anxiety or laughter—rather calm and perhaps a little bored. He sucked a long breath on his cigarette and peered out the window.

"I'm not sure he's dead," said Tulley suddenly, and the quiet meditation of the spectators rose with surprise and anger.

"Not dead?" One woman complained, her small voice bridging from mournfulness to fury with quiet haste. "Not dead? And what do you think's been smelling up the house all day?"

"I did not say he wasn't dead. I simply said I am not sure. If he is alive he should be given the final sacrament—assuming, of course, he is a Roman Catholic."

"He's be," Mrs. Mussolini assured him. "Mark's family is always be with the Church."

"In that case we should determine the matter immediately. Nevertheless." He looked down at Emily, whose head was resting upon her arms, her eyes closed. "I think we ought to get a doctor here right away. Yes. That would be much the best thing."

"There's one a couple of blocks from here," said a redheaded young man in front of me, going forward. "He's got office hours in the afternoon, but maybe if I tell him it's an emergency—you know, a matter of life or death—maybe he'll come over."

"That would be very good of you," answered Tulley, and the young man left the apartment. "Harry," Tulley called. "Would you please come here?"

Separating, the ladies let me pass through to the davenport.

"I believe the young lady is correct, Harry," he whispered, three fingers hiding his mouth. "I do not think he is dead."

"Is that so?" I said, smiling.

"Yes. A body dead long enough to give off such an odor," —he rolled his eyes upward—"rigor mortis and other symptoms should have set in. And yet—well, feel him for yourself. I mean, after all, he's cold enough I suppose, but none of us here, not even you, is qualified to determine. Perhaps we have been jumping at conclusions: circumstantial evidence, you understand. What would you say? You have much more——"

"I'd say, why don't you cut it out, Tulley?" Although he had been whispering, I spoke in normal tones and my voice sounded louder than I had ever heard it.

"Cut what out? One cannot be over cautious in——"

"What's going on here? Are you all crazy? Do you expect to go on with this?"

"Harry, I don't——"

"Just look there!" I pointed to the silken pillow. "What do you see?"

"I see, I suppose, just what you see or what anyone else sees. I'm afraid I do not at all understand what you might be driving at." He had become arrogant and so nervous that his arms twitched and the fingers with which he hid his mouth trembled.

"I'm not driving at anything. All you have to do is look and you'll see there's no——" But I interrupted myself and stared at the empty couch and, listening to the sudden frantic lurch of my heart, my eyes turned away, circling the room. I could not say it. I could not tell him the truth: *there is no one on the davenport, Tulley.* Because in Tulley's single eye, in the double eyes of everyone else, in Emily's bent weeping head, and in the jet of candle flame, there *was* someone on the davenport. All I might say was that I did not see him. And my head with these confusions began to swell and ache, and furious I pushed through the cheesecloth load of fat flowered flesh and ran into the other room.

"You rotten kid," I said to Mark, swiping his head with my hand. "You little rotten bastard." But he did not look up, nor did he move in any way except from the motion of my thrust. And if he had responded, I cannot think what I would have said to him.

"Take it easy, Harry," said Wallace smiling and offering me a cigarette. "Is there anything wrong?"

"And you, Wallace? And you?"

"What about me?" he asked, but I said nothing. "I won't believe that one more corpse can trouble an old gravedigger like you."

"Corpses never bother me."

Lighting the cigarette I went to the window and leaned against the ledge. In the street I saw the red-headed boy running from the corner.

"So Tulley's remembered you, has he? Where do you know him from?" But again I would not reply.

When the young man entered the apartment, he rushed past us into the next room. "He'll be over right away," I heard him say. "He was in the middle of cutting an abscess, but he'll come as soon as he's finished. Is there anything else you'd like me to do, Father?"

"No, thank you. It's been too good of you to do this much. You must have run all the way—why, you can't even catch your breath. But it has brought a splendid color to your cheeks." After a pause, he continued: "Perhaps it might be better if you ladies—and gentlemen, of course—would leave the apartment until after the doctor has come. You understand, there would be no point in crowding things, etcetera." There were several faint grumbles and a quick rumble of protest, but a steady stream of emergents issued through the door. "Ah, but what shall we do with this young lady?"

"She's come have tea with me. Miss Morrison, you come have tea with me. It's better for the stomach after such sadness."

"My dear lady, do be reasonable. Go and have tea with your friend."

"Miss Morrison, it's———"

"Leave her alone," I shouted. "What difference can it make?"

When Mrs. Mussolini had gone, Tulley shut the apartment door and drew a wooden chair beside Mark.

"I can't understand why Emily is carrying on that way," said Wallace.

"Ah, then you are acquainted with the young lady? Perhaps she knew the poor boy."

"I don't know," said Wallace.

Abruptly Tulley turned to Mark. "Do you feel like talking now?" But the boy did not speak. "However did you get any results out of him before, Mr. Pembrook?"

"I didn't."

"But he must have told you where the key was."

"No. He wouldn't do anything. I found the key in his pocket."

"Did you? How clever of you." Tulley pushed Mark slightly. "Try and talk, dear boy. Come to your senses. Can you tell me who the person is in the next room? Can you tell me?"

After a long silence that I did not expect Mark to break, the boy nodded. "Yes," he said, almost inaudibly. Tulley waited, but nothing more was heard.

"Well? Who is he?" Tulley clucked several times. "Come, come. Who is he? Is he a relative? Or perhaps a very dear friend? Is he? Dear boy, is he a relative?"

"Yes."

"Your brother, I presume. Am I correct?"

"Yes."

"And would you be kind and tell me his name?" And although Tulley continued to cluck and to insist Mark would not answer. Wallace moved along the couch until he was close beside Mark, then, putting his arm round his shoulder, he asked, "Is it Jamie, Mark? Is that who the boy is?"

For the first time since I had entered the flat, Mark raised his eyes: he looked to Tulley, then to me, then to Wallace, and at last back upon himself. "Yes. It's all over for Jamie, isn't it?"

"Very good. We know that much: his name is Jamie. Probably James, don't you think?"

"Yes, probably," said Wallace and smiled.

"And they're brothers. He did say they were brothers?" Tulley thought a moment. "Do you really suppose they are brothers? There is not the faintest resemblance between them. I shouldn't wonder, but then of course. Nevertheless."

"I'd imagine," said Emily quietly from the other room, "that he'd be in a better position than you to know who is or isn't his brother." When she had finished speaking she appeared in the doorway, her face white, her short mussed hair looking bristled and stiff.

"Yes. Quite right. Now, how old would you say he was or is, that is. Twenty? Twenty-one? And whatever is their family name?"

"Oh, leave it alone," Emily whined. "It's none of your business. Everything will be all right."

Rising, Tulley walked to the center of the room and frowned; his mouth rounded with offence and although he was about to say something, he suddenly swung away from us in a graceful whirl and went to the door. "I believe he must have arrived." He pulled the door open and bent his head into the corridor; I could see the women still gathered there pushing one another for a peek in. "Ah, yes, I thought I heard someone. Do come in," said Tulley.

The doctor was a short man with freckles and a large thick rust-colored moustache as soft looking as mink. Standing near the door, his legs slightly parted, he regarded each of us separately as if trying to determine which was the deceased. Raising his eyebrows he removed a pair of rimless spectacles from his breast pocket and put them on.

"How long about has the patient been dead?" he asked, not directing his question at anyone.

"Well, to tell the truth, Doctor," replied Tulley, "we are not at all certain he *is* dead. Of course none of us, not excluding Mr. Sutton, is in any position——"

"I'd say the smell——"

"Yes, well—nevertheless. Would you come into the next room and . . . Dear lady, do move aside."

Touching Emily's elbow he pushed her out of the way.

"Candles and everything," said the doctor as he disappeared through the doorway. Following him, Tulley looked out at us and nodded before he closed the door.

"I want a cigarette," said Emily. "I left my bag at Mrs. Mussolini's." Wallace gave her one and, smoking, she walked slowly round the room. "Why? Why, if he isn't dead . . ." She turned toward Mark and leaned over him. "Are you so anxious to be rid of him? Don't you know how good he is? Would you be so pleased to have him die?"

"It wouldn't seem that way," said Wallace.

"No, it wouldn't. But he's sick in the next room and this one has decided he's dead—bang! Just like that! If he wasn't sure, why did he light candles? And if he was sure it was only because he wanted him dead."

"Maybe he *is* dead," I told her. My eyes wandered through the window, beyond the fire escape, down into the street submerged in a late-afternoon emptiness. A blade of sunlight, cutting through some unseen space between buildings, lay across the center of the street transient and unoccupied until a long black tom lazied into it, curled up, and went to sleep.

"Just as I thought," shrieked Tulley, pulling the door open. "He isn't dead at all."

"No, of course he isn't," said Emily.

"Are you all the family?" asked the doctor, coming into the room.

"No," said Wallace. "None of us. That is, except for this young man here—the brother."

"Your brother is very sick. Frankly, I would say it's a question of hours." Unaware that Mark paid no attention to him, he went on talking directly at the boy. "In cases like these, I can only recommend you to a specialist, although, well——"

"Just what is wrong with him?" Tulley asked.

The doctor thumped his heart. "His ticker," he said.

"We ought to get him to a hospital right away," Emily suggested.

"I wouldn't risk moving him, if I were you. We'll do all we can here, but as I say . . . Well, you can't be too optimistic. Still, you should contact a specialist. I know a very good man who'll come out right away if you mention my name."

"Don't bother," said Mark quietly, looking up once again. "Don't bother to do anything. Jamie's dead. There's nothing to do."

13

"I'm so tired of sitting here. Why don't we all go down for a drink?" said Wallace, and the full extent of time came back to me: through the window I saw that a suggestion of twilight had sprung violet veins into the sky. How long ago had it been late afternoon? How long had I been standing beside the window exposing myself to incidents in time, incidents that took no time at all because I had not responded to them, because, emptied of any possible reaction, I had remained as passive and beside the point as a shelf whose surface is recklessly loaded with a hundred temporary objects.

"I'm so tired of sitting here."

And it occurred to me now to be tired of standing here, to shake the disorder from my surface: and although I tried, the confusion was only reshuffled, not cleared away.

Said Emily: "Everything will be" someone in time had gone to phone the specialist "all right if we're all" and he had come, speared by a Vandyke his chin entered first "together is the most important thing and he'll be" together they were in the other room. *There is no question of it:* "fine of course" *he cannot last the night; observe the extreme reaction* but only Tulley had observed and pulsed broken antiquities at short intervals and through the course of lipless days.

Said Emily walking from room to room, from apartment to apartment, misery melted into cheer: "Everything will be" *ne nos inducas in* "all right" she kissed Mark's plaster brow "we must all be together and take care of" the ladies in the corridor followed her and shook their heads "him and everything will be" *observe the rapid thrusts which* "all right." The words, the sighs, the tears of women angry that whatever was not in the room was not dead: women who know a soft-boiled egg cooks hard in two-point-so-many minutes want death to be death, and reasonable.

Said Emily, arms round Mark: "He meant no harm" *my services will be included with those of Dr. Jacobs* "by it; in his unhappiness, in his grief, he thought Jamie was" the Vandyke was followed out by the back of the silver head "dead, and he did what he thought was right. He was alone; at least, you see, Wallace, he thought he was alone; but he isn't—he has all of us, hasn't he? We'll make Jamie better, and he and Mark will be happy again."

Wallace smoked a cigarette and looked tired. Mark had relapsed into silence and immobility upon the purple coverlet. And Tulley was silent in the other room.

"Why don't we all go down for a drink?"

I moved away from the window and sank to a wooden chair. "That's a good idea."

"Oh, no, you mustn't go," Emily warned. "You mustn't leave. It's very important to be together and stay here and work toward Jamie's recovery. I feel it strangely inside: it reminds me of when I was a little girl—that I was ever a little girl! I used to have a wish, not exactly a wish, more like a dream because it came to me at night, in bed. (Do you remember my room at home and the gray steel bed?) I'd lie there at night just before falling asleep and I'd think of all the people I loved and I wished all of them could be with me in the room and we would all lie there in a half-sleep, living forever because we were all together. That's how I feel it's important——"

"I'm sure you'd feel a lot better if you'd come down with us and have a drink."

"That's impossible, Wallace. You heard what the doctor said: he's going to show me how to give the injections, and then those other things are going to be sent over."

"But why are *you* doing all this?"

"Someone has to tend to Jamie."

"And for no reason you're getting all upset and messing yourself up with what's none of your business."

Circling her head vaguely, she considered Wallace's statement, and it worried her, the worry showing softly in the movement of her eyes and forehead, in the strain that puckered and relaxed her lips.

"It *is* my business," she told him. "He's a good friend of mine."

"Mark?"

"No, not Mark—Jamie."

"I had no idea. How do you know him?"

"We met ... we've never spoken." Her lips pressed together in secrecy.

"Well, what did you do—make faces at each other?"

"In a way, yes. We just looked at each other. But it's not only for Jamie that we've got to stay here: it's for Mark too. He's all alone; he has nothing else in the world."

"That's very kind of you, Emily. You're always so kind. You oblige the dragon at the bottom of every pit."

"Oh, don't be mean." She pushed herself close to him, her shoulders touching his, her hand reaching to his arm. "Please understand. You'll stay here with me, and Harry will stay too."

"I don't know what anyone else is going to do," he said, "but I'm going down for a drink."

"Did you say you were leaving, Mr. Pembrook?" asked Tulley, coming from the bedroom.

"Yes."

"If you would be kind enough to wait one minute, I will go down with you." Walking to Mark, he tapped the boy's head. "Young man, it is extremely important that you answer some questions—not for my sake or yours, but for the sake of the person in the next room. Do you hear me? I honestly implore——"

"He won't answer you," said Wallace.

"He *must*. I am afraid my doubts as to a blood relationship between the two of them are mounting, and if this James is not his brother I could not very well give him the final sacrament, not knowing whether or not he is baptized. Absolution is the best I can do, and that is done. Still, if the boy is entitled to extreme unction, we should do everything to find out." And he turned back to Mark. "Please, poor boy, can you not understand how imperative it is for me——"

"I'll take care of him," said Emily. "He'll be better. I'll watch them both, and when Mark sees there's hope he'll be better. But don't worry him now."

"I assure you, my dear lady, that I have no intention of worrying him, but every baptized Roman Catholic is entitled to extreme unction when——"

"Oh, that's unnecessary," Emily laughed. "That's only for people who are going to die. Oh, Wallace, wait! Are you really leaving? Will you come back after you've had your drink? Harry and I will be waiting."

"No, Emily," I told her. "I'm going too."

"You're going too, Harry? Everyone is going; we ought all to be together and yet everyone is going . . ."

Except for the slow puzzled shaking of her head, she was absolutely still as Tulley followed us into the corridor and closed the door.

Unlit, the white glass balls hung from ceiling chains, like dead bulbs of memory, and the only light was the early-evening dimness coming through the tavern windows in heavy shadowed slabs.

"Won't they ever turn the lights on?" Wallace asked.

"Perhaps the management has a sense of romance," suggested Tulley, indicating a pair of adolescents kissing at a nearby table.

But Rebecca's darkness was uncomfortable rather than romantic. A blue and smoky twilight perverted everything: the tiled floor hushed away under the sawdust, the painted freaks above the brass-and-mirror bar faded into the wall, and the people were softened and distorted out of definition.

"Rats," Tulley said. "Rats: or perhaps mice. I believe that is the most likely explanation; wouldn't you think so? I mentioned the possibility to both doctors, but neither of them said anything about it. In buildings as old as that one, there are sure to be nests in every room, in the walls, you understand."

"And you suppose they all come to die, rot, and stink like mad at Mark's apartment?"

"It might be their graveyard. After all, it is at the top of the house, closest to heaven one might say." With a start of self-consciousness, he raised his hand to his neck, which seemed this evening particularly long, for on the way to Rebecca's he had unfastened his collar and stuffed it into his pocket. "What else could it be? It is such a special, unmistakable odor, and if the poor young man is *not* dead—of course there is one other possibility: a supernatural or miraculous one."

"What do you mean?" asked Wallace.

"Any number of things. Perhaps the boy *was* dead and by some Divine Restoration is returned to life; then again it might be an outpouring of Evil. Or, on the other hand, the odor may not be coming from this James at all but may be a quality surrounding him, induced by I do not know what——"

"Or, finally, it might be rats."

"Rats, yes."

"But what's even more interesting," said Wallace, "is the difference in Mark's face. I've seen shock make some awful changes in people, but this is almost incredible. You know, it's things like crow's feet and wrinkles and hollows and bumps and slightly disfiguring movements that give expression to faces, but now Mark seems all smoothed out: flat faced and absurd looking. It's amazing, isn't it, Harry?"

"Yes." The word leaped out and back like a lizard's tongue: an automatic response to a stimulus; and when the stimulus was gone, my need or desire to communicate went with it, and I slumped inward, away from the others, bewilderment and self fogged behind Rebecca's twilight. Tulley's, even Wallace's interest was extraneous, a concern with a fray of threads hanging from the hem of a robe; but because I could not see the robe, the fray of threads was suspended in space, tied up with nothing, locked in emptiness like the moon. I took several wild stares round the dimness, picking out other isolated and unconnected things: the kiss of adolescents, the phosphorescent GENTS, a tray of beer glasses moving past me, the white glass balls who ceiling chains had darkened away, and Tulley's finger uncircling from his gin glass, reaching into his pocket, taking a box marked "Crescents" in gold, easing several cigarettes forward until their gold tips pointed to nose.

"*Crescents!*" cried Wallace. "The pickings must have been good from the alms plate today."

"Mr. Pembrook, that is not kind."

The cigarettes were lit and the strong brown fumes

twisted upwards and merged upon the window, rocking back and forth before they disappeared.

"But if you say it was over a week ago," Tulley considered, "that Harry saw him and noticed this curious change, and if we assume that the change is due to shock at the illness of the other boy, then this James must already have been badly off, in which case how could so good a friend—or brother, if you prefer—have left him alone and gone airing himself in parks in the middle of the night? And that, unfortunately, brings me back to the question of whether they are *really* brothers. Whatever their relationship, you must understand"—his hand started to his neck, then dropped—"I am entirely sympathetic. But if they are not brothers, certain other elements become involved: not only, as I said, could I not administer the extreme unction, but there would be this James's family to think of. I am deeply sorry to say this, but perhaps we were wrong not to have brought the police in as the hasty ladies suggested."

The sudden lighting of the tavern momentarily silenced Tulley. And after the first crushing brightness in my eyes, not only the surroundings, but myself, clarified; I moved outside confusion, slid down the nonexistent robe, and tangled myself among the fray of threads. As I listened to Tulley continue his nosy probings into the flat on Crawford Street, I felt warm and dry-eyed like a child who has, after coming to misfortune, cried the emotion out of himself and assumes since the emotion is relieved, so must be the misfortune. In this way, my active interest in the conversation was based on something I can almost never do: lie to myself.

"If Mark says they're brothers," I said, "why don't you take his word for it?"

"Because Mark is in no condition to know what he is saying, and he did not explicitly say they were brothers. He merely answered, yes, when I asked if they were."

"Well, he's told Wallace they were brothers."

"Has he, Mr. Pembrook?"

But Wallace did not hear the question: his eyes were closed, and his entire face seemed in a way shut, as if the tired look I had noticed in the afternoon had intensified and brought with it—not sleep, for one fingernail lightly plucked the edge of the table—preoccupation.

"*Has* he, Mr. Pembrook?" Tulley repeated, putting his face close to Wallace's and raising his voice. "Has Mark told you before today that they are brothers?"

Wallace's eyes opened, but not his face, and he said quietly, "Yes."

"In that many words?"

"Most of Mark's poems," Wallace began, straining himself out of preoccupation into alertness, "are about Jamie, so of course I was curious to know who Jamie was. He wouldn't tell me at first, but when I asked again he said Jamie was his brother."

"Well, there you are!" Tulley clapped his hands. "If they were *really* brothers he should certainly not have hesitated to say so at once."

"Actually," said Wallace, "he didn't seem to hear the question when I first put it to him."

"Ah, well—but still, if there were any sort——"

"Dammit, Tulley," I said. "If you're that curious, maybe

you can check up at the bureau of records and see if they *are* in the same family."

"Excellent!" he cried, one eye fixed on me, the other on Wallace. "I've done that before, you know. I never have any difficulty because of my—my collar. Of course I couldn't very well go tonight, and then tomorrow is Sunday: closed, certainly. Dear, and then Monday may be too late—will surely be too late. James will probably be dead."

"It would be still better if he was," said Wallace. "Then we could hold a séance and contact him direct instead of depending on record bureaus."

Tulley's eye widened and he quickly poured the remaining gin into his mouth. "May I presume that you are interested in the *hereafter?*"

"You may," Wallace replied, leaning forward and beginning to smile. "And you?"

Tulley laid his lips together, paused thoughtfully, and looked sharply round to see if any strangers might be close enough to hear; then he spoke in a whisper. "It would be inconvenient if this were to be generally known, and I trust to your confidence. Being a friend of Harry's, Mr. Pembrook, I can rest calm that you will not betray my trust. Nevertheless. I am extremely interested in making contact with those who have passed into God's keeping. Since I realize this is not a completely orthodox approach to theology, I seldom reveal this part of my life to others."

"Are you trying to say that you hold séances?" asked Wallace. "That you're a medium?"

"Those are such unfortunate words: séance, medium. To me, they smack of heresy. I should prefer to call my contacts *sittings*; and myself—I am merely a clergyman, even in relation to the hereafter. But if you mean by your questions whether I am effective in reaching the departed, I must say yes."

"You never told me that, Tulley," I said.

"No, I imagine not, Harry. It is only during the past months that I have begun to take an active interest in my sittings. I mentioned before that I have taken a room uptown: a very modest place, I might say, in a quiet old brownstone. And it is there I keep my cats and make my contacts. I can tell you I have been extremely successful in my several attempts."

"I'm terribly interested," said Wallace. "I've never been to a genuine séance. Do you have a special spirit or do you just take potluck and come-what-may?"

"Oh, no, no. I have only one acquaintance, although very often he reaches others for me. He himself is an elderly gentleman named Haq, an Egyptian judge who died in 1939. I believe he died of plague, although on the subject of his death he is most vituperative and claims the British poisoned him. But otherwise he is a most charming man, gentle, kind, well mannered. Often when I cannot get up to the room for two or three days, he takes the trouble to feed the cats."

"Does he indeed?" roared Wallace, and I was caught up in his laughter.

"If you doubt my word, Mr. Pembrook, you are welcome to come to my room and speak to him for yourself. You may come at any time. Just give me a day's notice and I should be delighted to introduce you to Haq." He snapped his frowning face from Wallace to me. "You too, Harry, although——"

"Not interested, Tulley. Thanks."

"No, I did not suppose you would be. Spiritualism—if one must call it that—is next door to faith, and faith is far away from you, isn't it, Harry?"

Instead of answering, I looked down at my beer glass, and seeing it empty, I turned round to call the waiter. But I did not call, for my eyes rested across the room upon the barstool where I had sat the last time I'd been to Rebecca's; and I remembered that I had been thinking of Tess, and the contradiction arose once more: the body in bed, the triply-mirrored angry girl before the dressing table. I suppose, without forming a decision, I had known until this evening that I would not see her again, that I would kill the intrusion before it was fully born. Yet now the thought of Tess comforted.

She would gossip, be trivial, would not involve herself even to the extent of having seen Jamie. She would have no patience with faith or spiritualism; she would see only what can be seen, not what is usable. She is different from Tulley's delicate encroachments, from Emily's clouded concern, and even, although it is so difficult to believe, from Wallace. She is like me and like my cat, negating complications, aware of ourselves as a compact of space within an infinity, acting in terms of drive and not noetic-poetic emotions.

"What did she say his name was?" Tulley wondered. "The old lady who came to call me today: she told me Mark's family name." He thumped his finger on the table. "Ah, yes: Akero. Mark Akero. It sounds Spanish, wouldn't you say? Mark and James Akero. . . ."

14

Instead of dawn, a thick pale mist pushed the night away. Smearing over the streets, rolling into open windows, it lay everywhere and waited for a hot morning sun to dry it up. Beneath the mist was deep quiet, emphasized by an occasional distant sound as clear and sudden as a light: the clatter of a milk wagon, the whistle of a faraway tug, the high pure scream of a bird. Now, fitting beside the window where I had been for hours, observing what there was to see, I concentrated on these sudden sounds and on the silence, and breathed deeply when the faint sweet-smelling breeze rode across the mist, touching my face, cooling my eyes.

Although I had not slept during the night, I was not tired, or rather not sleepy, merely numb, except in my legs, where an indefinite ache crept through the bones. The flesh of my face was as tight as if pulled back at the ears, and my eyes seemed to have dissociated themselves from my system and were functioning in a detached unphysical manner, hardly blinking. I could, I suppose, have slept now, having thought the matter out of mind, but sleep was no longer important or necessary: nothing, in fact, was necessary but to sit forever at the window giving my face and body to the breeze, and resting in the permanence of early-morning mist. And as I sat I imagined nothing could alter, that somehow I had managed myself out of time and circumstance, out of relativity, out of night and day, into an unchangeable intransient reality, like a work of art.

But I was wrong of course: mist and breeze were slowly interspersed with tubes of sunlight, and my nakedness was backed away from the window when a yawning pajama'd neighbor rubbed his lids and looked across the way at me. Those clear and intermittent sounds of silence blurred into the more general noises of hurried living, and Kitty, with a scratch on her nose and a little blood back of the neck, returned through the window, landing with a thud at my feet. Squatting beside her, I scratched her belly until her eyes closed and the long orange tail swung up and down with elegance. Suddenly bored, she looked at me and stretched, then lifted herself and walked into the kitchen to see what she might find to eat.

Again I looked through the window and saw the last tatters of mist melting in the sun; the day was already hot. I dressed in a pair of rumpled army tropicals and a polo shirt and felt immediately uncomfortable, so after I had put coffee up to boil I picked a book from the shelf and sat down once more at the window. The book was Wallace's second novel and I began to turn through it, looking for the lines that had made me laugh aloud. But now all these comical people seemed to be saying nothing funny—in fact, perhaps because I read them out of context, their speeches were rather sad. Finally I stopped seeking to be amused and read the lines seriously: they became grandiose and tiresome: all the pointless sentences, the detached episodes, had curdled and staled. I could understand so clearly why Emily, although she says she loves Wallace's books, is always puzzled by them. What she refuses to comprehend in life, she can still less comprehend in fiction: a total lack of arrangement. How can she laugh at the incident of Peter's head being smashed by a falling chandelier immediately after his wedding when she believes firmly that Peter loved his bride, that marriage is eternal, and that death is tragic?

I took my coffee cool and very light, but without sugar, and gave Kitty a cup of milk, which she lapped indifferently, strolling away after each sip as if she could not decide whether it ought to be drunk. Unwound, my watch was frozen to four o'clock but I assumed it must be after six and, without finishing my coffee, I put on a pair of moccasins and left the flat. On the landing, before his door, Mrs. Collini's little boy stood in his undershirt and watched me.

"Where you gone?" he asked and stuck a finger in his nose.

"To the moon," I said.

He appeared satisfied until I turned down the stairs, and then I heard him call, "No, you're not."

"Yes, I am," I shouted back.

"No, you're not, cause there ain't none in the morning and even if there ..."

But I was already in the street and did not hear the rest.

I walked the other way from the funeral parlor and went round the corner on Inshore Street where the sun was blocked away by the tall wide buildings. But even so the concrete was warm enough to heat my soles, and the slough of motionless air drew the sweat from my body. All the shops were closed on Inshore Street and no one was about: desertion hung in the air, stretched past the 25-CENTS-A-NITE hotel, into the solemn green of the park beyond. At Rebecca's I paused and looked through the window to see if Tulley and Wallace sat where I had left them last night. But the place was dim, empty, shut; chairs were stacked upon the white steel tables; nothing moved but the reflection of my face in the mirror behind the bar. And looking at myself I felt a sensation I can only describe as longing, a dull but persistent desire, a nostalgia half bled of sentiment. But what it was I longed for I could not decide. My mind was reaching back to a memory, a recollection at once within and without me, going back behind myself; and arbitrarily my thoughts rested on Crawford Street: *there*, because memory was specific not merely a falling-back across tattooed legs and a violet-haired woman and visions of Tess.

Inshore Street was the path which least resisted the sensation of longing, so I followed it, not to the park, but southwards until it broke into three other streets: I took the one running left. I went as far as Wimple Road, a half-mile alleyway that lies like a moat between fortresses, for on either of its sides are factory blocks and behind them, invisible from where I stood, the slum. I was alone here, the high soundless walls rising round me, pressing in against my nostalgia; I looked to left and right a long while before I realized that what I longed for was the murmur of the factories, the steady noise of production. But today was Sunday, and those who worked the machines had gone away. I regarded the opaque windows that, from the taxi, I had seen lit yesterday afternoon, and the cold brick chimneys which had smoked into the summer sky. And what I desired was to see this half-mile hulk turn live again, to whir and smoke and blast with an occasional pale uninteresting uninterested face appearing at the window to look down at me and then over my head across the fortress to the slum and over that, perhaps, to the river. I longed for all this within my head and throat, and more than that—*entirely*, as if in it were release. I longed as a woman must to take it into me, snap my legs round it, and when finished, drag over to the slum, to Crawford Street, and then later—to the river.

It must have been a quarter of an hour, with the sun rapping at my head, that I thought such idiocy, giving myself to it seriously as though despite the fact that *there ain't none in the morning and even if there*—I had gone to the moon. But eventually, wherever I had gone, I came back again, and the nostalgia slowly subsided until the factories had no further fascination.

Once away from Wimple Road there were more people on the street, some in fine clothes going to early Mass, others loosely dressed with the easy look of Sunday morning. Moving among them, my dissatisfied mind returned to Wimple

Road, repeating the experience, and as I listened to myself I heard another voice lacing through mine. It was Wallace's, saying nothing in particular or rather indistinguishable things, and I tried to listen: in fact, I even paused on the street to hear better, but I could not. The only definite thing was his face, but even that alternated between his smile and the closed expression of fatigue or preoccupation I had seen yesterday. And I heard myself ask, Did you see Jamie, Wallace? Have you seen the boy who isn't there? The reply was splotched and incoherent, but as he talked his face weakened: I believed Wallace had seen Jamie, because if he had not, he would have said so.

Flump.

An awning dropped above my head and shaded the sun away. Turning, I saw I had stopped in front of a candy store; a short man with the stump of a cigar caught between his teeth stood in the door jamb and looked at me.

"I'd like a drink," I said.

"Yessirree." He backed into the store and I followed him. It was cool inside and I sat down at the fountain, leaning my arms upon the marble bar.

"What'll it be?" the man asked taking a glass from underneath.

"What's good for a warm morning?"

"Well, if we had any, I'd say iced coffee's the best. But a nice chocolate cream's almost as good."

"All right."

Two or three grains of ash fell from his cigar into my glass and he half-raised his eyes at me, but I pretended not to notice and turned my face to the window. Against the wall an electric clock ringed with neon showed a few minutes to seven, and I wondered, as my eyes ran round the neon, what I might do with the rest of the day.

I finished the soda slowly, dreading the idea of going out into the hot street; and then I did the only possible thing: I telephoned Tess.

15

In the beginning all my senses are remote, unintelligible, afloat: there is chaos at my eyes and ears and along the length of my flesh. Next I feel hot pinpoints peppering from face to trunk to legs, and I see a spotted blaze and then a flat pale sky extending evenly to everywhere, and from the rush of wind, sea, voices, I pick out Tess.

"Lousy kid! Why don't you look where . . . You think you own the place? Oh, you're up, Harry. That kid ran by and shot sand all over you. No, don't do that, you'll get it in your mouth."

Sliding her fingers across my lips, she brushes the sand away. And as she leans forward her breasts squeeze together and half out of the bathing suit, and her face is directly above mine. The black hair, before pinned up to be shoved in her cap, is now released and flashes streaks of copper and gold in the sunlight.

"Was I asleep long?"

"Over an hour, I guess. It's so hard to tell time on the beach: everything always seems like an hour. You slept so nice, with your mouth open a little and little *ka-rumphs* coming from ... Adenoids? Is that what makes the snoring noise?" Lowering her head she kisses me. "You have such a sweet mouth, Harry." Then suddenly grabbing my shoulders: "Come on, let's go in the water. Last one in is a dirty rat." She tosses her hair up, pins it unevenly, and fits the cap over her head.

"Just give me a minute, Tess. I'm still asleep."

"No, you're not. Come on."

"Take your cap off. I want to see your hair floating on the water."

"You men, you're crazy! If I don't wear ... How would you like to go around with a girl that's got wires instead of hair? Now, come on, get up, Harry!"

Climbing to my feet, I sense the cool breeze that comes from the water. Round us the beach is less crowded, and where blankets had lain are now only empty bottles, waxed paper, cucumber skins. Between us and the calm blue bay, two boys sit fashioning a mermaid from the wet sand.

"It's beginning to empty," I say.

"Sure, it must be after five already, and there's a nice wind coming up. It'll be a wonderful evening." Unexpectedly she touches my arm, swings away and races toward the water, her disappearing voice flagging back to me, "Last one in ..."

I run past the two boys, over their mermaid, and as my feet touch a receding wave, I see Tess vanish beneath the surface. Walking out further, I wait until I am covered to my chest before submerging. Beneath, after the initial breaking of the cold, I paddle until my nose is along the bottom, scraping above speckled clamshells and the sparkle of sand. The sea is yellow here and vast, and I have no desire to rise out of it but to remain until the sun sets, moving slowly along, the cool velvety water stroking every part of my body, pushing me forward or backward, straining with its gentle touch upon my shoulders. Round me minnows glide in clusters like clouds, executing their motions with the grace that is found only underwater where all movements are refined, where my arms and fingers are unnaturally plastic, inhumanly delicate, and I have the impression I can twist them like deep-sea flowers into any shape.

Then my breath is gone: a chain of bubbles rises from my mouth and streams through the yellow water to the surface. At last I am forced to rise and, coughing for air, I look round the bay for Tess: further in I see her white cap and begin to swim toward it.

"Jesus, Harry, I thought you drowned! You must've been under for two minutes or more."

"There's a nice world down there."

"Oh, it's all right. Only the people are too slimy, don't you think?"

"Let's swim out."

"No, I want to float. Here, take my hand. There, that's it. Isn't it lovely? You know, Harry . . . Say, can you hear me?"

"Yes."

"Floating always gives me such a feeling: I like it and I don't like it. I mean, isn't it funny about water? I can put my hand right through it like this, and yet it's strong enough to hold my whole body. And then I always think . . . You know the story how Jesus walked on water? Well, it seems kind of possible in a way."

"If he was bird-weight."

"I don't know. Anyway, that isn't what bothers me. Here I am floating and it's so unrealistic, like being in a dream or a fairy tale, and it's peaceful and calm, like my body went away. But then what happens? I stop floating and I drop my legs into the water and I look up to see where the beach is. And I get . . . Because there's such a peculiar feeling when I see the world looking so faraway and fake: all just a big front like scenery in a play. And then I get all mixed up and don't know which is real, the fakeness of floating or the world. Oh, I'm talking crazy, huh?"

Our hands are folded together tightly, resting upon the water. "So I think I'm dizzy those few seconds until I can straighten myself out because I get so nervous not knowing which is what." She sighs deeply. "But I guess it's the world that's real."

"I guess it is."

"Yeah, but still the feeling is funny." We float in silence a while, the small waves carrying our bodies, lilting us into a sensation of weightlessness. My ears now are submerged and I am not certain that what I hear is exactly what she is saying: "It's so nice to talk to you this way: in a serious way. You know, I love you, Harry."

Instead of replying I let her hand go, and force my legs

down. "Let's swim a little," and with a thrust I glide her away from me. Then I look round the bay, shoreward, to see the distant artificial world, and Tess's suggestion moves in me: is floating the reality or is it that wide flat painted front? And although the distance back is short, it seems for an instant that I can never swim it.

"See what I mean?" Tess yells to me. "Do you see?"

Jumping to the surface I swim to her, churning a madness of water into her face.

"Harry, oh, stop, for crying out loud! Stop or I'll ... I can't breathe. You're such a stinker." She takes a full mouth of water and spouts it into my face.

"You whale," I roar. "I'll fix you for that."

"No, Harry. Oh, Harry, *don't!*" Her scream vibrates as I tear the cap away; pins come away with it and the long bundle of hair tumbles round her shoulders, the tips touching the water. "Give it back to me! Give it back!"

"I threw it away."

"You couldn't have. Harry, that cap cost me a dollar twenty-five at ... Please——"

"It's all right. It's in my trunks. But you'll have to swim without it."

Putting my hands to her shoulders I push downward until her face has vanished and floating above is the circle of black hair spreading ring-like on the surface, thinning until each strand is separate and each an independent life. I release her and she rises.

"What do you want to do, kill me?" she blusters, hair deflating round her head and face. Angrily she starts away.

"Where are you going?"

"I'm going to sit down and relax. You're a bastard, Harry. You know, I didn't even . . . I could've drowned."

I follow her on to the beach; she walks ahead of me rapidly, her hips dancing in the bathing suit. She falls to the blanket, throws a towel round her shoulders, takes a comb from her bag, and begins to fix her hair, muttering *damn damn dammit*. Looking up at me suddenly, she begins to laugh, her body bending.

"What's so funny?"

"You better take my cap out of your pants. You look abnormal."

"Here."

"Thanks. Well, I hope you're satisfied now. Just look at what you've done to me."

I sink to the sand and bury my hands in it. The sun is still warm but already distant and harmless, no longer a violent white blaze that pales the sky but rather flushed and adding color to the sky. Round us families continue to pack away their things, begin to feel the discomfort of sand in the corners of their bodies, start to drag across the beach to the lockers and exits. The two boys who had fashioned the mermaid are gone but she remains, endures, while the growing waves swing closer to her, lashing foam to her tail.

"You know, I'm glad what happened last week happened," says Tess, four hairpins in her mouth.

"What do you mean?"

"When I said all those things. I know you didn't like it, but it made things different than before. I said to myself, well, maybe he won't call me again, but if he does it'll be different between us, more friendly than it was. Two people, when they keep on seeing each other, can't help getting closer, mixed up in each other's life. But anything I thought about you, I always felt I had . . . I mean it was like holding myself in all the time. What I said in the water, I couldn't have said it last week."

"What did you say?"

"That I love you."

"Oh."

"Does it embarrass you, Harry? I didn't mean it to. I just . . . Oh, you know."

"Yes, I know." I feel myself weakening, thinning, becoming insubstantial and defensive. The phrases necessary to cut the conversation cannot form in my head: I listen and consider and sense the swooning of my mind and an image of an empty davenport twitches before me.

Tess smiles, shrugs, continues to pin her hair up. "I would ask you if you love me, but I guess I know I better not." There is no anger in her voice, nor self-pity, nor even resignation, but only a kind of half-certain dare. "Weren't you *ever* in love, Harry? Maybe when you were a kid?"

"No."

"How can that be? I mean, everybody falls in love even for just a day or a minute and you . . . Well, you're past thirty already."

"I'll be thirty-two in the fall, in October."

"There, you see?" She puts two more pins in her mouth. "It's not *natural* not to fall in love."

The word hooks at me, pulls, and I feel myself coming back. "That's just it, Tess. It is natural not to fall in love because love is not a natural thing: it's something man made up—like the idea of God. And if you know there's no such thing as God, can you worship him?" Because she is silent, I repeat more loudly, "Well, *can* you?"

The force of the question turns her face bayward. "No, I guess not because ... Well, I think ... No, of course not."

"And it's the same thing with love: it's as manmade as if it had a factory number on it. It's *not* nature."

"It's manmade," she considers. "I don't know. Nature didn't invent permanent waves or dresses. Don't you believe in them either?"

"That isn't the same thing, or maybe it is the same thing, but smaller. Nature gave us hair and bodies: why fancify them? It's the same thing with sex; you fall in love so you can sugarcoat a screw and pretend it's more than a simple function. Sure, I could say I love you——"

"What do you mean, Harry?" she interrupts me, angered. Her hair is pinned up, tight round her head like a soft black helmet. "What do you mean? You could say you love me just to sugarcoat the screw. But all that counts *is* the screw? Is that it? Well, I'm getting sick and tired of being nothing but a screw. I don't know what's wrong with you, but I guess something must be—maybe you don't have enough vitamins. I don't care who made up love but it's a good thing for the heart to feel. I'm not an animal like a dog or a mosquito: I don't lay eggs or go sniffing around the streets for a screw—you hear! And now I feel—I guess I must've fallen for a dog or a mosquito. That's what you are, Harry. And here I am offering myself—and I'm a *person*—to an insect. How would you feel if I just stopped seeing you? I guess you wouldn't care much. You'd go find someone else to screw at the end of the week. Is that what you'd do? Tell me, Harry, would it matter if you never saw me again?"

Within me once more is the sensation of longing like a pressure on my chest; all the corners of my life seem to be folding inward, joining at the center: one complaint laps over another—love touches Tess and Tess touches Jamie and Jamie touches—or doesn't touch at all. I turn my face away and look to the north, down the long stretch of emptying beach and over the bay, which is deep blue, the color of the sky, so that the horizon is indistinguishable. The sun is pink now, suggesting evening and another hot day. What else is there to look at: the unequal buildings back of us, the line of green rocks that wanders into the sea, the gulls, the invisible ships? I look at anything to take my mind away from the longing that changes subtly into fear. But I cannot look at Tess, to whom I have come for answers but who has given me only questions. I want her to lean over me now and touch me, kiss me, untie anxiety, tell me that floating is unreal, that Jamie is unseeable. Everything is ruined: my head is destroyed: my balance is gone. The water, the wind, the sky smell like corpses; Tess has taken me nowhere but yesterday.

"Well, Harry, aren't you going to answer? Would you care if we never saw each other again?"

"Yes, I would care."

There is nothing more to look at. I close my eyes and drop my body into the sand and watch the colors pass before my closed lids: those nuanced tones—half-yellows, half-reds—I hate so much. And it is a long while with the sea breeze growing stronger that we remain so in silence.

"You know what, Harry?" Her voice is tender now.

"What?"

"You know what let's do?"

"What, Tess?"

"Let's swim out to the end of the rocks. They're flat all the way out and soft as a bed. And you know what we'll do there?"

My eyes are open and I see she has removed every pin from her head and the damp hair hangs to her shoulders.

"Do you want to, Harry?"

"Yes, yes. Let's go."

We both jump up and begin the run to the water's edge, smash outward and dive, and beneath the surface we swim beside each other, limbs moving frantically. It is no longer yellow here, rather green, but the water is still velvet and still soothes my body and distorts my arms and all of Tess into deep-sea flowers. She rises first and I follow, never resting, swimming toward the end of the rocks, our arms and legs battering foam high in the air, and all is gone but the end of the rocks. We are almost there, but we do not slow our movements as if getting there depends only on speed; then at last, before us, is the final green ledge dripping with moss and weed and barnacles.

I touch the slime-rock, dig my fingers into a niche, tear the green away, and lift myself. My foot slips along the stone, then rests in another crack, and when I have reached the top I give my hand to Tess.

"Isn't it faraway?" she sighs looking round, her breath coming in catches.

It *is* faraway. Back of us sea and sky reach toward each

other, touching out of sight; and before us is the fronted world miniaturized by distance; and underneath the sea heaves and retches. We sink into the moss and come close together, sensing each other from the cold wet touch of toes to our mouths. But although everything seems right, something is wrong. There could be no better place: civilization is left behind, and if this is not the jungle it is greener and wetter, and sun and wind are upon us, and sea is smashing to our feet.

"What's the matter, Harry?"

"I don't know. I can't."

"Why not?" Her eyes are wide and terrified. "It's because of me, of what I said before, isn't it?"

"No. I don't know. Yes, partly."

"Harry, please. Tell me what's wrong. Everything was so good before. I'll cut my tongue out if I've ... Please, don't look like that."

"I'm all right. Don't press me."

Her head sinks back into the moss, black tangling with green, and she is beautiful lying there, isolated and with a bewildered face.

"Look, Tess...."

"Yes, Harry?"

"Will you come somewhere with me? We'll swim back and change, and then will you come with me?"

She nods and we slide from the rock into the bay and slowly we begin the swim to shore.

16

"Jesus, Harry, what a smell!" she said as we passed from the cool crowded street into the dark corridor of the tenement. "What is it?"

"I don't know—maybe dead rats." I started up the iron-railed staircase, motioning her to follow. We had spoken very little since leaving the beach, and even then only of inconsequentials: bus fare, stopping for a hamburger, proper change, enough cigarettes, the growing wind. And most of the journey to Crawford Street Tess had occupied herself with painting her face and arranging or rearranging the thick damp bun that sat back of her head. Not once had she asked where we were going or why I wanted her to come, and it was not until we reached the landing beneath Mark's that I paused to explain.

"It may be crowded up there," I said, indicating the floor above with a tilt of my head, "or there might be only two or three people. In either case, Tess, they'll most likely be acting miserable."

"Why? What's happened?"

"You'll see in a minute." The sentence came easily, yet when it was said I found an inevitability glowing round it, the beginning of a despairing sureness within myself, for the phrase suggested what I had already started to feel: that Tess would be able to see Jamie. But, perhaps because of the soft numbness of physical exhaustion throughout my body, the certainty affected me less than I might have expected and left me merely with a sense of flat unworried resignation. "Promise me one thing: to be honest and tell me exactly what you *see* in the apartment."

"Of course I promise, Harry."

She smiled and we climbed the last flight. All doors were shut and the floor was deserted; only one shredded ribbon of gray light trailed to the landing and that from the window at the other end, outside Mrs. Mussolini's flat.

I rapped lightly at Mark's door, then waited, then rapped again more heavily.

"Maybe no one's there," said Tess.

"No, there must be . . ." and I turned the knob and pushed the door open.

Mrs. Mussolini, wrapped in black, stood directly before me, her eyes undecided as if a moment ago she had not known whether she ought to open the door. Like a mannequin of shriveled wires her body stood in the wide dress of laces and satin, a costume left from another mourning and another world, brought into the present by a safety pin, a blue patch. On either side of her, half hidden behind the flare of satin, was a thin blonde child with a serious face.

"The friend of Miss Morrison," said Mrs. Mussolini, and backed away. "If I know it's be you, mister, I open the door right away, but I think it's was neighbors with noses again. Miss Morrison she's like all of company." She looked at Tess and frowned. "You close a door, yes, miss, please?"

"Are you alone?" I said.

"No. Mark is here." She pointed behind her. "In another room with his——"

"And Emily? Miss Morrison—is she here?"

"She's just go down make telephones. All day she's went five times for telephones. Up and down a staircase: bad for the heart. And after what happens? Like poor other boy."

We all looked to the bedroom; pale yellow streaks of candle flame leaped again and again through the doorway. And Mrs. Mussolini nodded her head.

Back of us the door pushed open and Emily came in. There was a smile at her mouth, rather more like a laugh but soundless or controlled, and her eyes were unnaturally large as if she were forcing them—their color too was strange, perhaps from the flashes of candlelight, for they were waxen. Like an apology her fingers traveled down the disarrangement of her skirt and blouse—buttons were unhooked, the skirt had swung sideward, a seam was torn from her armpit up round her shoulder—but the disorder was intensified by her short jumpy movements.

"He'll be all right. Yes, he'll be *fine*—he'll be all right! I'm so glad you came, Harry. Is Wallace here? No? I've just been down to phone you both; I've been down *dozens* of times to phone you at the funeral parlor and they called up to your flat but you weren't there. Where were you? And Wallace hasn't been home since before noon; when I spoke to him he said he would be *right* over. I hope nothing's happened to him. And I waited for you for *hours* last night. You said you'd come back and I expected you every minute—but you didn't come. We were so disappointed, weren't we, Mrs. Mussolini? But you've come now and that's good. Is this beautiful girl a friend of yours, Harry?"

I introduced them and Emily took both Tess's hands in hers. "I'm so *very* happy to meet you. But may I call you Tess? And you must call me Emily."

"Sure," said Tess, easing herself loose.

"You're very kind. Would you like to come in and see Jamie? Oh, he's going to be *well*, you know, isn't he, Mrs. Mussolini?"

The old woman's lined unhappy face was full of doubt as she nodded her head. "It's better you take Miss Morrison home, mister. She's not sleep, all night sit there next to boy."

"Nonsense, Mrs. Mussolini. It's my job to worry about you, not yours to worry about me. And just *look* at the children! It's almost eight o'clock and they haven't had supper. I'll bet you're hungry, poor things, aren't you?" The children retreated behind their grandmother and jerked their heads meaninglessly. "Of course you are. You haven't had a thing since noon."

"Yes, I go now give them eat," said Mrs. Mussolini, then turning to me she spoke narrowly, threateningly. "You be better see Miss Morrison should rest." And although she had obviously meant to say more, she swept her grandchildren forward and left the room.

"Not that *she's* had any sleep," said Emily, delighted. "She was here with me all last night and most of today, but there's been so much to do: transfusions and medicines. I've even been giving Jamie injections. Oh, he's going to be *fine*, you know. I'm sure he'll be coming to consciousness during the night or tomorrow. And won't it be wonderful! He'll give me those deep beautiful looks again and tell me that more than two weeks ... Oh, but you don't want to listen to me talk; you want to see him."

I hesitated, my legs unwilling to carry me into the room, my heartbeats freezing me with their sudden reckless gallop. Half pleading, half futile was the look I showed to Tess, and my arm made a gesture of uselessness.

"Come, Harry," Emily urged; and I followed her through the doorway.

At the foot of the davenport, sitting cross-legged on the floor, was Mark. He nodded once, sharply, then leaned sideward, rested his cheek against the couch, and watched us.

"How are you feeling?" Emily asked him warmly.

"Why don't you go away and mind your own business," he said softly, his mouth hardly opening.

She turned to us and nodded sympathetically. "You must understand him. He doesn't realize yet that he's not alone and that Jamie is going to be well. The terrible sadness has made him"—touching her head secretively—"not seriously, you see, just for ... *Look* at all these things!" She pointed to a tall steel apparatus surrounded by bottles and thin rubber tubing. "For blood, and in order to feed Jamie. The oxygen was brought this morning but we decided he did just as well without it."

"The dead don't breathe," Mark grunted.

The davenport was as empty as it had been yesterday, more so in fact, for now the silken pillow was removed; behind, beneath the drawn window shade, the two thick candles continued to burn. Tess's face remained unchanged in the candlelight, and as I observed her I felt no emotion: my heart was calm and with perfect apathy I waited for her to tell me that Jamie was there.

"He's beautiful," she said quietly.

"Yes, isn't he?" Emily agreed. "I told Harry that was just the word for him—*beautiful*. And he's beautiful inside too."

"Is he your brother?" asked Tess.

"My brother? No, closer than that." Turning away she walked to the window and put her finger through a line of carbon on the shade. "These *candles!* They shouldn't be here at all. I'm sure they eat up all the air in the room; even the doctor said it wasn't a wise idea to have them, especially so close to Jamie's head. But Mark insists. And he's in *no* condition to argue with."

"You're supposed to put up candles for the dead," the boy said.

"Why does he keep saying he's dead?" Tess whispered.

"It's his mental state. At first I thought it was because he wanted Jamie dead, but how *wrong* I was! But when Jamie is better, when he becomes conscious, I'm sure Mark will snap out of it. And now with transfusions and feedings and the hypodermics to stimulate the heart, he'll be fine. Don't you think he already looks better than yesterday, Harry? Isn't there more color in his face?"

"I couldn't say."

"Oh, I *know*. It's so difficult to tell in the candlelight. Tomorrow I'm going to pull this shade up first thing in the morning and let the sun and air in. That's the best thing. Wouldn't you say so, Tess?"

"I guess so. I don't know." She paused. "I think the best place for sick people is in the hospital."

"The hospital? Yes, but . . . And besides we couldn't part with him even for a *minute*. He couldn't be better treated in the hospital than here. We're so close to the doctor that he's visited Jamie three times today, and he said he'll be coming again before bedtime. Oh, and the priest was here today, Harry, before, in the afternoon, and he said . . . but I'll tell you that later . . . not here, you understand. He was *very* impressed with the way Mrs. Mussolini and I were taking care of everything. He was here when the doctor came, and even the doctor said . . . but then that doctor is an idiot anyway."

A dry forced laugh broke from Mark. "Tell them what the doctor said. Don't you want to? He said it was almost unbelievable that Jamie had survived the night. That shows you what an idiot he *is:* Jamie's been dead for days."

Emily's hands sucked into each other tightly and the strain of the clasp shook her entire body; with every spasm she seemed to be saying *no* to Mark.

"Let's go into the other room," I said, and she relaxed with the suggestion. The three of us went out leaving Mark as he had been, at the foot of the davenport.

"I wish there were something to offer you," Emily began softly, but as she continued to speak the feverish excitement rose once more in her voice. "When I went down this morning I bought some things but they're all gone now. I can't imagine where it all went, but then so *many* people have been coming in to sit with us, to comfort us, to be all together. I could put up some coffee, if you'd like. Or perhaps tea? Anything? Although there's really nothing left— a cracker or two. Would you give me a cigarette, Harry? Thanks. I can't remember where I put mine. They were over there on my notebook. Have you ever seen that notebook, Tess? It's like a symbol of my work. When I walk down the street with it under my arm everyone knows who I am. 'She's a social investigator,' they say. It sounds horrid, but it *isn't*. It means I come to help the poor, to find what they need and to keep their bodies alive enough to hope. So many families in this very building are my problems. No, not here—they're not part of my work. In a way, you know, I feel Mark is more my work than Jamie—oh, it's all so mixed up! Jamie is so beautiful; not *glamorous*; I mean I don't believe people are good because they have beautiful faces. I know I haven't a beautiful face, but that isn't the beauty that counts; true beauty is what goes all the way down, what makes a man and woman shine and fly like angels. It's not only for my sake that Jamie's life is important—not only for my little black notebook. It's for Mark, because he *loves* Jamie. Oh, you mustn't think, Tess, that——"

The steadily mounting bewilderment in Tess's face was almost as clear as a sound, and Emily interrupted herself to lean forward and touch Tess's arm.

"No, you mustn't think wrong things about them. They're brothers, and young and all alone in the world with only each other. And that's"—her voice dropped to a whisper—"what I didn't want to say before in the room. When I told you the priest was here and he said something. Oh, but do you know what else he told me? You mustn't tell this to a soul; it's a *deep* secret. He makes séances: *sittings*, he calls them. What do you think of that? Wouldn't you love to go to a séance? When Jamie is better, we'll all go and have a *won*derful time. Who will we contact? I was thinking I'd like——"

"But what did he tell you," I asked, "that you didn't want to say in front of Mark?"

"Oh, about *that*. Something terrible. He wants to check on records to see if Jamie and Mark are really brothers. He says that if they're not, then the nearest of kin ought to be notified. I told him he mustn't, that it was wrong and mean and worse than a dozen mortal sins. Who could say that anyone could be nearer of kin to Jamie than Mark? But I think he wants to go anyway. Harry, you must see him and tell him how wrong it is. I told him it would be a *terrible* thing, that it would show coldness and hardness in his heart that he couldn't recognize such a closeness between them. You must talk——"

Pausing suddenly, Emily jumped from the couch as the door to the flat swung open: two women looked in.

"How is he?" one asked.

"Much better. He's doing splendidly. I'm sure by tomorrow he'll be fully conscious."

The two women exchanged a gaze of apparent curiosity, which hung parenthesized between them until Emily spoke again.

"Why don't you come in? Please come in. We're all——"

"No, thank you, dearie: not now. We've got supper to fix, but we'll peek in later on if it's all right with you." And the door closed.

"You see," said Emily, "how everyone is upset and concerned? You must make sure to come back in the morning, Harry. And you will too, *won't* you, Tess?"

"Gee no, I can't. I understand how . . . There's a smaller staff at the office in summer on account of vacations, so it's not fair to take off."

Tess looked at her apologetically, but Emily was no longer interested.

"I wonder what's become of Wallace," she said. "Do you know Wallace, Tess? You would love him. He's remarkable —the kind of *person* everyone would like to be. He does such wonderful things, always traveling around and having such a good time, doing so much with his life. And I've done so little with mine. Wallace says I'm always distracted from life. I thought a lot last night about what he said yesterday, that being here was no business of mine; and yet, I don't know, I'm always like that. But, Harry, do you know what I thought last night? I thought *being* here is right; *leaving* would be wrong. Everyone feels that; that's why everyone comes in. Even if it is a trap with a dragon; sometimes it's more important to be eaten up than to avoid the trap. But I don't know if that's right, If only I could just *live*. What is it to *live?* Oh, what time is it? I've got to give Jamie an injection. These are new ones, from this afternoon: every hour until the doctor comes, and we'll see what happens."

Quietly and efficiently she moved round the flat, gathering glass vials, a hypodermic tray, a small electric sterilizer, but I was less interested in what she collected than in her rapid decisive movements as she went about the work. And the greater her preoccupation, the more emphatic did she become as if all her flaccid indolence was being girdled into a column of rigid action. The strength she implied was perhaps different from the comforting warmth I had seen her offer to Mrs. Mussolini, yet it ran parallel: visible because her self was given away, given over, implicated in someone else.

"You ought to have been a nurse, Emily," I told her.

"A nurse," she repeated.

"Or a doctor. You're so good at tending people."

"Am I? Maybe you're right. But then in a way I am a doctor." She laughed, standing motionless in the center of the room, the sterilizer in her hand. "But I don't like my job. I want to quit my job. I don't know. . . ." Putting the hand with the sterilizer to her head, she went into the bedroom.

Tess's eyes were lowered, set on her folded hands, and her large lids were shadowed with blue in the darkening room.

"She's really taking it awful, isn't she? Do you think he *will* get better, Harry?"

I shrugged. "I can't say."

"Harry, what did she mean"—her voice was now a whisper—"when she said that Jamie was closer than a brother? He's not her boyfriend, is he? I mean, he's so young."

I avoided the question by leaving my chair and crossing

the room to the unpainted table beside the door. Upon it was an unshaded lamp with a bulb screwed into the top of the plain copper stand. I pushed the switch, but because it did not light I shook the lamp until it flickered and finally lit, washing a stream of white up the wall, across the ceiling, throwing a long silhouette of Tess upon the back wall near the window. When I started toward her I saw Mark standing just inside the room.

"She's giving him an injection," he said, a small unpleasant smile lifting his mouth at the corner.

"We know," said Tess cheerfully. "Would you like to sit down?"

"I'm not tired."

"You don't have to be tired to sit down. It's just more comfortable." She tried to laugh, but failed. "My name's Tess Ballantine, just in case you're wondering."

"I'm not."

Their conversation ended and I sank to a wooden chair beside Tess and listened to the sounds coming from the bedroom. "It won't hurt," said Emily once or twice. Gradually I ceased listening because fatigue took my mind away; it was a better fatigue than the mere nervous lack of sleep from last night, for it was a physical, consuming exhaustion due to the long afternoon at the beach, a weariness that dampened my mouth and made my head drop. I think I was asleep when the door banged open, a noise that brought my mind to consciousness but left my body torpid.

"Well," said Wallace, "what a depressing-looking lot you are."

"Wallace? Is that you? I'll be right there." And she sang

softly, *it didn't hurt, did it?* and emerged from the bedroom. "Oh, I thought you were killed or that something disastrous happened to you."

"No, I've managed to survive the day, but the heat was astonishing. I heard it was the hottest afternoon in five years. But it's cooled off now and there's a marvelous breeze and all along the street everyone is telling everyone else, my God, I thought I'd die. Did you think you would die? It never occurred to me."

"No, not the weather," said Emily vaguely. "You said you'd be right over on the telephone and that was before noon."

"I didn't say that. I said I'd come as soon as I could. Do you know what I did? I went to Connecticut—to the woods back of an academy for young ladies—and I wrapped my arms around a tree and listened. You see, I met a witch last night who told me if you put your arms around a good solid old tree and listen, it'll unfold its secrets to you. But either this tree had no secrets or it wasn't interested in parting with them. Well, anyway, what kind of secrets could the tree possibly have except perhaps about the young ladies at the academy. Don't you all like Connecticut? It's a state with a plan: laid out to order."

"But now that you're here, you'll stay forever."

"No, I can't stay forever. I'm meeting the witch again this evening. Don't complain, Harry. She's a very young witch. So I can only stay a minute, Emily."

"A minute?" she repeated absently, considering the word; then, abandoning consideration, she began to speak rapidly, raw delight coming again into her voice. "No, not a minute. You'll stay on and on. There's so much to talk about. Jamie is going to be well. He's much better today; a decided improvement. Everyone's noticed it."

"That's fine," he said, and looked across the room at Mark whose smile was gone. "Are you becoming more sociable?"

"Shouldn't I?"

"It would make you a most undesirable companion if you didn't. But why don't you come sit down instead of standing there like a misused butler. Over here, by the nice lady. Would you like a cigarette?"

Mark came forward slowly, each broken step tightening a muscle in my stomach, for with every movement he seemed about to topple over. But at last, arriving at the couch, he sank beside Tess.

"There, that's better," said Wallace. "Oh, come, don't look so miserable. Tell me, have you written any great poems lately?"

"That's all over," he replied quietly.

"No, it isn't. Perhaps it's all over for this week or this month, but in a little while it'll be fall, and that's a good poetry season. And your Poet will be busily at work again."

"My Poet?" He shook his head. "Nothing's left now, nothing but expenses: bills for other lives. And after that there'll be nothing—no poetry, no Jamie, no bills. Only life and a little money."

"Is that all?" Wallace laughed. "Only life and a little money! What more would you like?"

"Nothing more. If I'd wanted more I could have had it." He paused and sighed, his head shaking again. "I should have taken him away in the middle of the night and buried him somewhere secretly."

"And what would that have solved?"

"It wouldn't have solved anything, but it would have left me without everyone's questions and curiosity, without people running in and out: like all of you and neighbors we never had anything to do with. And without her, that crazy one." But Emily was unaware our attention had suddenly turned upon her. Seated on the small wooden chair beside the window, her arms folded, she was privately involved, for her face altered every moment, showing anxiety, pleasure, discontent, a silly vacuous-looking delight, as if she could not decide upon a proper emotion and so was trying them all, one after the other, in rapid succession.

"You ought to be happy," said Tess, "that people care so much for your brother and you that they want to know how things are."

"Oh, what do *they* know!" he yelled angrily, his face flushing. "What do any of you know? None of you knew him. You didn't know how hateful Jamie was. Everyone says such nice things about him, and she, that crazy one, she thinks he was beautiful inside, but he wasn't—he was rotten. Do you want to hear how rotten he was? *You!*" he screamed to Emily. "*You!* Do you want to hear?" But, emotion still shifting her face, she was not listening to him. He stood up, walked to her, and shouted until she lifted her eyes. "*You you you you!* Do you want to hear?"

She smiled gently. "What?"

"Do you want to hear how beautiful Jamie was?"

"Yes. Tell me."

"I'll tell you: he was the most selfish person I've ever known."

"No, no," Emily hushed him. "You mustn't——"

"He *was*. Maybe sickness did it to him; he was always sick. The whole world was himself and his sicknesses, lying here alone and isolated, bitter and jumpy. The radio or newspapers were only ways of finding new medicines—see there in the cupboard, hundreds of bottles and packages, hardly used. The money my parents left, each month's allowance was spent mostly on patent medicines. He never wanted a doctor: no one must come here; we must be alone." Shoulders rounded, head forward, fingers playing on his palm as he talked, he was like a small testy miser counting a stack of false coins.

"Poor thing," nodded Emily.

"*Poor* thing. He liked being sick: maybe sickness did make him rotten but it was also his excuse for being that way. He was never convinced I loved him—and I had, for so long. He was jealous of everything I did that didn't concern him, even sleep: waking me a thousand times to complain or say something mean. Or he'd hide my books so I couldn't read. If I'd get angry at him he'd tell me I was ungrateful. Don't I encourage you with your poetry? Don't I help you to develop your Poet? I live for you. It was *all* selfishness: another way to possess me. When I went out during the day or in the evening——"

"But you shouldn't have gone out," said Emily firmly. "You should have stayed with him. It's your duty."

He barely noticed her now, for his intensity was concentrating more and more upon himself. "He said he understood, but he didn't. He said he knew a writer must live and experience, but if I was too interested in anyone or anything he'd get angry and then be sick for days, not able to move. Watch out, Mark. You'll forget about me. You'll let me lie here and rot, and you'll end up nothing, nothing, a dishwasher or a baker's boy. How long can you love someone like that? And he knew when I shopped. But it was your fault—last year in the spring: the goings-away. Just to hurt me, that's all. Darkness, waking in the middle of the night because he *didn't* wake me, and finding you'd sneaked away, and not coming back for three or four days. Like last week, after the second attack, but then it was too late to hurt me. Where did he go? I can be independent, Mark. I can find work and do without you. Coming back sick and vomiting, but happy for my pain. You wanted to die in my agony. Oh, rotten—stinking and rotten and selfish and cruel."

"*No!*" Emily shrieked. "No more. It's not true." She jumped from the chair, her shoulders jerking with fury. "It's not true. *You're* stinking and—not him, not Jamie." And with clumsily frenetic gestures she ran into the other room.

But he was completely unaware of anything except himself. Limping back to the sofa he sank again beside Tess and he began to cry harshly with a tearing sound in his throat so that when he spoke the words seemed ripped from him. "He knew I wanted him to die, and he weakened through my wish. Will you haunt me, Jamie? I'll come back and bother you as long as you live and I'll never let you write another word and your Poet will freeze in your heart. Guilt guilt guilt for killing him. And what did I know of Death? Of someone coming from earth to torture me? You will; you are. You're right; there's nothing. Except the candles—when did you put them there, in the cupboard, back behind the bottles and everything? Will you never let me write another word?"

His weeping grew louder and, spontaneously, he leaned sideward to Tess, who drew herself to him, put her arms round his shoulders, and held him tight against her. And his next words were muddled in a mouth full of sobs. "But once I loved you. And there's nothing else."

Deeply moved, Tess looked as if she too might cry, but instead she cleared her throat with a soft squeak and said, "He'll be all right. He'll live." As she turned her eyes away from Mark toward the other room she seemed to be wondering about the relevance of her comfort. But it made no impression on Mark who had given himself entirely to the crying and to the swollen incomprehensible syllables that bubbled at his mouth.

A situation is invariably suspended when the person who dominates it decides to cry, for tears are a most effective arrester. Those round him may comfort or abuse, commiserate or mock, or simply be impatient, as Wallace was, to reset the circumstances into motion. If I knew Mark better or liked him more I might have felt relieved: I trust in the halting power of tears, in their ability to check not only the immediate situation but the emotion that induces them —distress is dangerous only when it moves.

"Oh, come on, Mark," urged Wallace. "Try to cool off."

"No, let him," said Tess. "It's better."

"He's got more reason to rejoice than to cry: he can start thinking about himself now."

"It doesn't happen like that. It's not . . . What you feel in your heart you can't turn on and off like an electric light." Tightening her grip round Mark's shoulders, she held him closer as if encouraging the tears.

"Of course you can. You *must*. It's all distraction."

She shrugged and raised her brow to show she had no interest in arguing the point. But, beginning to smile, Wallace continued to talk to her. "And distractions are death: you've got to exorcise them. Otherwise you end up like Emily —*with* distractions but *without* life. Did you see her: all upset over someone she doesn't know or anyway hasn't spoken to, when she ought to be off somewhere *doing* something. She isn't living, she never has. It's been that way for Mark before, but now——" Interrupting himself he leaned toward Tess. "Are you frowning or does your nose itch?"

"I'm frowning."

"Why?"

"Because you're very insulting. And it's not even true. She is so doing something. I think it's very personal to say she ... Everyone does different things and I guess for some people there's just as much of a kick in staying in a cave as for others in going around the ... Say, I once heard about a man who locked himself up in a windmill for years and years before he was sure he was alive. So you see, it depends. Life is—is just living, and even if you ruin your life you can still be *living* as much as anyone else or maybe even more." With a severe nod she added: "You can do whatever you want with your life."

"I know what I'll do," said Mark quietly. Unnoticed he had stopped crying and now his hands were rubbing against his eyes. "I'll let it live itself out. I'll feed it, warm it, obey its instincts, keep it going as long as possible, and then ..." He moved himself along the purple coverlet, out of Tess's reach.

"That sounds sensible but limited," Wallace laughed.

"I'd like a cigarette, if you've got one," said Mark.

"So would I," called Emily from the bedroom, and she came back, seating herself once more upon the wooden chair.

Everyone lit a cigarette and, under the thick whirling wave of smoke, seemed half-asleep. On the wall back of the couch were painted our long perfect shadows, occasionally smudged when a finger of candleglow leaped in at us, haloing the outlines.

"Feed it, warm it, obey its instincts," Wallace murmured, then looked up at Mark. "Well, that's got to be done. But what will you do when you're not doing that—and with the burden of Jamie off your back?"

"Nothing."

"Why are you talking this way, you sillies?" Emily asked with a laugh, the high pitch of her voice heightened by an uncertainty that had not been there earlier. "Jamie's not a burden and he's not off anybody's back. And isn't that a dreadful way of putting it? He'll be fine. The doctor was here——"

"Oh, for Christ's sake, Emily!" Wallace complained loudly.

Her mouth drew together, wrinkling as it rounded. "Please don't yell at me."

He had turned from her and was pushing back his sleeve to see the time. "I'm afraid I'll have to go," he told Mark.

"Will you come again? I'd like you to."

"Yes. Perhaps tomorrow."

He was almost at the door when Emily called. "Wallace. Wallace, don't go," she said flatly; he smiled and shook his head. "Why don't you stay? We can talk and smoke and maybe have tea. Wallace!" Her voice was weak now, but piercing. "Wallace! Stay!"

But he was already gone from the flat.

BOOK THREE

17

I was twelve years old the first time I saw a dead man. He was lying back of a park bench at dawn and both his legs were tattooed from ankle to groin: I saw because his trousers were several yards off beneath another bench.

Where I had been coming from or going to I can no longer remember, but since the park was only several blocks from home I passed through it often and frequently saw men, and occasionally women (always in shapeless black coats and overwide shoes and queer frayed little hats embellished with a broken feather), sleeping there. I might not especially have noticed the man had his trousers been on, and even so what attracted me was no concern for his health but the red and purple tangle of flowers painted on his legs. Coming closer I examined them with curiosity for

I had never before seen such an extensive tattoo, and it was not until some time had passed that I realized how extraordinary the situation was. It must have occurred to me at once that he was dead, but this came with no impact: I accepted it readily, without fear or squeamishness, and when I had finished looking at the legs, I went to a public phone in an all-night cafeteria and called the police. My voice then had not yet changed and because the officer I spoke to kept calling me *lady* I would not tell him my name. Several days later mention was made in the newspaper of an unidentified man found partially naked; he had been strangled—and a woman who had telephoned the police from Haley's Day-'n'-Nite was being sought for questioning.

Since that time I have seen many cadavers—most often of course at Mr. Trevor's place and during the war—and although I had known some of them in life, perhaps had even been attached to a few, I could experience nothing but indifference toward their corpses. I will not argue with those who feel it necessary to glorify the living, but it is the height of absurdity to languish or emotionalize over the dead. Still, as I say this, I look back to myself this afternoon when, alone, I sank into a white steel chair in the embalming room and, for the first time in two years, became immediately conscious of the three large drawers in the wall behind me. Two were empty, but in the third I knew was a forty-two-year-old heart attack named Mrs. Greta Opienski.

My consciousness of the corpse was neither detached nor professional: I was afraid of Mrs. Opienski, as if a remnant, an embolus of life, still lay in her frozen bones and might suddenly burst her from the placid white wall. It was ludicrous, yes, and sitting there I recognized it as such, felt my thoughts as unlikely and nonsensical as the question Mark put to me a year ago: "Has it ever happened that you buried a soul without a body?" What I feared was Mrs. Opienski's potential, her possibilities, and yet all potential was gone now: it had decreased gradually from birth when there was nothing else, until now when there was nothing at all.

Perhaps to reassure myself I stood up and walked to the solemnly divided wall and, bending, pulled open the bottom drawer. Within, as Frank had left her, she lay tubed in a hospital gown, her swollen arms sentimentally folded across her chest. Was there an embolus of life in this? Was there even a trace of potential left in Mrs. Opienski's bones? And although I knew that the answers, the body, everything pertaining to her was negative, the swell of irrational feelings forced me to react so that my throat tightened, my fingers chilled, and throughout me the sensation of longing began a tickling crawl like the beginnings of a sneeze. I bent closer to the woman, knelt beside the drawer, and drew my head down waiting with intense unrecognizable desire as I had stood yesterday morning on Wimple Road longing for the Sunday-dead factories to blast smoke and machines. In this way, longing, anticipating, attending an impossibility, I kneeled beside Mrs. Opienski—until the door opened. "What's the matter with you?" asked Frank.

Standing up, I told him, "Nothing. I was just courting the lady."

"You ain't a bit comical, Mr. Sutton. What kind of talk is that?" Removing his panama, he hung it behind the door, then pulled a cigarette from his lapel pocket and lit it. With the cigarette swinging from his lip, he said, "You staying late tonight?"

"No, why?"

"It's going on six-thirty."

"Is it? Then I guess I'll go upstairs. Take good care of my girlfriend—although you won't have much time: she's going home in an hour."

With the sound of his clicking tongue behind me I left the white chamber, went through the dark corridor and into the front office where I hung the *Please Phone* sign and passed into the street, locking the door after me. Once outside, I had no desire to climb the steps to my flat, nor did I have the inclination to go anywhere else, so I leaned back against the bricked space between the funeral parlor and the door that leads upstairs—and I thought of Mrs. Opienski and my unconsummated courtship. Perhaps, after all, it was only the result of nerves sharpened by sleeplessness, for despite the beach-induced fatigue and the fact that I had sat up all Saturday night, I was not able to sleep last night, not even to doze, but had lain until morning overexhausted and yet untired, pinned into an abrasive consciousness by thoughts that could not have been mine, that were, actually, not even thoughts but images flashing in at me: movements to observe, conversations to hear: Crawford Street Emily the beach Tess Wimple Road Wallace. Back round over round back: staring, trooping, talking into my passive hulk of sleeplessness; confusion unclarified by repetition. And Jamie; and why; and what. Why can't I see him? Why can they? What spot in my eye is blind? What twist in my brain prevents the impression from coming through?

And worst of all, the question that scratches sleep away, that tosses and twitches my body through the night—*have I acknowledged the blindness as mine?*

"But, Harry, is that you?"

Tulley was upstairs, leaning out my window, one finger pressed against the end of his nose.

"Yes, it's me."

"Do, please, come up—and trust to God the building will stand without your support."

Only then did I notice the comical angle at which I stood, one shoulder pushing prop-like against the brick wall. Relaxing with laughter I went through the door and up the staircase where Tulley's presence became immediately distinguishable: powerful suffocating fumes of Turkish tobacco had driven the air from the corridor.

"Have you been here long?" I asked as I entered the room.

"A while, yes." He was still at the window, his fingers busily folding a pair of gold-rimmed reading glasses into their case. "I peeked in your office as I passed but you were not there."

"I stay in back most of the afternoon. It's much cooler."

"Yes," he agreed absently, then paused and made a dry sound with his mouth. "You've nothing at all ... That is to say, I looked into the cupboard and found it bare."

"Oh, I'm sorry. I had some vermouth, but I finished it the other day. I wasn't expecting you."

"It is of no consequence. I never touch vermouth anyway." He put the spectacle case into his breast pocket.

"What were you reading?" I asked.

"I was not reading; I was merely thumbing. Mr. Pembrook's book. It was beside your bed. Of course I'd seen it here before, but having met him now, the book takes on added meaning. Mr. Pembrook is a very charming man, but I am afraid he is of little depth. This is to be seen as well in his book."

"I used to think it was very funny."

"I must take it away with me sometime and read it properly. Nevertheless. Tell me, Harry, have you been to visit the unfortunate young people since I saw you last?"

"I was there yesterday evening."

"And I in the afternoon."

"Emily told me you were."

"Ah, yes. Miss Morrison's interest in the case is extremely satisfying. She is a most generous and sympathetic person, and I believe quite intractable, but it seems so late in the day to begin hoping for James's recovery even though he has outlived expectations. When I was there yesterday the doctor said there was no possible hope of any change but for the worse. And still she persists in saying the boy will live as if her own life depended on it. It is symptomatic of a noble heart, but I am truly afraid. . . ." He sighed deeply and took the package of Crescents from his pocket, offering me one.

"She seemed less optimistic on the phone today," I said.

"She called you?"

"Yes, several times. She wanted me to get in touch with her office to say she was sick. And she asked me to tell *you* something."

"*Me?*" he said with affected astonishment.

I nodded. "I'm to try and talk you out of going to check

on the relationship between Mark and—and the other one. Emily says it's worse than a dozen mortal sins; it would show coldness and hardness in your heart if you couldn't recognize the closeness between the two boys."

"She told me that herself." He tugged at the bottom of his black jacket, then turned stiffly round to the window; his hand and cigarette were held out before him, the rising twists of brown smoke being sucked quickly out the window. "About that, Harry. There is something I should like to tell you." But he hesitated before continuing. "I was down at the bureau of records this morning. You must understand: it was not with the idea of making difficulties for the young man, this Mark, that I went, nor—and perhaps you are thinking this unlikelihood—from idle curiosity. Certainly I am completely sympathetic to the two of them, whatever their relationship. Nevertheless. We are all born with a proper name, with ties, connections to others—connections of blood; and it pained me deeply to think that this boy James would die, as it were, anonymously. But more important than that is the question of the sacrament: how could I give it to someone about whom we are all so uncertain? And, believe me, Harry, I *want* to—but with conscience I cannot.

"Well, to get on. Despite Miss Morrison's warnings and implorations (not to mention my own self-accusations) I went this morning to do my unpleasant bit of investigating. I never have any trouble with such bureaus; our city is always most gracious to clergymen. After some conversation with various supervisors, a clerk was advised to bring me whatever information there was on the family Akero.

Several folders were brought to me, and I seated myself off in a corner.

"But do you know, Harry, I knew at once I would not look at the papers. It was the most curious thing: not that I had lost interest, nor still less that I felt it was none of my business. I simply knew I could not look through the documents. Whatever was in them would have been irrelevant, beside the point: the two young men *are* nearest of kin, be they brothers or be they whatever they may be. So I sat for a quarter-hour shuffling the papers, pretending to read, but not looking at them at all; then I returned them and left the bureau. Once outside, and perhaps later, I was sorry I had not taken a quick peek, which I might have sealed forever in silence. But it was too late to go back and besides, if I had, I should probably have done the same thing again. And since this morning I have been plagued by the conflict: shall I or shall I not administer the extreme unction?"

The gravity with which Tulley stated his problem was extravagant, and although I thought of telling him so, I decided not to, and merely asked: "And do you think you will?"

"I don't yet know.... I rather think not.... And there seems to be so little time left."

I shrugged, a gesture I realized was pointless, for Tulley had not, at any moment, looked at me as he talked. Then we were silent until he cried, "Oh, look there!" Joining him at the window I saw his mouth split into a smile. "Isn't that your cat coming across the street?"

Kitty's long orange body strolled to the walk before the house. Seating herself beside the lamppost she stared up at us while Tulley called *here psss psss psss psss—do come here, charming thing*. At last she began the series of smooth sudden leaps that brought her to the sill.

"There we are," said Tulley taking her up and stroking his long easy fingers across her back. "What a ravishing little creature you are. Ah, what surprise! *Mais est-ce qu'elle est enceinte peut-être?* But come here, Harry, and squeeze her belly. Do, I insist! You are to be congratulated."

"If she is, Tulley, I assure you that I'm uninvolved."

"But still, it *is* beautiful. My cats lead such sheltered lives: they have taken an involuntary oath of chastity. I think cats are magnificent animals, Harry. Do you ever notice how they fold themselves up and stare into space with incredibly philosophical expressions on their faces? Imagine three of them doing it at once. They *know* something: I am positive that an enormous truth lies behind the eyes of every cat. I often wonder what it could be."

"Don't be ridiculous, Tulley," I laughed. "All they've got behind their eyes is a mass of soft pink pulp. That's what I like about Kitty—she's all real and palpable, and she doesn't pretend to be anything more."

"How crude!" He shuddered. "Soft pink pulp. There is more than that, Harry. Just look at her now. Do you mean to tell me there is not a thought in her head?"

"Well, if there is, it's all about food. And I'm not thinking of much more myself. Would you like to eat something?"

"No, thank you. Have you already forgotten my eating habits? Late tea in the late afternoon and nothing further until just before bed. But you go along and prepare dinner for yourself and for little-mother-to-be—and don't trouble about me. I shall be running away in a minute anyway. I want to go over to Crawford Street; do you think you will come along, Harry?"

"No," I said, crossing into the kitchen. "I won't be going there anymore."

"I should think it was your duty," Tulley called; I did not answer him. "I said, I should think it was your duty," he repeated, but since I maintained my silence, he said nothing else.

There is no window in my kitchenette; instead it is lit by a rust-colored bulb of figured glass that plays a dim pink lightning design up and down the walls and makes the room seem even more unpleasant than it is. For several minutes I strained my eyes as I rummaged through the dark cupboards, coming upon half-used boxes of cereal, months-old sauces growing jungles of mold, and the usual inedibles that clutter the pantries of uninterested housekeepers. Finally I chose a packet of dehydrated soup and a can of salmon large enough to share with Kitty. I had opened the fish and was putting the soup on when I heard the loud unbroken blast of a car horn from the street.

"Ah, good evening," shouted Tulley. "How do you do?—Harry, your friend is here, Mr. Pembrook, in a taxi."

The horn was still growling when I came to the window. "Why don't you tell him to cut it out?" I said, and Wallace put his head in to stop the driver.

"What are you doing?" asked Wallace.

"I'm about to eat. Do you want to come up?"

Mrs. Collini's little boy had emerged from the house, approached the cab, and was observing Wallace interestedly.

"Do you want something?" Wallace asked the little boy.

"Do you want something?" the child repeated.

"I've come to see my friend." He frowned and added, "Mr. Sutton," as if offering a credential. Then he turned his face upward, but before he spoke the child opened a wild toothy mouth and screamed with laughter.

"He's gone to the moon. He went yesterday."

"I'll be right up," said Wallace impatiently and dismissed the taxi.

When I drew my head in and started back to the kitchen, Tulley followed and paced round the pink-lit room, then paused behind me while I stirred the soup. "I should appreciate it, Harry," he muttered, "if you said nothing to Mr. Pembrook of my visit to the bureau of records. It is not that——"

"No, of course I won't, Tulley."

"You are very good. Nevertheless." And he left the kitchenette as Wallace's footsteps sounded across the landing.

"Who was that little bastard?" said Wallace coming into the flat.

"My neighbor's kid."

"If parents were reasonable they'd lop their children's tongues out at birth and not sew them back in for twenty years. But then if parents were reasonable they wouldn't have had the kids in the first place."

"Mr. Pembrook, that is not kind, even in jest."

"I didn't mean it in jest."

"Then you are doubly wrong. Children are our one constant hope."

"Perhaps yours, Tulley. My only constant hope is myself.

Think how much better adults would be if they hadn't been allowed to speak when they were children. The Greeks knew that. Didn't Pythagoras found a school where novices were compelled to silence? Maybe that's what I ought to do, start a school: Daddy Pembrook's College for Young Men and Women. How long do you expect to be eating, Harry? I'm going over to Mark's; will you come with me?"

"No, but Tulley will." I entered the room with my pot of soup and seated myself beside the window. "Tell Emily I'm sorry I couldn't come but I caught cold or have a headache. Tell her anything." But, in fact, I did have a headache and spooning the hot soup into my dry mouth seemed to make it worse. Still, I continued to eat, hoping that a full warm stomach might put me to sleep when the others were gone.

"She's terribly annoying these past days," said Wallace.

"I hate to be pestered that way: Wallace come, Wallace stay, Wallace here, Wallace there. I'm sympathetic about all this nonsense but just because she gets pulled in isn't any reason to drag me along, or you, or anyone."

"Misery loves company," said Tulley, nodding.

"Oh, this *misery* of hers! It's just another way of avoiding herself. When someone gets broken-up——"

"If you will permit me to interrupt you, Mr. Pembrook, I should like to say that the misfortune of our age seems to be the inability of most people to accept a deed of profound kindness and unselfishness as such. In my work I have often come across perfect strangers helping each other for no further reason than a desire to aid a fellow-sufferer or as an expression of God-given sympathy implicit in the human soul. You must forgive me if I say it is highly un-Christian of you to say what you have. I should think you would feel more obliged to comfort Miss Morrison in the sorrow she has taken upon herself than to analyze the motives that led to the action. It is perhaps necessary to remind you that one of the concepts upon which our life together is based (and remains possible) is that we must love our neighbor as ourselves. And what better way is there to show this love than to take another's burdens as our own?" From the beginning Tulley had assumed, as he often does, a rhetorical tone, and as he went on, his voice grew louder and flatter and became less a part of him than a separate entity like a recording playing behind him, spinning out patent wisdom while he pantomimed before it, his good eye becoming gradually as impassive as the glass one, his mouth laboring up and down, *chop-chop*. When he finished he flushed self-consciously as if he had just noticed the recording back of him, and, crossing the room nervously, he picked Kitty into the crook of his arm. "You must come see my cats some time, both of you. One is Siamese, you know, and almost perfectly blue; it relaxes me to look at her." He hesitated, stiffened, and went on. "When I spoke to Miss Morrison yesterday I mentioned my sittings and she was very anxious to come to my place some evening when this is all over."

"I'd like to also," said Wallace. "If it's going to be genuine. I've had enough of ouija, hands-on-the-table, and automatic writing."

"They can be quite effective too."

"But everyone's always pushing the things around so they'll get the best answers. With your friend though—what's his name?"

"You mean Haq?"

"Yes. I suppose if Haq comes floating around over us, it'll be hard to cheat."

Wrinkling his brow, Tulley said nothing; he merely stared at Wallace and tried to detect the exact tone of his statement.

"What I mean is," Wallace told him, "if we're all sitting *here*, and things are happening *there*, then it would be obvious that physical laws were not appropriate."

"Why, Mr. Pembrook!" Tulley was incredulous. "I must confess that until this very moment my doubts about your faith were continually mounting."

"Were they?"

"Oh, yes. Listening to you talk, and then I have run quickly through your book over there and I *have* seen the other one on the shelf—but to suddenly learn that you can embrace the possibility of the miraculous! Well, I am quite inarticulate with joy." His sincere and simple delight was horrible to watch.

"Oh, dammit, Tulley," I shouted. "He's kidding you."

His joy suspended itself but did not vanish. "Is this true, Mr. Pembrook?"

"I once knew a man named William Harte," said Wallace. "Don't interrupt, Tulley: wait a minute. I was friendly with Mr. Harte from the time I was about fourteen until eighteen or nineteen. He was a retired merchant seaman come to live in Chicago, and I think when I met him he must have been more than seventy-five, yet most people took him for a much younger man. Of course time has changed my picture of him: I remember him as tall as a tree with white hair thick, and wild as a flood of leaves. His face was clear and unwrinkled and not like most seamen's faces because it was pale and, though perhaps tough, looked soft when you weren't up close. I was interested in foreign countries and Mr. Harte used to take me up to his room and show me pictures of the places he'd been and the souvenirs he'd brought back. Well, one day when we were at his place I said something about God. I can't remember what specifically, but when I'd finished, Mr. Harte rumbled, 'Oh, *That One!*' 'What do you mean?' I asked him. And he said a very curious thing: 'I don't like Him one bit—not at all.' I laughed, and I still think it's funny: most people either don't believe in God or else they worship Him, but they aren't usually at odds with His personality. As it turned out, God and Mr. Harte were incompatible; the sailor believed fiercely, had no patience with any doubts on my part, but his belief vented itself only in hate. He wouldn't explain why he felt that way, but I observed that he spoke of God with the same familiar contempt and disdain with which one speaks of a personal rival. And it was due to this note of jealousy that I eventually realized that William Harte was annoyed with God not because he envied Him His infinite power— Mr. Harte wouldn't have known what to do with so much magic. It was simply that God was immortal and he was not. When I confronted the old sailor with this he denied it violently, so I assume I was right." He stopped abruptly, and although his face had been lowered while he talked, he now looked across the room, his eyes squinting.

Stroking Kitty, his whole body curved forward attentively, Tulley said, "Do go on, Mr. Pembrook."

"Go on with what?"

"With the story. I mean, I do not understand the connection. That is to say, what is the point of your little anecdote?"

"There is no point. I was a pallbearer at Mr. Harte's funeral."

18

Then they were gone: suddenly: leaving me alone and uncertain in the middle of the room.

I listened while their voices circled down the staircase and out the house; I heard the blur of evening noises take away Tulley's tone of firmness and Wallace's laugh.

Staring across the room and through the window at an angle, I saw the side wall of the church opposite just as a light was switched on. From the back door of the church a fat old man emerged, dragging a swollen burlap sack behind him; when he had pulled it almost out of my line of vision, he paused, lifted his cap and scratched his head, then passed from sight. I wanted to move closer to the window to follow him but the impulse was not strong enough to set me into motion and I continued to stand in the center of the room.

Like the departure of the others, like a sign of desertion, my headache had gone, leaving instead a strange empty sorrow. And even Kitty had vanished from the room, slyly, at some unknown moment. For a long time I stood without moving, as if snooping round the flat like burglars were a crowd of unpleasant thoughts and sensations that, should I remain motionless, might not notice me and go away. But they stayed, becoming aware of me, opening drawers and cupboards in my head, rummaging through the valuables.

Finally I managed myself to the window, but the old man from the church was gone and the light was off. My fingers, playing across the sill, stumbled on a box of Crescents, empty except for the smooth strongly scented tinfoil, which I removed and flattened into a plain of silver—and I told myself it was better I had not left with them. Lying has always been an effort for me, and every minute at Mark's, although I say almost nothing, is obviously a lie. And if the desire to look again upon the davenport was strong, it could not disguise the anticipation of my feelings should I once more see the thick yellow candles flaming for no one. Crushing the tinfoil into a ball, I dropped it out the window, saw it carried slightly by the breeze to fall between two women who looked up as I drew my head in. I walked idly to the kitchenette, snapped the light on and off several times, and then lay down upon the bed where, after a moment, I knew that sleep would not come, for I felt my senses opening to the caravan of images that had traveled into them all last night. To drive it away I focused my mind on Tess. That is something I often do when I cannot sleep: imagine a woman into my bed, concentrate on a slow progression of passions, extend details endlessly—the only end being in sleep. And so tonight I took Tess, and when she was naked I found her body oiled so that I could not grasp her, and she kept oozing away, out of my arms. "Lackety," she said. "Kickrack placemore: nodiddle."

It was impossible to shut her mouth upon the nonsense or to keep her from sliming from me, and I was no nearer sleep. I opened my eyes, took a cigarette from the night table, and after a while I went downstairs.

The warm streets had begun to fill with overfed people, hungry for the breeze: beef-armed men in undershirts lounged before their doors making jokes with neighbors' wives who sat on small straight chairs, their doughy buttocks pouring over the sides. I have seen these people luxuriate in the evenings of three summers: gossiping and flirting and examining passers-by and turning, as the twilight deepens, from pink to lavender to blue. Generally I pass them slowly, amused by their interested stares, but tonight I felt only embarrassment and hurried to the corner where I turned upon Inshore Street and started to the park.

There, the crowds lumped beyond the railings and on to the curb—space stuffed with them and with their chatter and the chatter of the leaves. I went *pardonme excuseme whydontchalookout* down the wide center lane, stopping at the fountain, but its rim was filled with younger people, most of them alone and intense-looking. Back of me, on the other side of the fountain, a guitar chord shivered tentatively and three or four girls began a song about ghosts. Walking to them I stared: they were all short-haired and ugly, mouths puckered, faces drawn to whisper harmonies —so I turned away, back across the park through the *dont-push sorry* path I had come, to the exit where, just within the park, I saw the old man. Leaning against the rail he was posed in a cone of lamplight beyond which nothing could be seen. His bright angry eyes were set on me, and the mouth, surrounded by the thin scattered rag of beard, sagged an instant, then shot back up.

Pausing before him, I shook with two sudden violent impulses: to scream at him or to take hold of his eyes and flip them like pennies with my thumb.

"A poor old man ..." he said as if describing a pain, and I was furious.

"Do you know who I am?" I asked.

"My boy, for me all men——"

"I don't mean all men. I mean me. Do you know me? I was here the other day with a friend who'd gone to the aquarium with you."

At first he said nothing, but then, although his face in no way changed, he nodded once. "Yes, I remember. He was a very impatient young man: decidedly squid. I haven't had a meal since that day—would you believe it? And I'll give you a piece of advice that no one else can give you, my boy. The end of all of us is the same, the very same indeed. And do you know what it is? The sea, I tell you. Water, water, everywhere ..." His gums slammed up and down fiercely, always about to touch, but never actually reaching each other. My anger, irrational and unmotivated except perhaps by his complacency, centered in my throat and rose with the words, "I'd like to ..." but I stopped.

"What is it? My advice is worth all the money of Ford and Rockefeller put together. When I say——"

Rolling up from my throat, over my tongue in a roar of fury, "Take me to the aquarium." Then my anger calmed into humiliation and I shook my head repeatedly. "That isn't what I meant to say."

"Not at night, child, it's closed. But tomorrow—if I live. And for what I tell you I don't ask all the money in the world. I ask no more than a crust of bread, though what I say is invaluable."

"I don't want to go. I was joking." I reached into my pocket and found three quarters.

"Mercy on you." He put his hand to my shoulder. "You've found grace in knowledge. There's blessed little . . ."

I crossed from the chatter of the park to the quiet of Inshore Street. And I walked blindly, aware of nothing but isolation and the insanity of my actions with the old beggar. Not until Wimple Road did I regain a sense of whereabouts, and there only because it is bare of lights and streetlamps, and night is thick and conclusive. I ran back to the avenue and followed it south, went round several unfamiliar corners, and found myself where I suppose I knew I would. Opposite, above, I saw the two windows of Mark's flat: one half-dim half-lit by the shadeless lamp, the other streaked by two solemn yellow lines. And I knew that Emily —if she had intended to—had not succeeded in extinguishing the candles or opening the bedroom window. Standing there I felt no desire to go upstairs, for this compromise with distance was comfortable and I leaned against a building and smoked a cigarette.

Down the street from which I'd come someone ran unevenly: at first rapidly, then pausing and moving into a quick heavy walk, and then running again. When she turned the corner, she ran several yards past me before bringing herself to a stop.

"Oh, God, Harry. Oh, oh! Why didn't you say something?" Finding it difficult to get her breath, she waited off the curb, gasping.

"I wasn't sure it was you."

"Honestly, it's awful—will it happen? It can't possibly. And how they are up there. They're all so funny, Harry. I don't understand."

"What's the matter?"

"I went to the doctor and he was having his dinner and I thought, oh God, how can he eat at a time like this? But he'll come over before dessert. Aren't you sick? Tulley said you were—you had a headache; I don't know—something."

"I thought the air might do me good."

Now shadowed, now lit by the thin light of distant lamps, she gave me the impression of collapse: her arms hung relaxed but motionless, her face was jowled, and beneath the floppy drape of the stained blouse her breasts seemed to have dropped away.

"Maybe Tulley cares; he's so nervous beside the bed. But all the rest of them—the neighbors—aren't they funny, Harry? They're nice people; they're all concerned; but how can they accept things just like that? Why don't they fight against it? Do you just let someone die? Even when you love him? Is that what you do? Don't you put your foot down and say, no, he's going to live and we're going to be happy and sing and love and give thanks to God? Or do you just sit and say, how terrible, too bad, isn't it a shame? Isn't death a terrible thing? Why do people die, Harry? Do they always die? Does every single person die? Can't we stop each other from dying: my friend, it's all horrible and miserable and endless suffering, but don't let it end, don't leave, don't go away. When you're alive you can hope for better things, but when you die—is it all? Oh, come up, Harry. Come upstairs."

"No. I don't want to go up."

"What do you mean? You must! Please, Harry." The slow uncertain motion of her hand taking mine sickened me, but I did not shake her hold away, rather I let myself dissolve into the contact, becoming less myself than the cold wet connection of our two hands. "Will Wallace die too?" she wondered suddenly. "I don't like him anymore, Harry. I'm not mad at him, but I don't think I like him. You know, isn't it funny, I don't think he notices me—or only the way he notices a tree or a house. He doesn't notice anything. He's so *hard*, Harry, as hard as nails. Do you think he ever cried? He's so lucky; it would be beautiful to live as he does or to *be* Wallace. But it's not beautiful to be outside him."

I was surprised to see her turn away, not because I had expected her to plead with me to come up, but because I was unaware she had let my hand go. Neither of us spoke as I followed her into the building and up the staircase; the smell of decay was still sharp, yet less distinguishable, having merged into the condition of the house like the scrawled walls and the odor of hall toilets. On the top floor, light fell into the passage from Mark's partly open door; Emily pushed in ahead of me and before I entered she was gone, into the second room.

And in the doorway to that room was Mrs. Mussolini, kneeling, her lace-and-satin mourning dress lifted above the bulbs of her knees. Round her neck she had a thick silver cross and from her hands swung a rosary of ruby beads, which she counted while her mouth raced out a series of soundless prayers. Several other women stood about her, heads lowered somberly, and among them I recognized the fat woman of Saturday, whose frizzled hair was no longer in curlers.

"So you've come," said Wallace from the couch.

"Yes. I didn't want to, but I met Emily in the street and she insisted——"

"Well, what were you doing in the street if you didn't want to come up?"

"Just strolling."

"It's a good night for it too."

Beside him sat Mark holding a book in his lap and reading silently, his lips trembling in a faint familiar way. Now and then he lifted his eyes, looked round with amused indecision as if he did not know whether he ought to say something particularly comic, and returned to the book. Suddenly he raised his head and laughed, slapping Wallace's knee forcefully.

"It's much better than the first time," he said. "I can see so much more in it." He laughed once more, conclusively, and continued to read.

"I'm so flattered," said Wallace. "Do you know what he's done? He went to the library this morning and took out my books. *Oh*, what now? Persephone's come up for air."

Emily was looking out over Mrs. Mussolini's head and motioning to me. "Would you like to see him?" she whispered.

"No."

"Do come in, Harry," Tulley suggested, appearing behind Emily, and closing his eyes he added, "I have done it," but it was a great while before I understood the reference.

Because I did not move, Emily called again, impatiently, lips pressed together like an insistent mother's. Finally, stepping across Mrs. Mussolini's legs, I went into the room and stood between Tulley and Emily. But I did not dare to look: instead I stared into the candles until my vision tripled and blurred, and my eyes pulsed with flame; then I lowered my head.

"Say he'll live, Harry. Why doesn't someone make him live?"

"The doctor's here," Wallace shouted, and the three of us turned. Mrs. Mussolini, pulled by a couple of women, rose from her knees, nodded slowly, and backed away, the rest of the ladies retreating with her.

Wet brown eyes bloated behind rimless glasses, the doctor fixed me in a look of searching thoughtfulness, and his tongue ran back and forth across his upper teeth, clearing away his dinner. He nodded rapidly to Emily and Tulley, and walked by.

"We'll see what there's to see," he said.

Rather than turn to watch him, I left the room and sat down beside Wallace.

I can't tell you what a pity—

Honest to God my heart —
I ask oneself why do such things —
I lit a candle for him just this —

They stood lumped together before the wall, Mrs. Mussolini a bit away from them, her fingers stroking the beads, but she muttered no prayers.

"It's better he was," she said. "She's not sleep from Saturday for taking care. Rest—she's need rest." Pausing, she regarded Mark, her face moving to a look of disgust. "You someone else; no more the same. Where went the heart—the poetry?"

He turned a page and smiled.

Then the whispers came, rushed, harsh, shivering from the bedroom like the candle flame, chilling the women to silence. When I began to decipher the whispers, they disappeared except for Tulley's intermittent *ah yes ah yes ah yes* coming with chantlike regularity. But that too ended and it was some time before the doctor's loud whisper *that's that* and Tulley's incredulous whisper *do you mean just this very second?* Then in a normal voice, but with fogged and reverent finality, Tulley said: "Nevertheless."

Then: silence—and everyone leaned forward a little, even Mark who, closing his book, placed it soundlessly upon the floor and as he waited bit his lower lip, his face exactly as it was a year ago. But his expression was gone almost at once, for Emily screamed, a dry imperfect scream that did not slice cleanly through the silence but, rather, permeated it, replaced it. Everyone began to speak. Mrs. Mussolini and the other women came forward then swept back.

"Don't do that!" Emily shrieked. "He isn't. He isn't."

"Dear Miss Morrison . . ." purred Tulley, but his voice broke.

When she passed through the doorway and paused just beyond the threshold her face was powder white except where blue blotted the eyes sunk back in their sockets. Although we were all watching her I thought at first she saw no one, but gradually I understood that she was perfectly aware of the circumstances. Circling her head slowly she stopped at every face in the room, offering each the same careful deliberate smile that suggested that behind itself whirled a mouthful of poisonous secrets to be loosed not now, but presently. She stared a long while at Mark, who turned away with a self-conscious twitch, but she looked only momentarily at Wallace, who mirrored back a smile just like her own. When she saw me she crossed to the couch and waited until I gave her my place.

A series of faces had been floating by the outside door, and once Emily was seated, another group of women entered, joined the first, and together, led by Mrs. Mussolini's solemn black figure, swung wave-like into the bedroom. There were the sighs, the choking sounds, the sobs.

Only a kid after all—
I ask you Lily is it worth it—
That's how it is—
Life's like that—
O Mother Who watches—

"Excuse me," said the doctor and, coming to the sofa, clattered out a general round of sympathies.

"What are you having for dessert, doctor?" Emily asked.

"Why—Why . . . chocolate pudding." He moved one step back.

"With whipped cream? Will you have it with whipped cream, doctor?"

"I be . . . I don't know. I believe so." He turned to Mark. ". . . Since there's no further need for me . . ."

"You'll send the bill?" said Mark.

"Yes, certainly."

"Make sure you do."

"There's no need to talk of it at——"

"No, there's not," he agreed. "I only want you to be sure." He smiled calmly and as the doctor left the flat, one short laugh jerked from Mark's throat.

"What about the remains?" said Wallace.

"What about them? *He'll* take care of it all."

"I won't be able to do that personally," I said. "If you want to make arrangements you'd better phone and ask for Samuel Pry. Here's the number." I drew one of Mr. Trevor's cards from my breast pocket.

Reaching his arm back of Wallace, Mark tapped Emily's shoulder, but she did not respond. Tapping again, he called, "*Hey!* Will you go down and phone the undertaker?"

"No."

"Oh, go on. The air will do you good."

He was touching her neck now and, with unexpected speed, Emily swung her head, reached her hand up, pinched his thumb, and held the flesh while the boy shouted and tried to pull away. "Go to hell," she said quietly and released him.

"What's the idea?" he cried, stamping to his feet, one

hand massaging the other. "What happened to all your kindness and good humor?"

"Worthless good-for-nothing!"

"Are you going to phone or not?" he demanded, but she was silent. (Only then I noticed Wallace's smiling face between them, turning from one to the other.) "All right, I'll go if you won't," Mark threatened. "I'm going. I said I'm going." Realizing at last that she would not stop him, he started to the door quickly and furiously.

"Wait a minute," Wallace said. "I'll go down with you. We can stop and have a drink somewhere."

When they'd gone, I sank beside Emily. "Yes," she said, then leaned over and drew her face close to mine, so close in fact that I could see nothing but her eyes, separate, isolated, detached, like those of the old beggar. But unlike the beggar's, there was no ferocity in hers, merely a staring blinkless calm—a look I might have expected had I found her on a ship mid-ocean as she gazed into the consuming water—altogether different from the expression I have come to associate with her. Her eyes were shadowed and sunken but they were alive and firm, and seemed not to belong in Emily's crumpled bearing.

"We must think about the funeral now," she said, scratching her head and drawing away from me. "We have to see him off in style—it's a very important thing. I want your friend Tess to come. Do you think she will, Harry? She's so awfully sweet; do you know her long? Why haven't you ever introduced us before? You should have. Did you hear what she told Wallace last night? Do you think what she said was right? I thought about it a long time after you left—is life *any*thing or *some*thing? I know she works, but maybe you can make her come to the funeral. It would be so nice to have her."

"I'll ask, but I——"

"What's today? Only Monday? It seems like weeks. I guess then we'll have it Thursday or Friday, or maybe even later than that."

Dropping back against the wall, she closed her eyes and cupped a hand over one breast. The ringers were still moving lightly even after she'd fallen asleep, and through her partly open mouth breath came heavily and with a groan as if she were trying to speak.

"Is she asleep?" whispered Tulley, coming out of the bedroom.

"Yes."

He dragged a wooden chair across the floor and seated himself before me, his hands folded upon his lap, his tongue clicking softly. Never have I seen Tulley as pale as he was tonight, nor each feature so explicitly telling—especially the mouth, bent with melancholy like the mouth of a tragic mask.

"What else could I do, Harry? I am not hard; I am deeply pained by such things. Looking at him just now . . ." I had to lean forward in order to hear him. "I felt only personal sadness. It is wrong for me to talk this way perhaps. I believe I shall cry—forgive me."

"It's all right, Tulley. Would you like to go outside?"

"No. I shall be fine in a minute, I promise you. And you've seen me cry before, haven't you? My heart is monstrous and sinful, and that boy is pure. You can see purity in the whiteness of his face, in his pale silk hair. Oh, Harry, it is most abominable of me! I am all fire inside and I am doomed. No one's faith goes deeper than mine, and each day I repent, regret everything I said the day before: to be in eternal error. Control, we live by control, by locking up the unlockable: sometimes it runs out and touches earth. I shall bite my lips a thousand times tomorrow. How could I deny the boy what was rightly his? And the tightness is mine. Why should it hurt so? You live only on the earth, Harry; perhaps that is why I am so fond of you. For I am, you know: terribly. I missed you deeply the months we were apart."

"You could have come to see me. I was always there."

"I was embarrassed; I had acted a fool. Do *not* tell me no. Nevertheless. That boy in there lived above the clouds; it is so easy to see. Somewhere in the middle—not for me I say this; but for you—somewhere in the middle between clouds and earth. An impossible place, with only its impossibility to recommend it. Impossible? And yet I think most men are there—not you, Harry, nor I, but these others: forsaking earth for myth, then myth for earth. Why have I a mouth of blasphemy? A mouth where sinfulness is poured in and out. Truly, punishment is implicit in the crime. And how can one confess one's crimes? Ought one to do as the Jews do: stand altogether before their God, yet hide themselves behind the series of prescribed sins, and confess all the sins committed or not but perhaps with heavier accent on those one *has* committed; and confess not to man but to the only final Understander? Ought I to beat my chest and cry *Ashamnu Bagadnu Gazalnu Dibarnu-Dophi* . . . ?"

Ecstatically, far away from genuine consciousness, Tulley

pounded his breast and cried the Hebrew, his eye rolling among its tears. He was like this when two ladies emerged from the bedroom and were caught shock-still by his atonement. I poked his thigh and he was immediately quiet.

"He's upset about the poor kid," I told them, and they nodded faintly and left the flat.

"I have been too silly. Please forgive me, Harry. Such things rarely happen to me and . . . yes. Nevertheless. On the way over here this evening Mr. Pembrook told me that there was a young lady here last night; he called her a talkative young lady but a very attractive one. It seems she was not in agreement——"

But he was checked by a burst of laughter that hammered in from the corridor and was, after a moment, followed into the room by Wallace and Mark.

"What is it?" shrieked Emily sitting up; then seeing them she slumped back and frowned.

"The funniest thing just happened," said Wallace. "As we were coming up the stairs we saw two women standing——"

"Did you have your drink?" Emily asked.

"Just a little one. We had to hurry back because the man said the wagon would be right over. But listen to this: the two women were standing in the cor——"

"Is there anything to be done before they come for him?" she interrupted again.

"No, not a thing. The man said you were to sit tight and listen to my story."

But she had already turned to Mark who, still laughing, stood in the door jamb of the bedroom. "When will the funeral be held?"

"Wednesday." His laughter was silenced into a smile.

"Wednesday? But that's the day after tomorrow. You can't possibly——"

"Wednesday morning," he said soberly, and as he backed into the other room he added, "First thing in the morning——"

"How can that possibly be?" she wondered, and looked to Tulley for an explanation.

But Wallace spoke first. "Will you please be quiet and listen? Apparently the two women were coming out of——"

"No," Emily screamed, one hand lifted to hide her mouth. "No no no no no no no. No one wants to hear your story."

His cheeks flushed, Wallace stepped rapidly across the room and took hold of her shoulder. "Now, look, Emily. I don't know how long you intend to go on with this disgusting performance, but someone ought to tell you where to stop. I've had more than enough from you during the——"

"And I've had more than enough from *you*. Where do you think you are? Laughing and telling jokes in a house of mourning with a dead boy in the next room. You've no feelings at all."

"I've got feelings but I don't enslave myself and everyone around me with them. And I don't believe in mourning. I hope when I die people come dancing on my grave; I hope my flesh is devoured by vultures and my bones ground into fertilizer. It's pointless to feel about anything but the living, isn't it?"

"The living? What do you know about the living?"

Her voice was high and thin and excited; she shook Wallace's hand away and shuddered. "You don't know anything about them. And do you know why? Because they're all in traps, all fallen in—but not you, Wallace. You take care and pass them by; you don't even look down; you don't even notice them. Selfish, selfish bastard. Where's my book? Where's my notebook?" She jumped up, looked round wildly, and then ran to the table at the other side of the room. "Here it is: the black book. The list of the fallen: a guidebook to fallen angels—only they've fallen higher than you. I love this book; I love my people."

"Well, for Christ's sake," said Wallace. "Then why are you always complaining about what hell your job is?"

"Because it is. No, it isn't. Because I thought I wasn't living."

"And now you think you are? *Hoop-la!* Just like that! In the words of the black-haired young lady of last night, living is just living."

"Yes, that's it. That's what it is. It's falling in, not carefully avoiding. She's right—and I was always on your side against myself. I don't like you anymore, Wallace. Believe me, I don't. In my heart, I don't." She paused uncertainly and waited, but he said nothing; instead he bent over and lifted his book from the floor. "What do you say to that, Wallace? What are you thinking?"

He did not hesitate before he answered. "That not only are you fallen and eaten, but you are partially digested."

Her confusion was so evident that I stood up and went to her.

"I want to go home, Harry. I don't want to stay here anymore."

19

We found a taxi along Anderson Street and I told the driver Emily's address. The ride is not a long one no matter which way you go, but I was glad we drove beside the East River, where, with our window down, a cold damp breeze fluttered in. Since we'd left Mark's flat I had been expecting, or perhaps hoping, that Emily would cry, but her intention was otherwise, for she lay half-asleep throughout the journey, one hand again upon her breast, her lips moving lightly.

"I'm so glad we're here," she said abruptly when we turned off Third Avenue to her street. At her building, she started out of the cab, made a short skip-jump off the running board and went quickly to the house.

"Wait a minute, Harry. I want to see if there's any mail." Down the corridor she unlocked the postbox, found a single letter, and without looking at it, shoved it into her bag.

"You can read it if you'd like," I said. "I won't mind."

"No. It's from Sidney: square envelopes. He writes such boring letters, always the same. 'Dear Sis, the weather is too hot or too cold these days. I hope you're okay or better. Barry and Tom ask for you all the time. May's going for another checkup at the doc's—backaches all the time. Betty, Carolyn, and Henry are swell, and Gloria has more callers than you can shake a stick at. If it's not too much trouble do you think you can spare an extra sawbuck this week? I'd be much obliged to you.' It's a good thing it hasn't rained since Saturday. I left all the windows open when I went to work. I didn't expect to be away this long."

"No, I suppose not."

"Is that what you suppose, Harry?" She laughed and gave my nose a small painful pinch. When I groaned, she kissed it and apologized. "I don't know what's wrong with me. I feel absolutely drunk. Do you know, if someone asked me now where I'd spent the weekend, I wouldn't be able to say. Where *did* I spend the weekend?"

She was still trying to recall when we entered her flat. The living room was partially lit by the bright lamps of the apartment across the court, and, dancing to the windows, Emily posed herself in one beam of light and stood on her toes, looking ridiculous.

"Calm down, now," I said. "If you're hungry I'll fix you something to eat."

"Hungry? No. But I think I'd like a chocolate. Do you want one, Harry? Oh, what *will* become of my figure?" Switching on the floorlamp, she arranged herself before the mirror and examined her image. "Harry! Harry! I must have lost ten pounds since Saturday. Just look at me. I'm a dream." She spun round to the mantelpiece and put two chocolates in her mouth.

"Look at the dust!" she cried, sweeping a finger along the mantel. "Mountains of it. Dust dust dust. That's what you get for living in an old house. Lord, but I like high ceilings. Don't you? All life is a movement toward high ceilings— higher and higher: because coffins have the lowest of all. Who do I sound like, Harry? Guess who!" Moving to a small table beside the sofa, she wrote something in the dust. When she had finished, she studied it a moment, then erased it with her thumb and wrote again below.

"Come see what I've done. Do you think I'm naughty?"

In a wild vague hand she had scrawled *Godfugitall*, and as I read, she pushed me aside and added *nevertheless!*

"*Godfugitallnevertheless!*" she recited thoughtfully. "Harry, do you think it's possible God might be a woman— some gorgeous empty-headed creature who just pokes around the universe wagging her hips and things? I certainly told him off, didn't I?"

"Who?"

"Wallace. That little man Pembrook. Sleep with him, did you ask? I would sooner take to fireplugs: no, swans or bulls." Dropping herself upon the sofa, she adjusted her skirt, spreading it round like the folds of a gown; thumb and second finger rode down imaginary pleats. "There are some things I want you to tell me, Harry."

"Sure, anything."

"Phone numbers. I want phone numbers for Wednesday

morning. I want Tess's number—such a sweet girl. And I want Tulley's." Squinting, she lifted her hand and looked at the position of the fingers, fixed as if between them wriggled a trapped insect; she shuddered and dropped her hand. "Isn't he peculiar? I always feel like he's going to rub against my leg. He's queer, isn't he? Is that possible? I ought to ask Mr. Pembrook some time. Oh, well. What's his number?"

"He'll probably come to the funeral anyway."

"Still, I want his number. Maybe we can have a séance: that is to say, a sitting, at his place. Well, what is it?"

"I don't know. You can reach him at the church."

"And Tess?"

I gave her the number of Tess's office.

"Two-three-six-four. No, I won't forget it. Doubled inside and outside. Thank you. I think I'll take a shower and go to sleep." Falling back she closed her eyes, then opened them a moment later, surprised. "Are you still here? But you were supposed to be gone long ago. Go home, Harry. What are you waiting for?"

I was about to tell her, but the words shaping on my tongue suddenly embarrassed me: *I want you to cry*—embarrassed me because I knew I expected more from her tears than a pause in agony: a frail worried chamber of my heart hoped that tears might float her sick emotion above this obliquely unhappy state, might make it visible, and therefore harmless.

"I ask you again, young man. What are you waiting for? I don't feel like it tonight. Oh, Harry, remember the time? And with Sidney at the garage. What a hussy I was. Am I the hussy type? And you, you ne'er-do-well!" Her head plumped from side to side, slowly, repeatedly. "Go home, Harry. Let me sleep. What are you standing there for?"

"If you want the truth——"

"The truth! Yes, always the truth."

"I'm waiting for you to cry."

Her head stopped moving and she looked up at me placidly; it was a while before I heard the thin faint shriek in her throat. Then her eyes and face squeezed together with enormous effort—and she was crying, deeply and uncontrollably, the sounds no longer from her throat but scooping up from her chest.

"Will you be all right now?" I asked.

She nodded.

"I'm going home, Emily. If you want me to come back, call the funeral parlor; I'll tell the old man I'm expecting a call."

She nodded again and raised her head for a kiss. "Do you still love me?" she wailed.

I could hear her crying even from the landing below, even from the lobby of the building: a noise as profound and inclusive as the scream she had yielded up at Mark's, displacing everything, leaving room for nothing else.

Although he sat upright at the desk, Samuel Pry was asleep when I looked through the window, over the laurel-capped urn, into the fully lighted office. His mouth twitched constantly, perhaps indicating a dream—a dream of song or laughter. For long ago Samuel Pry was a vaudeville comic, and while he knows his day of glory is over he yet clings secretly (and not-so-secretly) to his art. That, for example, is why he insists on being addressed by his full name: it implies a deviation from the commonplace, it suggests celebrity. And Frank has told me he has caught Samuel Pry several times at the altar in the chapel snapping his heels together, making faces, and singing dirty songs to the rows of empty chairs. Of this, of course, Frank is very disapproving and often suggests I talk to the old man about it.

The thought of Frank doubled my pleasure in gazing at Samuel Pry, in fact, sweetened the sleeper beyond his waking capabilities, for if he is usually pleasant, he is always voluble. So it was because of himself both asleep and awake that I decided not to disturb him. Taking the key from my pocket I let myself into the office; the old man's head rolled; I was still; he straightened. Crossing the room, I slid the enormous ledger off the desk and from the back of the volume tore a page, blank except for a couple of telephone numbers I had once scribbled at the bottom: one number was Tess's, but the other I could not associate. I wrote a short note explaining that I might receive a call, and when finished I started to prop the sheet up against the ledger, but I stopped, drew the book back to me, and opened it.

The entry was incomplete, as Samuel Pry's always are, waiting for me to fill it out in the morning. But the name was there, and reading it left me hollow and chilled: *he is here where nothing lives but myself and an old sleeper*. Between me and Jamie, between the oaken door and the steel door, was only the twisting unlighted passage through which I walk a hundred times a day. And tonight I walked it too, tonight I entered the cool dry darkness of the white chamber and was alone with Jamie.

I intended to keep the room dark, and I might not have dissuaded myself had the curious feeling not risen in me—a strong sense of reality, a sudden vision. I felt I had after many years returned to a place where my enemy lay coiled; I felt him opposite me, waiting, as I was waiting. My hand reached out and snapped the light on. The tables were empty, the chairs were empty, the three cold drawers were unfilled, and each corner of the room was still: he was nowhere: he was everywhere, like the beggar's sea. *Jamie Jamie everywhere ...*

And as I sank weakly to the white steel chair, he was no longer my enemy: either I had ceased to fight or I was already vanquished. My eyes closed, I bent my head and I began to mutter the name *Jamie* over and over until it rattled without effort, without meaning, off my tongue. After a while I added the word *please*, but if I was expecting anything to happen, nothing did, except that a sensation of longing oppressed me again, the desire for a still thing to move, for a dead thing to live, for my quiet painful heart to pump into my ears as loudly as Emily's weeping.

"Jamie," I whispered. "Jamie please Jamie." And although so many other words hung in my throat I could not release them.

And when I lifted myself and switched the light away, when I started back into the corridor, I knew that it mattered.

20

I cannot remember sleeping, but I must have—perhaps just before dawn, because in the morning my mind was stuffed with a dream.

The boulevard I walked upon was broad and treeless, and on either side high thick un-windowed buildings stood set back from the walk. Everything within the dream was made of the same dull substance: a cold gray perfectly smooth stone: of this was the sky, the street, the buildings, even myself—the lone stroller on the avenue. A tomblike effect resulted, for while the heavy stone world extended indefinitely behind itself I was vaguely conscious of something beyond, perhaps only a flood of bright clear space. Nothing lit the scene, but there was light, a dim even light of the same consistency and color as the stone: it might have been the material world illuminating itself, but without casting light because there were no shadows.

Only the rational man can know confusion: the dreamer never stops to speculate or analyze or to learn the motivations of the unmotivated. So there was no bewilderment in my mind when I walked calmly upon the boulevard; the road would stretch as far as it would and I would go as far as I went. Then: the long high fine scream from all around me: not a human sound, nor animal, nor of life, but a cry from the cold gray stone, from the essence of the dream, from my fingernails and armpits, from everywhere like another aspect of the light. People were on the street—people unconcerned and gray, fashioned from the only available element. They strolled as I did, and we passed each other, uninterested, faceless. At the corner, which was not a corner for the street did not end, Tess stood with her face toward the sky, her body tortured and twisted and wound. As I watched, she unwhirled to a normal state, turned her eyes from the sky, and strolled away. Then I looked upwards and saw the moon, saw its light frosted upon the world: and it was falling slowly in a straight line not to earth but I think just round the edge. And everything was ordinary now. Sadness tightened all my muscles and it was an incredibly miserable effort to lift my arm and wave goodbye to the moon. Gripped as I was in melancholy, no relief came when I knew that the moon would not drop away but would hang suspended, swooping like a pendulum.

In the morning, gloom cushioned my limbs and made every movement cumbersome and disagreeable. Pushed by habit, however, I dressed and had coffee, smoked a cigarette, wondered when I might be inclined to straighten the flat, and, noticing that it was not yet eight o'clock, I began to wash dishes. Perhaps I expected to limber up with activity, but instead I was more conscious of the exaggerated slowness of my body; even my ears were dulled, for the clatter of crockery and cutlery reached me as rubber-thuds. I left the sink and took to the broom, but that too was useless because when my mind peered through the curtain of dream, it saw that I was not collecting dust, but merely raising it and letting it fall again. Ultimately I dropped the broom and smoked another cigarette: and in the smoke and dust of the stale room, the idea formed. It was not an idea, really, nor did it have shape: its nature was general: a pulse of energy thrusting me toward flight, toward escape.

At nine o'clock I went downstairs, unlocked the door of the funeral parlor, sank to the chair behind my desk, and continued to yield my torpidness up to the growing pulse of energy. Finally I took the phone from the drawer and dialed Mr. Trevor's uptown *studio*.

"Trevor's Funeral Parlor," Mrs. Timothy said with early-morning cheer.

"This is Harry Sutton. Has the boss come in yet? I'd like to talk to him."

"Yes, indeed, Mr. Sutton. He's upstairs. I'll connect you."

Three clicks, a moment of silence, another click, and Mr. Trevor's voice dripping through the wires. "Harry? Good morning, Harry. I've been meaning——"

"I'm going away."

"You're going away? Where?"

The question only puzzled me an instant. "I don't know. I'm leaving."

"Is anything wrong, Harry? If there is . . ." A tone of sympathy followed by a pause of understanding. ". . . you can feel free to tell me."

"Nothing's wrong."

"Then why——"

"I called to tell you to get someone over here because I'm leaving."

"But your vacation doesn't begin until the twentieth. I thought all that was arranged."

"I'm not going on vacation. I'm just leaving. You'd better get someone over here right away."

"But, Harry, that's impossible. I can't manage to find anyone on such short notice."

"Send Sarah."

"Sarah's going to summer school. I don't know if——"

"I'm leaving at ten o'clock." I hung the receiver on its stand and replaced the telephone.

As soon as I had shut the drawer the telephone began to ring, but I ignored it, and eventually its fuzzy persistence ended. The melancholy which had edged out of the dream still wrapped my body, but had become tolerable: I had adapted myself to it, had accepted it as normal along with the rising thump of action. Each seemed to be working against the other, and I, as the host of both, had to reconcile myself to their opposition. In this way I sat at the desk, suspended between a force that recommended movement and one that deprecated it. My mind had turned so far inward that it was not until I found my fingers stroking the rough-edged ledger that I remembered what was lying in the embalming room. But the memory did not alter my mood, for somehow, somewhere, during the night, Jamie had sunk behind himself, had turned into a spook that haunted other worries, that floated fantastically through things unconnected. And my only comfort was the pulse of action that would soon drive me away.

The telephone rang again and continued to ring, rang until I left my desk and went through the dark corridor into the white chamber.

Frank looked up at me and nodded. "Samuel Pry left a note; says about this kid Akero brought in last night. The family doesn't want him put out or brought home."

"Do what you want," I told him.

"But I don't know. What if it gets crowded, Mr. Sutton?"

"There's always room for one more."

"Yeah, but you don't like making the place look like——"

"I'll leave it to you."

His small eyes poked at mine. "Say, what's the matter with you? You sick?"

"No, why?"

"You look bad."

"I guess I'm tired. I got to bed late last night."

The bell over the outside door clinked its thin dull note and I turned away from Frank and went back to the office. The telephone still quavered and as I entered the room Mr. Trevor bent behind the desk and lifted the receiver. Not wanting to listen to his conversation I smiled to Sarah who was leaning against a bronze urn, her thickly painted mouth arranged in a yawn that looked permanent, her right hand dangling a magazine by its back cover.

"According to *my* clock," she said, her words inflated by the yawn, "it's the middle of the night, and all honest folk ought to be asleep."

But her uncle was awake, in fact violently so, and he gestured excessively—his arm looped the telephone through space, then whirled it to the drawer; his hands swept over his head and smoothed the two neat planes of hair away from their center-parting; his fingers chivvied down his pinstripe lapel.

And he spoke. "Well, Harry. Will you explain what you meant on the telephone?"

"I'm leaving right away."

"How long will you be gone?"

"I don't know."

"Not forever?" asked Sarah moving from the urn to a green plush bench.

"I don't know. Maybe."

"You can't mean to say, Harry, that you're just quitting me like that."

"I'll send you a card."

"But where are you going?"

"I don't know."

"I'd have hoped," said Mr. Trevor, and his pale lips labored extravagantly, "that in the years you've been working here, a feeling of confidence had come to exist between us. I see I may be mistaken." He smiled and put a hand on my shoulder. "Come now, Harry. Something must be troubling you. If you feel you can't tell me in front of Sarah, I'm——"

"There's nothing to tell. I just want to go away."

"No one *just* wants to go away, my boy."

"Sure they do, Uncle Clark," said Sarah, awakening.

"You be quiet," he snapped.

"Look," I began firmly. "Take your hand off me." He obeyed. "I'm leaving New York this morning. I don't know where I'm going and I don't know how long I'll be away. It hasn't occurred to me that I'm quitting your place, Mr. Trevor; I didn't think of that, but in order to leave the city I've got to leave the job. But maybe I will quit—I don't know."

"Those are the statements of a very irresponsible young man. All I can say is that I feel I've been deceived in you."

"Perhaps I've been deceived in myself."

". . . Leaving so suddenly, after all. It won't be easy to replace you on such short notice."

"And remember, Uncle Clark, I've got classes in the afternoon."

"I'll write you in a day or two," I told him, "and let you know if and when I'm coming back."

"Very well, Harry. Of course I can't promise you that after such behavior you'll be able to return to as comfortable and well paying a position as this."

I shrugged. "There are other funeral parlors."

"I won't deny that, but I wonder if all employers are generous enough to hire people without references."

We stared at one another; then, since I had nothing more to say, I went to the door.

"Harry . . ." His voice was uncertain as if he had not yet decided what to say and, in fact, he hadn't, for as I turned I saw his arm rise and drop—a gesture unaccompanied by words but more expressive than any other movement I have ever seen him make: it conveyed nothing more specific than anxiety. But when I faced him, his smooth professional factitiousness shaped itself into a clear and exact portrait of a painfully disappointed man.

The pages of Sarah's magazine erupted into a flutter and, folding the journal back upon an illustrated story, she began to read.

Then I was on the close smoky upper level of a bus that jerked along Fifth Avenue, through the crowded morning street, through the carts and bicycles and taxicabs. On my lap was a blue canvas overnight bag into which I now looked: a pair of underclothes, a pair of green and yellow socks (these had come in the mail over a year ago), a can opener. It had occurred to me when I slow-motioned round my flat wondering what to pack, then wondering if I had packed it, to take the mosquito-edged tie; but lost as I was between motion and enervation, the thought must have dissolved, as the thought of packing other things had dissolved. In fact all was dissolving: as I moved past an idea, a house, a street, it disintegrated. From the bus I looked over Twenty-third Street, yet the usual ordinal name implied the existence of two-dozen earlier streets—which could not be: they were dissolved: there was only *here*.

But because with each spasm of the bus the real and visible *here* turned into the demolished past, I could do nothing but think of the future: of ultimately. Ultimately I would leave the bus, take my canvas bag and descend into the avenue, leave the man across the aisle who picked his flushed berry nose and wiped the thick ingenuous finger on the window leaving another streak beside those smeared on by soot, by grease, by rain, perhaps by another ingenuous finger: indications of the past. Ultimately I would take a train out of the unforeseeable past and leave all behind me, totally dissolved, completely immaterial.

My mind rode across space, swept from state to state, traveled first west as far as Chicago, then back and south. I stopped at North Carolina, or rather in it, at the army camp near Pertyville during the war, and I remembered the woman. Her first name, if I ever knew it, is forgotten, but she was married to a man named Lieutenant Sadie. Her hair was beyond red, beyond copper, almost violet; and in the darkness it was deep blue. We met on the road, a bend from the highway, and I cannot recall that we ever spoke or even kissed—but we must have, for I know of her family and I can recollect the taste of her rouge. Off the road we backed among the trees into a darkness that was not moonlighted that autumn. And Mrs. Sadie showed me what she had.

We never made an appointment; sometimes she would be there, sometimes not, depending I suppose on whether another soldier had passed earlier along the bend. Ultimately I would go to North Carolina, I would come round the dark road to see if Mrs. Sadie, silent and violet-haired, waited for anyone.

At Forty-second Street I left the bus and walked to Park Avenue, to the station. Within Grand Central, sound was hollow; I followed the ramp and the corridor and the confusion of archways leading to the pale enormous marble circle where no matter how deep the crowds are, one has always the sensation of emptiness. I crossed to the window marked SOUTHBOUND and looked through the glass: eyes focused on something in his lap, the preoccupied ticket agent did not notice me.

"For Pertyville, North Carolina," I said.

He raised his eyes, kind clear fur-brown eyes, and he spoke a list of things that struck my head like stones.

Time single eleven-forty express return three-twenty-two roundtrip one-way coach local two o'clock or pullman, sir, or change at — —

Because I said nothing the ticket agent paused and smiled patiently; and as I turned away from the window I remembered something Wallace often says. "If only I could somehow overcome this involvement with little things. Try as one will, it's impossible to live grandly, to sweep across life, to avoid the misery of details and littleness. It's especially evident in travel: when I want to go from one place to another, it would be so much more satisfying if I could simply *be* there. Instead, there have got to be plans, tickets, reservations, unreadable timetables, and of course enough money to cover it all. Forty-league boots are what I should have been born with."

And had I those forty-league boots I might have gone south this morning into the nighttime road. But when the soft-eyed ticket agent listed the details involved in the grand sweep, I was aware I could go no further. Within the tenuous compulsion that had driven me to the SOUTH-

BOUND window lay no force for details. All I might have replied to *roundtrip or coach* was that I did not know; and it had not until then occurred to me to count the money in my wallet.

Pushing my way from the circle, I became embarrassed, for I suppose awareness was returning to me; I stepped out of my coffin, observed my bodily remains, and found them spinning—and spinning out of their orbit. All my life I have seen myself silhouetted against entirety and therefore I have understood how short my shadow falls, how infinitesimal my relationship to anything or anyone, and theirs to me. If man considers himself a creature unique, his uniqueness lies only in the ability to thus appreciate himself. Man is the animal with the lamp of conceit, and, having light, he believes he can illuminate a darkness too deep, too vast, too idiotly selfless to be disturbed an instant by a flame perhaps real but imperceptible. So he creates God in his image, so he creates himself in the image of God, so he is deluded—as he is distressed, for distress sits on the shoulders of delusion. And my unhappiness this morning was the result of behavior rooted in the prime delusion, in the greatest conceit: I was taking things seriously. I was in contradiction with what I had always believed. And worse, I could not see the way out.

The knot of motion was gone but my languor had not diminished. I thought of Mrs. Sadie on the moonless road and wondered if perhaps she too would not be there tonight. My face was flushed as I started up the ramp and I lowered my eyes to avoid the sight of the descending masses; from the side wall a row of red telephone booths rippled into my vision and I crossed back, entered a cabin and closed the door. It was a while before I could think of dialing a number.

"Holborn and Bradley," the woman lullabied.

I said nothing.

"Holborn and Bradley. Good morning!"

"May I speak to Tess Ballantine?"

"Just a moment, please . . . Oh, I'm sorry, Miss Ballantine is occupied just now. Could you leave a message?"

"No."

"Would you like me to tell her who called?"

"Tell her Trevor's Funeral Parlor."

"Trevor's—oh, gee! Hold on, I'll get her right away."

After a pause the operator whispered with excitement: "Must be an emergency. Tell her to take it on four . . . You got it, Tess?"

"Yeah," she said. "And get off the line, Estelle."

"I was just going to. My God, you'd think——" And she switched herself away.

"Is that you, Harry?"

"Yes."

"You called at a lousy time. I was just in the middle of . . . Can you phone back later?"

"No. I want to see you."

"When?"

"Now, right away."

"Now? But there's——"

"Please, Tess——"

"Is anything wrong, Harry? You sound funny."

"I don't know."

"You don't know?"

"I'm at Grand Central. It'll only take me a few minutes——"

"What are you doing *there?* Aren't you working today? Harry, what's *wrong?*"

"I'll explain when I see you. Will you meet me in front of your building right away?"

"Yeah. All right. I'll be there."

When I emerged from the subway into the wind of a shaded side street and went round the corner to the avenue, the notion shocked up and down my head. It had suddenly occurred to me that Tess might *not* be there—that is, she would be there, but I would not see her. At first, without knowing it, I laughed aloud: awareness came when a woman on the street looked at me, then, infected by my laughter, smiled.

It is four avenue blocks from the subway to Tess's building, enough of a distance for time to push a suggestion into a fear. Humor was gone; then terror went; every sensation, real or unreal, I had experienced this morning receded and I was charged with a single desire: to *see* Tess.

She was not there when I reached the revolving doors and peered through into the high white lobby; or at least I did not see her. I half—awaited a transparent touch or an unbodied voice: "Can't you see me, Harry? I'm right over ... No, *here,* not *there!*" What would I do if there were no Tess? if I spent my life in a room through which merely her voice drifted? if I climbed into bed and took nothing in my arms?

When she came out of the lobby, whirled through the revolving doors, I only stared, and the quake of relief was followed by a quake of nausea. I closed my eyes.

"Jesus, Harry, what's the matter? You look terrible. Harry, open your eyes. What are you doing?"

"I thought I wouldn't see you."

But I *could*, standing before me, long dark eyes wide with concern, breasts shaping out the bodice of the pale blue dress; my vision filled her into the transparent touch, into the unbodied voice.

"What do you mean?" she asked.

"Nothing. We'll talk about it later. Come across the street—it's sunny there."

"Honest, you're crazy today, Harry. It's warm enough without the sun." But her arm linked into mine and I led her to the other side. "Where do you want to go? Would you like to go over to the zoo? It's only a couple of blocks away and there's that restaurant. Do you know it? You can have coffee on the terrace."

"All right."

"Now, tell me what's wrong, Harry. You were acting funny even on the beach on Sunday, and then at that house——"

"Don't talk about me. Later! Talk about something else now. Tell me some gossip."

"Gossip." She considered the topic as we crossed Fifty-ninth Street. "That kid died, but I guess you know—that boy Jamie. Your friend Emily Morrison called me at the office this morning. She's a very sweet girl, but so nervous. Is she always so nervous, Harry? I told her I didn't know whether I could come to the funeral tomorrow. I mean, it's a shame about the kid, but I didn't know him or ... You think I ought to go? I'd feel kind of funny. She's a peculiar girl: she wants everyone to get as upset about it as she is. It's awful to see a kid like that die when he ought to have his whole life ahead of him, but everybody can't feel the same about ... You understand? But maybe I'll come; she kept pleading like the whole show depended on me."

"What did you think of Wallace?"

"*Him!* I told you I couldn't stand him. He does that one thing I hate in a man: he wears perfumed aftershave lotion. I know it's funny with me about that. For instance, you see all these types in New York that tweeze their eyebrows or wear make up. Genuine fairies. But they don't bother me at all. In a way, they're kind of cute, you know—like poetry: every time I see a fairy, I say there's a walking poem. But then I meet a man who wears perfumed shaving lotion, and my skin crawls. You know, I get this feeling of being an outraged woman and I just want to tear his eyes out."

Pleased that I laughed, she pressed my arm a little tighter. "It's true, Harry. I bet you think I'm crazy."

"No, I don't at all. I think shaving lotion is a wonderful reason for hating someone."

"Oh, I don't *hate* him." She paused and we entered the park. "This way—it's shorter. He's not the kind of person you hate, is he? He's just not so nice to be with. All that talk. Jesus, is he full of it! After we left the place on Sunday didn't you tell me you grew up with them; or did I dream it? I thought you ... It's funny, Harry, but I never would have guessed you ran around with characters like that. Oh, there's the place. See, and back of it is the zoo."

The lane brought us to the graveled terrace of the restaurant, and to an air of greenness. The steel tables and the wicker chairs were green, and seating ourselves further up, at the edge, we overlooked the heads of a row of new trees and a grassy slope riding round to the zoo.

"Look how empty the place is," said Tess. "But come here between twelve and two and you can't move."

Silent and unexplained, a waitress stood beside me: her face, the curve of her arms, the starched linen uniform, reflected the greenness. We ordered coffee; the waitress remained; we ordered doughnuts.

"Oh, damn," I remembered suddenly. "The bag."

"What bag?"

"I don't know where I left it."

"*What?*"

"I packed an overnight bag, but I haven't got it anymore. I must have forgotten it on the subway or in the booth when I phoned you. There wasn't anything important in it."

"What were you doing with an overnight bag?"

"I was going away," I said.

"Oh, that's why . . . But where to?"

"I wasn't sure. I thought maybe North Carolina to my old army base."

"But why? All of a sudden . . ."

"I don't know. There was no reason. I felt awful this morning." But what I felt now was excitement, for the conversation moved clearly toward where I had not thought to go, and I was carried along, half-within, half-without.

Silent and unexplained, the doughnuts and coffee were on the table.

"We can phone the lost-and-found," Tess was saying, "and ask if it was turned in."

"It's all right."

"But, Harry, you can't go——"

"It was an old sack and there was nothing in it but a can opener."

"A can opener?" She was disturbed.

"I don't know why. It was just there. Please don't ask me about it." I leaned back, sorry that the conversation had moved the wrong way; but, after a long pause, during which we stared at each other uselessly, she began to talk.

"That's what it is: it has something to do with that kid because ... Harry, I forgot to ask you when we left that place on Sunday. Remember, before we went up there you made me promise to tell you everything I saw: what did you mean?"

"I wanted to know if you could see Jamie," I said, more relieved than hesitant. "That is, if your *eyes* could see him."

"Naturally I could see him. I'm not blind, am I?"

"Neither am I—at least, I don't think so."

Her smile was uncertain and slightly defensive. "No, you're not——"

"But I've never seen him, Tess."

"I ... Harry, I was there when you saw him."

"*You* saw him, Tess; apparently everybody's seen him. But I haven't. I've looked and I've looked but I haven't seen a damn thing. When you all said he was lying on the davenport, it was empty to me. And last night, I stopped at the funeral parlor after he'd been brought in: but I couldn't find him. I can't see him, that's all. My eyes can't see him."

It took her a long time before she realized that I meant what I was saying, that I was not teasing her. And then shock washed the color from her face, drew her jaw down until her lips rounded, and left her nothing to say.

"Are you listening to me?" I asked, and she nodded without any change in expression. I told her everything I could remember, trusting in the impulse toward confidence and yet regretting it, for I thought it might frighten her from me. By the time I had come to this morning, a slow but steady stream of people were seating themselves at tables round us.

"Let's get away from here," I said, and she stood up, still speechless, took my arm, and we followed the path through the grassy slope and beyond to the zoo. When I finished speaking we were standing before the barred garden of two kangaroos. "Well, what do you think of it?"

"I don't know what to think of it," she said at last. "No wonder you're so upset. If it was me, I think I would've gone crazy." She caught my smile and added impatiently, "Oh, don't be dumb, Harry. It's just a question of being sensible about it. Jamie is there and you'll see him."

"But I've told you it's not only Jamie that bothers me. There are other things."

"What other things?"

"I don't know. It's all vague; it's everything—maybe you."

"*Me?*" Although she appeared startled, she could not conceal her satisfaction: lines of color drew into her pale face.

"You know, I thought I wouldn't see you again, after that argument at your place. But then this happened and you seemed like the only reasonable person to go to. I mean, maybe what I feel ... I don't know; it's all so mixed up in my mind and maybe Jamie is the least of it. Tomorrow he'll be buried and if I want I can pretend I *have* seen him. But I won't be buried tomorrow, and neither will you. Do you understand? I'm not sure I do myself. It's a feeling I have often these days: longing or desire: insane desire for the craziest things. Yesterday I kneeled beside a corpse, a Mrs. Opienski, and I think I was waiting for her to come to life. Maybe I'm mad, huh, Tess?"

"You're not mad, you're just all tightened up. Now, listen!" She became business-like. "I love you, Harry. About all these other things that are bothering you and you don't know what they are, I don't know. But about Jamie I do know and I want to go straight down to the funeral parlor now. We'll look at the body and you'll——"

"No."

"Yes, not no."

"I won't go."

"But maybe because I'm there ... Now that you've told someone about it. You know how people can be not sure of something until somebody else knows about it too."

"I don't want to look; it makes me feel terrible. No, don't press me. I really don't want to."

"But you have to."

"All right. But not now, later. No, tomorrow—at the funeral."

"You promise?" she asked, dissatisfied.

"Yes."

We had moved on past the kangaroos, past the bears

past the frayed lioness whose tasseled tail snapped in the dust, toward the scream of the monkey house.

"What you said, Harry, that when you thought you wouldn't see me again, but then you did—that maybe what you feel——"

"Oh, Tess...."

And we stared dryly at a hysterical orangutan.

21

We spent part of the afternoon at the zoo; we spoke little, and not at all of what mattered, for she was aware that the conversation would have to wait until tomorrow. So we looked at the caged animals, and now and then they looked back at us.

"Do you think she knows what's going on?" Tess asked as we stood again beside the cage of the nervous lioness. "Do you think she remembers about before?"

Afterwards we left the park and had a tasteless lunch in a large mirrored restaurant where tubes of neon ran along the ceiling and dropped color on the food. Then we walked again, without direction, following a street to its avenue, the avenue to its street. Once or twice we stopped for a drink and talked a little, but not about ourselves, yet everything seemed intensely personal as if from Max Turnip or Emily or large-nosed Madeline we could easily bridge to immediacy: but this did not happen, not when our hands touched, not when I kissed her. Within the framework of ourselves, we were parenthetical, and Jamie was silenced away.

It was after six o'clock when we reached her apartment.

"Don't my feet hurt!" she said, pulling off her shoes. "We certainly did walk. Are you as tired as I am?"

"I hope so. Maybe I'll be able to sleep tonight."

"You'll stay here, won't you? We can make a little meal out of . . . Or else, you know, there's a delicatessen around the corner. And then you'll spend the night here."

"No, I think I'd better be alone."

"Why? No, Harry, I'll be so nervous if you go. Honest, you know how you were this morning. Would you like it better if I spent the night at your place?"

"Don't worry about me. I'm all right."

"I didn't say I was worrying about you. I want to be with you, that's all."

"You'll be with me tomorrow."

"I want to be with you tonight."

"But if I don't sleep, you'll be upset."

"No, I won't. And besides, you *will* sleep. There's nothing to worry about now. Everything will be all cleared up tomorrow. You'll see Jamie and everything else will clear up. I promise you, Harry. Oh, I love you so much—I love your sadness."

A moment of silence came and went like a special heart-breaking cry, and I desired Tess in a fantastic way, in an impossible way, in a way that is make-believe.

"Tess . . . Tess . . ." into the flood of long black hair.

But in my bed, alone, undressed, I could not sleep. Misted evening light waved uncertainly into my room and I thought once more of Mrs. Sadie, focused my unwilling attention upon her as if everything within my head might form a circle round this one image, draw slowly toward it, until, reaching it, I would finally sleep. But breaks in the circle came not only from my mind but from outside, under my window, a fragmentary march of voices.

Kay says I ought to see a doctor—
Forty cents a pound and just last week—
Tru-huly Tru-huly Fair—
Just like that he said it if you won't—
With beaded bubbles winking at the brim—
I haven't got all day so if—

And over it all, honing my consciousness was fatigue; when one is overtired, one is no longer sleepy; when one is over-hungry, one has no appetite; and perhaps when one over-wants, there is no more desire—for my heart was flaccid, shapeless, and although my mind knew that I was tired, hungry, in want of Tess, I felt none of it.

Lifting myself from the bed I went to the window and stared through the fogged glow of twilight. Across the way, in a space between two buildings, sat Kitty, legs folded under the orange cushion of her body, the two unblinking eyes apparently fixed on me, reactionless, unemotional. The empty-headed stare annoyed me suddenly; the infrangible calm of her posture, the vacant interminable purr (of course inaudible from here), scratched at my spine. Standing there I felt that Kitty was one of the indefinable things come to bother me, and, reaching to the night table, I took the glass ashtray from beside the lamp and flung it as powerfully as I could across the street. It fell short of her, smashed noisily upon the walk, and Kitty disappeared into the alley. I stepped back from the window.

Now I noticed the condition of the room: it was impossibly neat; I wondered if I could have straightened up this morning before I left. I continued to think about it while I dressed but the only memory I retained was that of scattering things, not arranging them.

On the way downstairs I stopped puzzling myself about the flat and instead puzzled myself about where I might go. Tess frightened and attracted in rapid opposite flashes. Outside, I paused a moment before the funeral parlor: no light was on and the sign hung in the window: it was not yet eight o'clock. I wondered if, were I to go inside, I might see Jamie lying somewhere in the white chamber or perhaps already in the chapel for tomorrow morning. And then, what if the funeral took place and the coffin lid was nailed down and the body taken away, and I did not after all see him? There was a sensation of regret—not for myself but for Tess, for having told her. To me it could mean nothing: I could go on exactly as I always have: I *could* clear away the confusion and return. "I know what I'll do," Mark had said of his life the other night. "I'll let it live itself out." Like something beyond his control, like something outside himself. *Stand aside everyone my life is living itself out.* But even as I thought this I knew I did not want to live my life *out*; I wanted to live my life *in*, to accept confusion if it meant that, to see Jamie, to love Tess.

But the impulse was toward Emily, not Tess; not toward love, but commiseration. I went round the corner on Inshore Street and into Rebecca's, back of the bar to the telephones.

"How are you?" I asked.

"I'm all right. Who is this?" Her tone was suspended, hesitant.

"Harry."

"Harry? Where are you phoning from?"

"Rebecca's."

"But you're not in New York, are you?"

"Of course I am. Where did you think I was?"

"Oh, Harry, everyone's so funny these days. They told me you went away." Although a restless delight still sharpened her voice, she sounded calmer and her words came out more slowly.

"Who's *they?*" I asked.

"A girl. You see, I phoned you in the morning and she said you'd gone away, maybe forever. So I took a cab over to your place, and the door was open—not the way you usually leave it, unlocked, but wide open and your things were all over the place. I tidied up for you."

"Oh, it was you."

"Yes, did you notice how neat everything was? I did it. I put everything away so nicely."

"That was sweet of you."

"Was it? Yes, I suppose it was. Well, then I went downstairs and there was a girl sitting at your desk. I've never seen her before. And she told me what happened this morning. Is something wrong with you? Oh, I know what it is: Jamie. Isn't that it? You and I are together in this, Harry. I think only we really care. Then I said to the girl, I'd like to see him, but do you know, she said I couldn't, that the family had given instructions not to let the body be seen until the funeral. I think I'm just as much the family as anyone and I told her so. But it didn't do much good. And after that I went to see Tulley, at the church and he phoned the girl and told her who he was, but she didn't care. We're going to have a sitting tonight, Harry, and we're going to contact Jamie if Haq's in the mood." She laughed. "As a matter of fact, we must stop talking because I've got to go. Would you like to come along?"

"I don't know."

"Please come, Harry. It'll be so nice to be able——"

"Who else is going to be there?"

"No one. Just Tulley and me and you."

"Have you seen Wallace today, or spoken to him?"

"No," she said quietly, and there was a long pause.

"Would you like me to phone him and ask him to come?"

"If I wanted him, I'd have asked him myself. You must understand, Harry, that things are different now. I've my own life to lead. Not Wallace's."

"All right. I just thought——"

"If you want to come, Harry, I'll wait for you and we can go to Tulley's together."

I saw the three of us sitting in a circle in a half-lit room, Tulley, in a trance, murmuring to his Egyptian judge: the image struck me not so comic as sad.

"I'll be right over," I said.

Solid, thick, sepulchral, the brownstone houses stood clumped together as if incompletely cut from a huge ugly mountain. And the one where Tulley lives is like all the rest: heavy, cheerless, like a widow introspective and aged—and the dull light that tumbles out upon the walk is an indication of her secret living grief.

Emily in a black dress seemed appropriate to the street.

"He calls himself Mr. Geneva here," she said as we climbed the stoop, each stair bent in the center like a sagging bed.

Beside the stained-glass door, under the single bell, was a hand-written note fixed behind celluloid:

        Hendricks - - - long and short
        Applebaum - - - three shorts
        Axel - - - - - short and long
        Mr. Geneva - - - two longs

I plunged the button twice, and after a moment the door opened.

"Ah, Miss Morrison. And Harry!—such a surprise!" Giving us each a hand he drew us into the house. In a tight gray turtleneck sweater, Tulley looked unusually thin and unusually soft, and much more out of place in the stiff neatness of the foyer than he would had he been wearing his black suit.

"But I thought you had gone out of town, Harry."

"I started to, Tulley, but then I changed my mind."

"T-t-t-t-t!" he silenced, then in a whisper, "The name is Geneva here. Come along to my room now. It's just back of the staircase. Right around here, you see."

In the center of the room was a round table on top of which sat a Siamese cat whose eyes crossed as we entered. The other two cats lay on the studio couch and slept. Except for an ivory crucifix and the enormous picture of a woman's face, the walls were bare.

"Is that your mother?" Emily asked, indicating the photograph.

"Oh, no no. She was my landlady's mother; she died in this room, you see, while dusting. And Mrs. Bank was quite upset when I suggested taking it down. So I left it there; such an interesting face, if you observe closely—notice how the eyes seem to follow you."

Pushing the cats from the couch, I sat down and laughed.

"It happens to be true, Harry; but it is of no importance. Nevertheless. I must say I am surprised to see you here, not only because I was told you were away, but because . . . Did you tell him, Miss Morrison, what we shall attempt tonight?"

"And do you mean to say, Harry, that it makes no difference to you——"

"Why should it?"

"Well, I *am* surprised. But then I have a surprise for you too. We're going to have another member for our sitting tonight—Mr. Pembrook."

Emily said, nothing. Since I had met her, she had been smiling, a quiet insistent smile whose very insistence implied a certain wisdom. For an instant, with Tulley's declaration the smile seemed not to know what to do with itself, but then it resettled, comfortable and sure, and Emily sank to a wooden chair, smoothing the back of her black dress as she did so.

"After you left me this afternoon," Tulley was saying to her, "I went to see the bereaved young man. Fortunately I was saved the effort of climbing six flights because he was on the street—with Mr. Pembrook. My business was simple; I wanted only to offer my services in conducting a final prayer at the funeral tomorrow. 'Oh, no,' Mark said. 'There won't be any prayers. There won't be anything like that. Wallace will make a little speech and that's all.' Needless to say I found this improper and I said so. I tried to convince him how much better it would be for all concerned, but he refused to listen. Finally, much exasperated, I dropped the subject. And although Mr. Pembrook agreed with Mark, there is something about him that is warm and personally attractive. Don't you find him so? In any case, I asked him to come along tonight, making it clear, of course, that I directed the invitation *only* to him. I thought you might be pleased, despite certain unpleasantnesses last night; and he *has* expressed interest in my sittings. Nevertheless. But as for Mark, there is a frightful quality about him. Try as I will I cannot understand his attitude toward the disaster. Ah, but here I am, not having offered anything to my guests. I am truly afraid I have only these odd little biscuits— moonfaced, wouldn't you say?"

Bringing the plate from the dresser across the room, he

offered the cookies to us, then gave us sweet wine. "Unless you would like something stronger, of course. For myself, you know, I never take other than . . ." and he poured himself a drink.

"And now I must tell you the unfortunate part of my news. We will not be able to hold a proper sitting tonight. I had some words with Haq just before you came and, well, he is often this way with strangers. I am afraid he will not go much further than ouija."

"You mean with the alphabet?" said Emily.

"Yes, here you are." He unrolled a sheet of brown wrapping paper upon the table. "I have done the letters, as you can see, and the numbers from zero to nine. I hope he will be responsive; you know, ouija is child's play for Haq, but in many ways he is very—but, hush, we must say no more. If you notice, I have written *oui* on the left and *non* on the right: he prefers it that way."

The bell in the corridor rang five or six rapid blasts.

"Who could that be for?" Tulley wondered and the bell rang again. "Do you think it might be Mr. Pembrook? He might not have noticed the instructions for ringing. I'll run and take a look. Please excuse me."

When he had danced from the room, I circled my eyes round to Emily and, I suppose, in spite of all she had said, I was waiting for the familiar crack of her knuckles or the nervous anticipative pucker that would draw her lips. Instead, her smile persisted, and her motionless hands were folded upon her belly. When I nodded, I was startled to realize that I was counting on her strength, that I was even depending on it, that we were *together* much more than I thought, and almost as much as Emily said.

"I am grateful you did not bring Mark," said Tulley in the corridor. "I was so terribly worried you would."

"Oh, no," Wallace laughed. "I think we've had enough of him. Do you know what he did this afternoon? He got himself a job in a pastry shop as a baker's boy. And he has a pile of money, his parents' life insurance. There's so much he can do—but no, it's the baker's for him. Can't you imagine little Mark shoveling cakes in and out of the fire? And then, you know, one day he'll shovel him*self* in. But he won't die; no, not at all; he'll turn into a gingerbread boy."

He had come through the door while speaking, and as he finished his statement he looked round the room, pointed to the three cats who lay together back of the door, and greeted us all.

"Look at Emily," he said. "All in black. Whatever for?"

Her smile shifted peculiarly. "I don't suppose Mark——"

"Oh, Mark Mark Mark! Who cares about Mark? In the heat of it all you've forgotten Wallace."

"*You* haven't," said Emily.

"No, I haven't. I think I'm a lot more memorable than the baker's boy. I know his kind well; they make despair into a profession. Oh, maybe he *has* given up poetry and is burying all his dreams, but he'll think of something new next week. When people like that have nothing to believe in, they turn around and believe in nothing. Did you see the way he was laughing today, Tulley? The drearier he gets, the funnier he thinks it is—just like you, Emily." Laughing, he walked to her chair and bent to kiss her.

"Do you remember what I said to you last night, Wallace?" she asked as he moved away from her.

"You said so many things, and I've forgotten all of them."

I was so caught up with them that I almost answered for Emily, but I didn't; I looked to her and I waited. Her smile had dried from her mouth, leaving her lips pressed flat against each other. "You shouldn't have forgotten," was all she said to Wallace, but even that he did not hear, for he had turned suddenly to the table and lifted the sheet of brown wrapping paper by the corner.

"Ouija!" he shouted, shaking the paper toward Tulley like an accusation. "I thought we were going to have a real séance. I've done ouija before."

"I am terribly sorry, Mr. Pembrook," said Tulley. "As I explained to the others before, Haq is not in the mood——"

"Ouija is perfectly all right with me," nodded Emily, her smile righted back upon her face. "Isn't it with you, Harry?"

I hesitated. "I guess so. Yes. I don't know anything about any of these games."

"Majority rules," sighed Wallace, shrugged and sank beside me on the couch. Although the three of them continued to talk I felt myself moving slowly away, riding along something that would carry me as far as I wanted to go, as long as I remained will-less and available. It was a while before I realized the imaginary vehicle was only Wallace's shaving lotion; it did not repel me, nor did I find it irresistible, but as soon as I recognized it, it ceased to carry me away, and dropped me before the image of Tess. The fall awakened all the hungers I had earlier this evening known only in my head: I hungered for food, for sleep, for Tess——

"... for heaven's sake, Harry," Wallace was saying. "Don't sniff at me like that. If you tell me what you want to smell I'll oblige you immediately."

"Oh, I'm sorry, Wallace. No, I didn't—I mean, I don't—I'm sorry."

Four wooden chairs had been drawn together round half the table, and a saucer, lying face down upon the wrapping paper, had a large oily lipstick arrow painted on its back.

"If you will be kind enough to come sit at the table," said Tulley, "we shall begin."

Obeying him, we all took seats, and each put the fingertips of one hand upon the saucer. Tulley's fingers seemed to spray across the others; his arm was perfectly still; his face went long and pale, cheeks sucking inward, the lids over his closed eyes had a faint rapid twitch.

"Please concentrate," he said softly. "Try very hard. We are here for an extremely important purpose. Do please concentrate. Can you hear me?"

"Yes," said Emily.

"Be quiet, Miss Morrison. I am not speaking, to you. Can you hear me? I have brought some friends for you. It is of great urgency that we make contact this evening. Please do not delay. Please come at once." He paused, his eyelids twitching. "Haq, good Haq. Come to us. Are you in a French mood perhaps? *Tu veux parler français? Tu ne m'aimes plus? Viens, je te dis; viens!* Are you dissatisfied with French? Would you prefer German perhaps? *Bitte, süsser! Kennst du das Land*—oh, Haq, please do not embarrass me at such a moment. I implore you to come. Is there someone here who displeases you?"

Beneath my fingertips I felt the saucer shiver; slowly it began to move, then stop, then with a lurch begin again and slide up the sheet toward the alphabet.

Tulley's eyes were open now, and a flush was sweeping along his cheeks. "Who displeases you, Haq? Will you tell me?"

A violent jerk was followed by the description of wide circles that touched at each of us. I wondered who was doing the pushing but all fingers, as if simultaneously alarmed, hardly seemed to be pressed upon the saucer.

"He doesn't like anyone?" Emily asked, apparently pained.

"He is merely being wretched, Miss Morrison." The saucer stopped moving. "Oh, no, Haq, I did not mean you were wretched. I meant you were timid. We shall certainly give you time to familiarize yourself with the newcomers."

The saucer moved again, calmly but indecisively, picking at letters like bits of corn, spelling nothing in particular. Suddenly, in great haste, it described two wide circles and then the lipstick arrow began to point.

IAMHAQ it wrote and swung to OUI

"Ah, you have come. It is good to have you with us. Have you anything to tell us?"

NON NON NON and then BEWAREOFHAYSTACKS and NON NON

"What does he mean?" asked Emily. "Ask him if Jamie is there. Ask him if he can reach Jamie for us."

"Haq, would you kindly tell us if a young man named James or Jamie Akero is perhaps with you tonight?"

OUI NON OUI NON IAMHAQ

"*Please*, do not be evasive! Is the young man there?"

OUI NON JAMIEISHERE

"Oh, Haq, may I speak with him?" Emily called, and her hand went flat on the saucer.

IAM OUI

"What does that mean?" I asked.

"Perhaps we are speaking to Jamie now. Is this so?"

OUI NON IAMHAQ

"Well, is he Jamie or Haq? He couldn't be both," Wallace insisted.

"There are more things in heaven and earth, Mr. Pembrook, than are dreamt of in your philosophy."

"Haq, Haq," Emily pleaded. "Bring Jamie. I want to talk to Jamie."

IAMJAMIE

"Oh, it's *him?*" She shrieked. "Oh, Jamie, Jamie, then somewhere you live."

OUI

"Are you well, Jamie?" Wallace asked.

Emily turned on him furiously. "Must you always be such a damn——" But the saucer interrupted her.

IAMFINE

"Then you're quite recovered?" Wallace continued, and I noticed that, although his arm moved as the others, he had lifted his fingers from the dish.

IAMDEAD

"But somewhere you live, don't you?" Emily repeated.

OUI BUTHARRY

Until I saw my name spelled out upon the paper I had not considered myself part of the game, had not felt that the letters were related to me. But now, with a start, I pulled my fingers from the saucer, looked at them suspiciously, ran my thumb across the other four, and then pretended to put them back but, like Wallace, did not actually touch the saucer.

"What about Harry?" Tulley asked.

X Q D E R A B C D E F

"Ex-cu-der-ab-ce-def," said Wallace. "Is that code?"

"Occasionally Haq speaks in Arabic, and then of course I am simply lost."

"But this isn't Haq," said Emily. "It's Jamie. What do you want to say about Harry, Jamie? Is it important?"

N O T H A R R Y E M I L Y

"The message is for me?" she asked.

O U I I A M T H E S H O P W I N D O W

The saucer paused, Emily's eyes wide and fixed upon it; it hesitated a moment then went on.

H A R R Y I S N O T T O U C H I N G

"You did that, Wallace," cried Emily. "I felt you push the plate then."

Indeed, his fingers were once again upon the surface. "No, it wasn't me, Emily. It was the spirit within me pushing. Anyway, it's quite true: Harry isn't touching."

"No arguments, please," Tulley urged. "You will only succeed in displeasing Haq. And, Harry, please put your fingers back."

I obeyed.

O U I N O N I A M O U I N O N H A R R Y

"Tell us about Harry," said Tulley.

O U I L E T M E

"Let you what? What shall I let you?"

LETME OUI NON IAMHAQ

"Oh, no. Call Jamie back," cried Emily.

But the saucer did not move.

"Perhaps one of you would like to ask a question about the future? That is generally the first thing people prefer to do at sittings. Mr. Pembrook, is there anything you would like to know?"

"Think how terrible, Tulley, how terrible and dull it would be to know the future. But I'm sure Emily would like to ask a question."

"No. Nothing about the future."

"Go on, Emily. Ask Haq if you'll ever have your heart's desire."

"I know the answer to that."

"What is it?" Tulley asked.

"Oui non I am Haq," and she giggled, then reset her mouth into the smile.

"I want to ask a question," I said.

"Hooray for Harry," said Tulley. "Here we have someone who believes he has a future to ask about."

"No, I don't want to ask about the future. I want to know if he's human."

IAM

"You are human?"

IAMDEAD

"Well, do you experience anything human?"

OUI

"What?" But there was a long pause before it wrote.

SHALL

"I don't understand," I said, feeling the saucer twitch under my fingers. "You experience *shall?*"

SHALL

"But shall what?"

OUI NON IAMHAQISHALL

"And so shall I," I said, lifting my hand.

I fell asleep on the downtown bus: a half-conscious yet very deep and restful sleep, and I woke when Emily tried to step over me into the aisle.

"What are you doing?" I asked.

"I've got to get off at the next stop. I didn't want to wake you, you were sleeping so soundly."

"I'll take you home."

"No, don't be silly. Go back to sleep."

And I did, until the end of the line, until the stop at the bottom of the park. A corner of moon—I could not recall whether it was new or old—hung cocooned by mist and secure in the pale sky, and the damp cool night made me hurry toward home, my entire body rushing in the direction of sleep.

22

Sunlight and voices entered together, intermingled, at first inseparable; but as I shook myself to consciousness light and sound untwisted, and gradually the voices were distinguishable.

"... before but he didn't answer." That was Emily.

"I'll go upstairs," said Tess.

"Harry! *Harry!*" Emily called.

Pulling a blanket off the bed with me, I swung it round my hips and went to the window.

With a look of relief Tess smiled and rubbed a hand across her belly, then tugged at the waist of her dress. Her dress had nothing to do with a funeral: it was pale yellow and its neck cut round to her breasts. But beside her, Emily, who looked up with impatience, was still in black, and under her arm was the small black notebook.

"At last," said Emily. "It's almost ten. You'd better hurry."

"Were you sleeping, Harry?"

"Yes." I smiled. "What are you two doing down there?"

"We just met here," said Tess. "I was coming to call for you, and she was here already."

"Harry, get dressed. Don't you realize how late it is?"

"Should I come up, Harry?"

Emily touched her arm. "He'll meet us, Tess. Let's go in now."

"No, I want to wait. I'll come up, Harry."

"It's all right," I said. "Go on ahead. I'll be right there."

"But I want to come up."

Then I surprised her by saying: "Please. I'd like to go alone." And I surprised myself by adding: "Just this once."

Finally Tess permitted Emily to take her arm and lead her down the street. When they had gone round the corner to the chapel-entrance, I turned back to the room and began to dress. My mind, stuffed with thoughts, had not the time to think; in fact I had no time for anything—I dressed rapidly, forgot my tie, and put on moccasins instead of shoes. I ran down the staircase and out into the street; but I stopped before my office.

On the window I caught the reflection of Mr. Trevor's empty Packard parked across the street; and through the window I saw the empty office, deserted of every transient sign of life. I turned away slowly and went round the corner.

Outside the chapel the hearse waited and the two uniformed men leaned against it.

"Morning, Mr. Sutton."

"Morning, Mr. Sutton."

"Morning."

Someone had vomited in the foyer and although it had been brushed away, the smell remained, and lumpy pink lines were visible in the grooves of the corrugated rubber carpet. At my left was the chapel door; pushing it open a bit, I stared through.

The first half-dozen rows were filled, but further back, toward where I stood, it was more scattered. Emily, Mrs. Mussolini, Tulley, and Mark sat in front, back of the coffin, and just before it and slightly above, Wallace stood beside the lectern; he was talking but I did not hear what he said. Then there were the others, recognizably from Crawford Street: the red-headed youth, the bristle-legged lady, others. And of those scattered in the last rows, most were unknown to me; but some seemed familiar although difficult to place. One man, his face sagging with confusion, was especially perplexing; but when he cleared his throat with a thick sound I remembered him as Emily's friend, the lawyer with the TV set. And in the last row, close to the door, sat Mr. Trevor, Frank, and Sarah, who, like most of the others, wept.

Then I saw Tess, like a pale yellow light, sitting on the aisle, her anxious face profiled toward the oaken door near the altar, the door to the white chamber. Suddenly she edged in her seat and looked to the back, and I pushed the door open.

". . . so that visitations of death must be forgotten," Wallace is saying. "We are gathered here not to mourn or cry but to form a contract to forget what passes in this room."

I sink into the chair beside Tess and I take her hand.

"I love you, Harry," she whispers.

"And say to yourselves I will live, I will avoid what distracts me as death, and we will join together and make a daisy chain of happiness, of wonder, of pleasure."

Cray Cray Cray, cries the congregation.

And from behind himself he takes the rustling chains of the red glass censer and swings blue-brown fumes into the room. "Life is priceless beyond everything; dance naked in the streets; have no dream but the present; have no desire but *now*, to fulfill *now*. Hate what tells you there is other than there is, that there is more than you have, but have all. Have a leaf, a rainfall, a hard rod, or a soft circle—and leave the leaf when it dies, the rain when it dries, the rod when it softens, and the circle when it hardens. And love yourself as you would your neighbor."

Cray Cray Cray

Tulley rises and turns to the congregation. "If you might wish a final look . . . and may the Lord have mercy on . . ."

And the march begins with Tess's arm in mine and mine in hers, toward the unlidded coffin, beneath Wallace, who swings the ruby censer.

"I love you, Harry."

"Yes." I nod my head. "And I—I love you, Tess."

"I love you so much, Harry, and I always will."

"You *always* will? But always is today and ends tomorrow."

"But it never ends today."

It never ends today, smiles Emily.

It ended yesterday, laughs Mark.
It never did exist, says Wallace.
It never ends nevertheless, sighs Tulley.
and
Cray Cray Cray, does the congregation go.

"Oh, Harry, stay near me. Don't be afraid. You'll see him. You *will*."

SHALL

And we all shall, all shall trail by the unlidded coffin, Mark first of all, Mark pastry-eyed, then Emily, Emily dry-eyed and tear-breasted, then Tulley, then all: the thick young man and the bristle-legged lady and Mrs. Mussolini and Mr. Trevor and Sarah yawning and dehymenated, and then Tess, and then myself. Last shall I go, and last shall I see Jamie lying in the coffin with the rose silk pillow at his head.

"I see him, Tess. I can see him. My eyes can see him."

Cray Cray Cray

And Jamie will be there as plain as day beneath the lectern, beneath the tubes of sunlight tubing through the stained-glass windows, beneath—and lo! will Mrs. Opienski come floating above us swept by the factory hum from Wimple Road as Tess and I join before the silk, the pale, the sadboy body of Jamie, join hands lips rods circles souls forever always how the corkel eebementor gracks metafixus blay neztomanile asumny

Cray Cray Cray
Cray Cray Cray
Cray Cray Cray

AFTERWORD

ALFRED: A Memoir
by Harriet Sohmers Zwerling

He had met my lover, M., in Ibiza, where she remained after a painful and seemingly terminal breakup with me. Alfred fell in love with her, as he often did with women, in a wistful, erotic, but asexual manner, and she with him. She asked him to contact me on his return to Paris, and we met at the American Express mail desk. Small, pudgy, cherubic, with pale blue doll's eyes (lashless), pink skin, and a golden doll's wig, he aroused in me, after the first visual shock, a peculiar motherly feeling, as for some blind, helpless, and hairless kitten. That feeling remained all through the years of our friendship, in spite of my almost immediate discovery that this kitten had sharp claws.

When M. returned to Paris, for a while, to me, we three became a small family. Alfred's friend—the pianist—

remained always apart. His was a sacred precinct, guarded jealously by Alfred. He had no interest in Alfred's friends, or even, I think, in his work. A stone narcissist, he was in love with his piano and permitted Alfred to worship at his shrine.

Alfred became the essential go-between when my friend and I had our many passionate battles. One of us would always run weeping to Alfred and somehow he would always patch things up.

His benevolent participation in our relationship came to a painful end, however, when we hitchhiked to Salerno, where he and the pianist had rented a beautiful house with an amazing garden high above the sea. My obsession with M. had reached a peak of hysterical anxiety and we were both unhappy and fearful. Staying with Alfred was meant to be a healing vacation for all of us, in which, I hoped, Alfred would practice his emotional doctoring and help me to bring my hysteria to a more manageable level. He was always so practical and clear-headed about other people's love affairs!

Alas, this was not to be. After about forty-eight hours of misery, during which the friend never left his piano, refusing to join us even for meals, and I spent a sleepless night contemplating the pistol I had found in the drawer of my bed table, Alfred told us that we would have to leave. His friend just couldn't work with us around (those ungodly scales!). This was not an easy thing for us to do, since we were out of money and had planned to wait at Alfred's until somebody sent some; worse, it was a horrible betrayal by our healer, he who would put things right between us. But

Alfred was adamant, and off we went, thumbs and smiles, two young American girls on the road.

But somehow, as always, I could not stay angry at him, and Alfred and I became friends again.

In Paris, in the fifties, for a few years, we led a lovely life. M. and I lived at the Hôtel de Poitou, on the rue de Seine. I worked at the *Tribune* in Paris, hours six to midnight, six nights a week. Perfect schedule for the night person I was then. After work I'd take the Métro from the Champs-Elysées to St.-Germain and hang out, sometimes till dawn, at the Monaco, the Bonaparte, Deux Magots, Tabou, with Alfred, Elliot Stein, Ricardo Vigón, the marvelous international stew of young expatriates that walked the night from Montparnasse to St.-Germain and even to Montmartre. Then, home to the hotel and bed till noon. A great lunch/breakfast at Orestias or Chez Julien or the Beaux Arts and then the terrasses de café—Old Navy, Select, Dôme—until five-thirty and time to return to the rue de Berri for my night's work. Oh, the lovely hours spent sitting in front of a café noir, watching the world go by.

Alfred's nature was severely divided. He could be reasonable, kindly, a Jewish mother—or cruel, irrational, and malevolent, almost demonic.

One famous story about him in those days concerned a book party given for *Jamie Is My Heart's Desire* at Gait Froge's American Bookstore, on the rue de Seine. A trapdoor on to stairs leading to the cellar had somehow been left open and in the excitement of the party, an American woman fell through it, breaking her leg. As the shocked group waited for an ambulance, Alfred was heard to say, "Thank God, it was only Gertrude"!

My memories of Alfred leap from the fifties to the sixties here. I honestly don't remember if he was still around when my relationship with O. became the hot item of the Paris gossips. I see him next in New York, living on Sullivan Street with the cats, whose balls of hair rolled around the bare floors like tumbleweed. The pianist was gone. Walter K. was around, and O. and I lived on West End Avenue and saw a lot of Alfred, M. and her current lover, and certain literary types from *Partisan* and *Commentary* with whom Alfred and O. were both becoming involved—new stars in the New York intellectual scene.

And then, my life, traumatized by betrayal (to which Alfred was a silent but remorseful witness), changed direction. I gave up my always halfhearted involvement with women and went straight—totally and forever straight. No longer was Alfred the angelic mediator of my loves; now there were men in my life, and except insofar as all loves are the same, he was no longer an expert. In fact, he was highly critical of the men in my life. Of course, gay men and straight women have one important thing in common—a love of the male anatomy.

At that time, Alfred was involved with a hippieish young man named Extro—a self-invented Kerouac-style bad boy, handsome but dumb. We had many conversations about the values involved in relationships. Alfred always maintained that intellect had nothing to do with love. "I have my friends to talk to," he declared. I have since come to the conclusion that he was right.

And then he left for Morocco. I had wonderful letters. In 1963 my son was born. Alfred was Milo's godfather. He sent a colorful skullcap and a sheepskin—gifts traditional for male children in Morocco—and a beautiful godfatherly benediction:

God give him much courage, much strength, much laughter, an open heart, an endless appetite for life, the power to be silent or alone without pain, eyes good enough to catch sight of another's soul and suffering, a body which he need never make much of one way or the other, sicknesses which leave him healthier, wiser, and more grateful, a knowledge of the French language so that he can converse with his mother, the ability to love those who love him, honor without pride, self-respect without vanity, and above everything the wit to distinguish between the work of man and the work of God.

Milo must have been about two when Alfred returned for the first time. He called from the airport and asked if I could put him up until he found a place of his own. Of course —and there was my tanned (now wigless) darling, slimmer, harder looking, pale eyes glittering with madness.

He talked endlessly about the green Volkswagens that followed him everywhere, the ceaseless messages from extraterrestrials that were using his burning brain as a radio receiver. He accused me of bugging the little room in my apartment where he slept and of being in league with his tormentors. One afternoon, with Milo strapped securely in his highchair in the kitchen, I held a nine-inch bread knife in my hand, behind my back, and told the weird, wired, red-faced stranger, no longer my beloved friend, that if he did not "act sane" he'd have to leave my apartment. "I don't care if you really believe this stuff or not, I want you to stop talking about it. Pretend you're rational or go!"

I suffered horrible nightmares in which the Martian who had taken over my friend's mind ordered him to take or hurt my baby. He had to go.

And he did. Always brilliant at finding a home for himself, he located the St. Mark's Place apartment and was gone. And then began his odyssey from Morocco to London, to Paris, to Kennedy Airport (from which he phoned me, begging me to come see him at the motel where he was holed up), to the Chelsea Hotel (where his dogs chewed up the bedspread)—restless wandering to and from his adored Tangier, unnamable adventures in unidentifiable places. By then, he had come into his mother's money, which permitted him to pursue these harried trajectories.

I seem to remember him telling me, calling from JFK, that he had been evicted from Morocco as an Israeli agent. There were other stories, not quite so glamorous.

And then he was in Brooklyn Heights, on Clinton Street, in a lovely old garden apartment. It was summer. He furnished the place with gorgeous castoffs from the Salvation Army. I especially remember a long, silvery green velvet sofa. The garden, cool and shadowy with large trees and tall flowers, soon became unusable because of the accumulating piles of dog shit, but before that happened, oh, the lovely martinis with Dennis Selby, and Alfred reading to us from works in progress, especially the marvelous "Trois

Corsages," portraits of three women: myself, Susan Sontag, and Maria Irene Fornes. This manuscript has never been found, and, if I were prone to conspiracy-mania like Alfred, I would divine some scary significance here.

Alfred left the apartment only at dawn, or very late at night, to walk the dogs. He hated to see and be seen by people in the street. He would order deliveries of food and gin—large expensive steaks for the dogs, salads and light things for himself. Dennis and I brought pot for dreaming in the garden.

At some point I got a phone call from Extro, just out of jail I think, who was looking for a friend. He was overjoyed to hear that Alfred was in town, established in Brooklyn. Alfred seemed pleased, planning a sexual idyll with his old friend, stacking up on goodies to enhance the fun. But when Extro actually showed up at his place, Alfred found him pathetic, manipulative, and unattractive and sent him rapidly on his way.

I don't remember why, but I stopped going to Clinton Street, and Dennis did too. The Clinton Street apartment was abandoned—I mourned for that velvet couch—and the wanderer was gone again, this time to Jerusalem and his death. His godson is now a beautiful twenty-seven-year-old man. I have only one personal photo of Alfred, his golden wig shining in the sun of a Salerno garden. I sit on the deck of the house in Truro, on this Labor Day weekend, looking out over the bay and toward the rakish Sienese campanile that makes the peculiar skyline of Provincetown, thinking of Alfred.

1993

ALFRED CHESTER was born September 7, 1928, in Brooklyn, New York, the youngest of three children of a Russian-born furrier and his wife. At the age of seven, a case of scarlet fever robbed him of his hair, even his eyelashes, and for most of the rest of his life he wore a wig to mask his baldness. He attended yeshiva and Abraham Lincoln High School, and in 1949 received his B.A. from New York University. He then began graduate studies in English at Columbia, but after a year he moved to France, determined to become a writer. His first book, the collection of stories *Here Be Dragons*, was published in Paris in 1955. The following year his first novel, *Jamie Is My Heart's Desire*, was published in London by André Deutsch. Chester returned to New York in 1960 and became one of the decade's most prolific and provocative literary journalists, publishing criticism in *Commentary*, *Partisan Review*, and *The New York Review of Books*. In 1963, at the suggestion of the writer-composer Paul Bowles, he moved to Morocco, where he found, for the first time, something like happiness. In 1964 he published a second collection of stories, *Behold Goliath*, and in 1967 his masterpiece, *The Exquisite Corpse* (Black Sparrow Books edition, 2003). His final years were characterized by wandering, alcoholism, drug addiction, and madness. He died in Jerusalem, alone and alienated from his friends, on August 2, 1971. His literary executor, Edward Field, has edited two posthumous collections, *Head of a Sad Angel: Stories 1953–1966* (1990) and *Looking for Genet: Literary Essays and Reviews* (1992), and is currently preparing an edition of his letters.

BLACK SPARROW BOOKS
Also by Alfred Chester

The Exquisite Corpse
afterword by Diana Athill

Lyric and tender one moment, cruel and dizzying the next, *The Exquisite Corpse* neither celebrates perversity nor laments it; rather it projects it as part of man's never-ending search for a true self and for transcendent communion with others. In forty-nine brief, highly cinematic chapters, we meet a series of twisted but sincere searchers—Tomtom Jim and his naked, hungry family; Mary Poorpoor and her utterly "otherly" baby; angry John Doe and his sex slave, James Madison—each in flight from despair. As one surreal episode morphs into the next, these searchers change shape and their journeys change direction; names and identities come and go, storylines collide, and desires intertwine, all with the lightning-quick illogic of a dream. The result is a tragicomic *tour de force*, an upside-down roadmap to everyone's inner Sodom, a perversely moral masterpiece by a modern-day Marquis de Sade.

Chester is out to shock, to dazzle, to shake up, to offend, but at the same time he is seriously striving to record the implications of obsession, to document the tyranny and anguish of compulsive fantasy.... Like Henry Miller and William S. Burroughs, he is a born writer with a zestful imagination and a poet's gift for provocative images.
—The New York Times Book Review

272 pages · softcover · $16.95

www.blacksparrowbooks.com

BLACK SPARROW BOOKS
Selected Fiction

KENNETH BURKE
*Here and Elsewhere:
The Collected Fiction of Kenneth Burke*
Introduction by Denis Donoghue
432 PAGES · SOFTCOVER · $22.95

BANDULA CHANDRARATNA
Mirage
224 PAGES · SOFTCOVER · $15.95

ISOBEL ENGLISH
Every Eye
192 PAGES · HARDCOVER · $23.95

DANIEL FUCHS
The Brooklyn Novels
Introduction by Jonathan Lethem
832 PAGES · SOFTCOVER · $24.95

DANIEL FUCHS
The Golden West: Hollywood Stories
Introduction by John Updike
272 PAGES . SOFTCOVER . $16.95

Black Sparrow Books is an imprint of David R. Godine, Publisher.
For a complete list of Black Sparrow Books titles please visit our
website *www.blacksparrowbooks.com,* or write to:

BLACK SPARROW BOOKS
DAVID R. GODINE, *Publisher*
Post Office Box 450
Jaffrey, New Hampshire 03452

Printed in the United States
81673LV00001B/1-102